CANDLELIGHT *Supreme*

**"HELLO, LEGS." HIS INTIMATE VOICE
MATCHED THE INTENSITY OF HIS EYES.**

"Oh, no," she mumbled. She closed her eyes, thinking she was hallucinating, but when she opened them Murphy was still there.

"Sit down, Charlie, before you fall down," he suggested with a hint of a smile on his lips.

She stared at the man she had lived with years ago. How could this be happening? Finally she managed to say, "If I had known I'd be working here with you, I would never have accepted the job. I think I'd better leave."

"Scared?"

His low taunt sent strange tingles down her spine. "That isn't it at all. I just don't believe in dredging up dead relationships."

"Well, neither do I. But as you can see, we're both very much alive and anything can happen."

CANDLELIGHT SUPREMES

MURPHY'S CHARM

Linda Randall Wisdom

A CANDLELIGHT SUPREME

Published by
Dell Publishing Co., Inc.
1 Dag Hammarskjold Plaza
New York, New York 10017

ISBN: 0-440-16201-7

Printed in the United States of America

December 1986

10 9 8 7 6 5 4 3 2 1

WFH

To Our Readers:

We are pleased and excited by your overwhelmingly positive response to our Candlelight Supremes. Unlike all the other series, the Supremes are filled with more passion, adventure, and intrigue, and are obviously the stories you like best.

In months to come we will continue to publish books by many of your favorite authors as well as the very finest work from new authors of romantic fiction. As always, we are striving to present unique, absorbing love stories —the very best love has to offer.

Breathtaking and unforgettable, Supremes follow in the great romantic tradition you've come to expect *only* from Candlelight Romances.

Your suggestions and comments are always welcome. Please let us hear from you.

Sincerely,

The Editors
Candlelight Romances
1 Dag Hammarskjold Plaza
New York, New York 10017

MURPHY'S CHARM

CHAPTER ONE

This has *got* to be a joke! Charlie thought hysterically, looking around the medical office decorated with several lithographs of western scenes and framed medical degrees attesting that Dr. Arnold Grissom had graduated from U.C.L.A. with honors and had gone on to further studies in Boston and Baltimore. That was it. She'd misunderstood him, and if she sat back and listened calmly she'd learn just how wrong she was.

"Charlie, listen to me." The gray-haired man spoke firmly in order to regain her attention. "This is not some kind of game. You've gone against my orders time and time again, even though I warned you this could happen. You didn't rest long enough after that fall you took three years ago, and by not taking proper care of yourself, you're paying for it now." He couldn't allow himself to feel sympathy for someone who basically caused her own problems. He had treated dancers long enough to know if he wasn't firm with them from the very beginning, they tended to forget what doctor's orders meant. Then, when a serious injury brought them to his office, they pleaded with him to fix them up, but it was often too late. Charlie Wells followed his advice to the letter only when it pleased her, but she hadn't when it counted most. Now she was most definitely paying the price.

The dark blond woman sitting before him in a navy leotard and pink sweatpants wasn't beautiful in the conventional sense. One way to describe her was tall, lean, and leggy. Long legs were an asset in a dancer's life, but they made her look a bit too thin for her five-feet-seven-inch frame. Her mouth was full, her eyes a bit too close, and her chin a trifle pointed—but with the proper use of cosmetics, no one noticed. Only the physician in him could see what some people might call imperfections. He sensed that Charlie only saw them as another challenge to conquer—the way she saw life. Now she had the most important challenge facing her. He only hoped she would do what was required of her and not end up a cripple the way some dancers did because they refused to believe the rug could so easily be pulled out from under them.

"Whether you like it or not, you're going to have to take six months to a year off and allow that bum knee to heal properly," he told her, closing the manila folder before him.

"I can't afford to take that much time off!" she cried passionately. Charlie sat forward in her chair, her hands outstretched. "Please, Dr. Grissom, you're signing my death sentence. Do you realize how much of my day is spent dancing? When I'm not rehearsing for a show, I'm in classes or auditioning. We're not talking about taking time away from a job; we're talking about my life!" Her blue gray eyes shimmered with tears she refused to shed. She couldn't even begin to contemplate what the doctor's words meant. The show she was working in was a success, guaranteed a long run. Now

10

he was telling her she would have to walk away from the best break she'd had in a long time.

Dr. Grissom sighed. He understood her fears only too well. His wife had been an up-and-coming dancer twenty years ago when an ankle injury cut off her dream of stardom. Luckily she had the inner strength to turn her energy into opening a dance studio, which had been successful. In fact, Charlie was one of the students there. Deep down, he felt Charlie had that same inner strength if she cared to look for it. He didn't want to tell her that he wasn't sure a year's rest would be sufficient. But he was willing to give her the benefit of the doubt. In situations like this he always hoped his diagnosis would be wrong, after all.

Charlie gathered up her canvas tote bag. "I'll have to let Ray, the director, know he'll need a replacement," she said slowly, still finding it hard to believe her dreams and hopes were crumbling. "I've never left a show in the middle of a run before."

"It's for your own good, Charlie," he replied quietly. "And you know I'm here if you need anything. So is Sylvia. Remember, she's been through the same thing. Don't sit home alone thinking about this. Talk to someone and get the pain out of your system."

She nodded as she turned away and left the office. Right now she only wanted to go home and lick her wounds in peace. Still in a daze, she settled her account with the bookkeeper and walked outside. Her shiny red Honda was in the parking lot, and she climbed in and started the engine. She had felt confident enough to buy a new car this year. "Hope I'm able to make the next forty-three payments," she muttered as she drove away. Luckily she lived only ten minutes away and could

11

drive home without worrying about battling the busy L.A. freeways.

A short while later she parked the car in the cracked concrete driveway. She loved her house, which she had lived in for the past five years, and wondered how long she could afford the rent if she couldn't find a job that didn't involve staying on her feet for long periods of time. The tiny house looked more like an idyllic hide-away for lovers instead of a forty-year-old house. As she approached the front door, she could hear a deep-throated barking.

"Huggie Bear, you stop that," she scolded, unlocking the two dead bolts. The warning barks immediately changed to yips of delight as the dog realized his mistress had returned. He knew dinner was forthcoming.

She walked into the living room, dodging the excited Newfoundland as she checked her answering machine. Charlie winced as she listened to a message from her agent. She immediately dialed his number and ended up leaving a message with his answering machine.

While Charlie waited for Harry's call, she fed Huggie Bear and Snickers, her Persian cat. Once the dog was fed, she pushed him outside to the small fenced yard and concentrated on cleaning up the kitchen. Though she never had time to do much cooking or even eating in the room, she still enjoyed sitting in there instead of her living room. A poster of *CATS* covered a wall near the dinette set, and two framed photographs of Charlie dancing in a popular musical were on the opposite wall, next to the gas stove. Even the tiny curtain covering the window had ballet dancers printed on the white cotton fabric. It was as good a time as any to rearrange her cabinets, she decided. She had to do something, anything, not to think about Dr. Grissom's words.

Talk to someone, he had suggested. Once there had been someone she could tell everything to, but that had been a long time ago. A tiny smile quivered at the corner of her mouth and disappeared. She hadn't seen Murphy in years, but his memory still lingered and she had a pretty good idea it always would. It was said that a woman never forgot her first lover, and Charlie certainly hadn't. It was more than that, though, because he would have become a very important part of her life if she'd only had the sense to hang on to him instead of opting for her career and walking away from the best thing that could have happened to her. But it had taken all these years and a bit of maturing to make her realize that.

She missed Murphy, but she had no one to blame but herself for losing him. It was funny how life played tricks on a person. She'd heard he had left acting, but no one knew where he had gone or what he was doing. Charlie wouldn't even know where to begin to look for him, but she wished he was around to talk to; no one had ever understood her the way Murphy had.

Luckily, before she could grow too maudlin about the past, Harry called and agreed to stop by her house that evening. She wasn't looking forward to the meeting with her agent.

Having a couple hours to kill, she fixed herself a sandwich, realizing she didn't have to worry about calories now, and wandered into the bedroom to change her clothes. A rustle of feathers alerted her before the raspy words were spoken.

"Hello, hello, hello." A low, slightly gruff voice re-

13

peated the greeting as a blue-front Amazon parrot hopped excitedly along a manzanita branch doubling as the perch. Large, slightly round dark gold eyes watched Charlie—or at least her sandwich—avidly.

"Donnie, I should have named you Miss Piggy," Charlie teased, tearing off a piece of bread crust and handing it to the parrot. "You're an avian garbage can."

After eating her treat, the parrot stretched her neck out, emitting the closest sound to a bird's purr. "Good girl," she crooned, dropping her yellow head tipped with blue feathers to one side. She fanned her blue-green wing feathers, displaying the deep cobalt secondary feathers. "That's a good girl, Donnie."

"At least someone feels good around here." Charlie sighed, and dropped onto her bed, staring at the poster for *A Chorus Line* on the opposite wall. "Right now I feel very sick." She looked down at her legs. There didn't seem to be anything major wrong with the shapely limbs except for some soreness running along one knee, and a hot bath should take care of that. It also might help relax her.

"And how was your day, Charlie?" she asked herself brightly, walking into the bathroom and turning on the tub faucets.

"Darling, to be perfectly frank, it was sheer hell. Such a *ghastly* day," she drawled with a perfect English drawing room accent. "If I were a horse, I would have been shot." She poured a generous amount of bubble bath in the tub and wondered with a sorrowful sigh how it would feel to drown in a tub filled with bubbles.

By the time Harry showed up at her house that evening Charlie felt more like her old self. She had changed into a lilac oversized T-shirt, and her short hair was washed and blown dry into its customary tousled style that could either frame her face with soft wisps or be brushed back in a more conservative style.

"Hi," she greeted him with a hug. "Want a drink?"

The balding man grimaced as he settled his bulky frame in a velvety easy chair. "I guess you're not going to give me good news, so make it a double."

She nodded and headed for the kitchen.

"Charlie, that cat is on me!" he yelled after her.

"Harry, you know very well that Snickers wouldn't harm you," she called out from the kitchen as she fixed a scotch for Harry and poured herself a glass of Perrier.

He eyed the cat with the same disdain the feline showed for him. "That's what you think," he muttered, looking around at the hodgepodge of furniture filling the tiny living room. He remembered that Charlie called her decorating scheme "early garage sale." The ancient couch with its sagging springs attested to her lighthearted description. He looked up when Charlie stood before him, holding out a glass partly filled with amber liquid.

"Dr. Grissom's news wasn't good, was it?" he asked bluntly, after swallowing almost half his drink.

She nodded, her eyes wide with something that could only be described as pure fear. "He said the knee isn't improving and I'll have to take six months to a year off in order to let it heal properly."

Harry bolted down the rest of his drink. He wasn't surprised by her news, but it was still a shock because he knew how much dancing meant to Charlie. And after knowing her as long as he had, he knew better than to offer sympathy; she wouldn't accept it. He also felt

15

anger—not at Charlie but at the situation that hurt the woman he considered more a daughter than a client.

Harry swore loudly to hide the pity he felt for her. "Dammit, Charlie! You *knew* from the beginning how fragile your knee was and that you had to be careful!" he shouted, pacing back and forth. "But, no, you just had to get in this show, didn't you? You assured me your knee was fine. Then you had to lose your balance during that turn and screw it up again. Why can't you do what you're told instead of going on your merry way?"

Charlie felt the tension rising in her body. "There is nothing permanently wrong with my knee," she denied vehemently. "A dancer is used to pain, Harry, just the way an athlete is. We live with sprains and pulled tendons all the time. This is nothing new to me except that"—she hesitated, swallowing the lump stuck in her throat—"except that I'm out of the game for a while. If I rest and take care of myself, I'll be back in fighting shape in no time." She knew every word she spoke was a lie because that much time away from the dance world was certain death to a dancer. "Dr. Grissom was just using scare tactics on me. You know how heavy-handed he likes to be with his patients."

"I doubt very much they're 'scare tactics,' Charlie. You know only too well how delicate a dancer's legs can be." He sighed, hating what he was going to do. "Remember what happened to Leslie?"

She looked at him sharply, remembering a fellow dancer who disregarded doctor's orders and was now confined to a wheelchair for the rest of her life. The young woman had become bitter over her disability and refused to see any of her old friends. "That's a low blow, Harry," she said softly, blinking furiously to keep the tears back.

"Honey, I'll do anything to ensure you won't screw yourself up. I care too much about you to see you ruin yourself."

Charlie collapsed in the chair and dropped her head into her hands. "What am I supposed to do with myself if I can't dance?" she demanded, still refusing to believe the truth. "I don't have the patience to teach, and my typing and office skills are rotten."

"I have a few ideas. I'll let you know just as soon as I can," he assured her, patting her shoulder awkwardly. Like most men he knew, Harry was helpless when it came to a woman's tears. He ran a hand through his iron-gray hair and then settled it in his pocket. "You get a good night's sleep, and I'll talk to you in the next day or so. Don't get yourself too upset, or you won't be good for anything. I'll call Ray and tell him what happened, and I'll get back to you when I hear something."

"Sure, don't call us; we'll call you," Charlie said wearily, tipping her head back against the chair. She managed a weak wave as Harry left. She heard the sound of his car leaving and wondered when he was going to take care of that knocking engine.

Unable to stay down long, she jumped up and locked the door. From there, she walked through the kitchen to the back door and opened it to allow the coal black Newfoundland inside. "Hello, Huggie Bear," she crooned, hugging the dog that easily reached her waist. "Now, Snickers, don't upset him," she warned the arrogant Persian, who had entered the kitchen. The large dog stepped gingerly around the cat. From the first day the two animals met they had been cautious adversaries.

17

Not caring to sit and worry herself any further, she locked the house up for the night and huddled in bed with the television on until the early morning hours. But if anyone had asked her what she had watched, she wouldn't have been able to give a good answer. All she knew was that the part of her life that had been so important to her was gone—all because she happened to turn her head too quickly and lost her balance.

It was three days before Charlie heard from Harry. By the second day, she was bored out of her mind since she had kept close to the house in hopes of his call. Every time the phone rang, she grabbed it on the first ring in hopes it would be her agent with an idea on how to keep her from going crazy. But instead of calling her, Harry ended up paying her a visit.

"You must be bored," he announced, walking into the immaculate living room. "I bet I won't even find dust under the couch."

"Don't push your luck," Charlie muttered, watching him circle the room that didn't have one magazine or throw pillow out of place. "Are you bringing me good news, or is there a revolver in your pocket with my name on it?" she asked with macabre humor.

He shook his head. "You're not acting too optimistic, honey. You've got to have faith in me. I told you I'd come up with something. And I did," he added proudly.

"What would that be, since I'm not allowed to dance?" She refused to think that her knee would give out now when it had done so much for her over the last twenty-nine years. "You can't say that I can be a waitress since I'm not supposed to be on my feet a lot."

"Baby, you'll love my idea," he said with bold enthusiasm. "This is tailor-made for you."

Charlie gazed suspiciously at him. When Harry said she'd love it and it was made for her, she knew she was in trouble. "What will I love?"

"You can call it a paid vacation," Harry cajoled.

"Don't tell me . . . I'll be teaching ballroom dancing on a cruise ship in the Mediterranean."

He paused. "Not exactly."

"In the Caribbean?"

"You're getting closer."

Charlie pushed her bangs away from her forehead. "How close do I have to get before I win the grand prize?"

Harry's face split in a broad smile. "Thanks to me, you have an excellent chance to become the director of activities for the New Eden Retirement Community."

A pin could have dropped and sounded like a bomb in the heavy silence. "A director of activities for a retirement community?" Charlie echoed. "Harry, it sounds more like a camp counselor. That's not a very funny joke."

"It isn't meant to be. My aunt is a resident up there and mentioned they're looking for a new director. I called and spoke to someone on their board, and he suggested you drive up for an interview sometime next week." He looked very proud of himself. Charlie, however, looked as though she wanted to kill him. "I'm a dancer, not a social director," she argued.

His expression sombered. "Charlie, you're going to have to face facts. Right now you're well on your way to becoming an *ex*-dancer, and you may as well write off the next six to twelve months when it comes to prancing around on a stage."

Charlie walked the length of the room with short, choppy steps. "So I'm out for a while," she snapped, slicing the air with her hand. If she didn't remain angry, she knew she would break down in tears. Seriously considering this job meant she accepted the idea that her career was over, and she couldn't do that just yet. She didn't know how she would react if it turned out she couldn't dance again. "I'll do what the doctor says, and in six months, I'll go back to see him. I have some savings put by, so I'll be fine until then," she lied.

Harry shook his head. "That won't work, Charlie, and we both know it. It's only been a few days and you're already going crazy around here. In six months you'd be certifiably insane. Your best bet is to drive up to Santa Barbara and talk to the people up there. There should be no problem with your getting the job because of your background. I even bet you'll enjoy the place, and it's not as if you'll be marooned in the sticks. Ninety percent of the residents there are retired show people, and they feel more comfortable around people who understand their little quirks."

"Quirks? Is that the same as kinky?" She still didn't feel good about this so-called fantastic job. Harry had once waxed enthusiastic over a job for her that turned out to be a role as a dancing ear of corn in a frozen-food commercial. She hadn't trusted him since.

Harry shot her a look filled with exasperation. "You, of all people, should know that people in our business aren't your ordinary, everyday citizens," he said flatly, looking around at the decrepit couch and an easy chair decorated with a silk Spanish shawl edged with long black fringe. His eyes swept over Charlie's pale coral strapless terry jumpsuit that bared her beautiful legs and shoulders. Today she had let her slightly curly hair dry on its own, and instead of shoes, she wore a gold toe ring as a touch of whimsy.

"Harry, I can't work as some kind of glorified baby-sitter for senior citizens," she protested.

"Tell me something . . . How do you expect to pay the rent if you're out of work for more than six months? What if the doctor can't give you his final diagnosis for more than a year? Is that when you're going to decide it's time to figure out what to do with your life? And what if his decision is against dancing for good?" he demanded. Then he added more softly, "Charlie, the word is out that you probably won't be returning to work."

When distressed, her eyes turned gray, and now they were the darkest he had ever seen them.

"A washed-up has-been—is that what you're saying? Wonderful. I'm pronounced dead before the body is even cold."

He pulled at his bow tie that never seemed straight. Even after all these years, he couldn't tie one properly and refused to wear a clip-on. "You've got an excellent chance at this director's job, Charlie. You know I wouldn't suggest you unless I thought you could do it. If you gave yourself a chance, I think you'd even enjoy it." Now he was pleading with her. She had always been his favorite client, though he never tried to show favoritism. But there was something about this woman who was always so filled with energy and light that he couldn't help seeing her as someone very special.

Charlie had made a lot of mistakes in her life and was

as stubborn as hell, but she knew when to back down. At the same time, she knew when to inject a bit of hope. "But then I'd be letting *them* down if the doctor says I can return to my dancing." By now she strongly sensed her dancing days were over, but she still couldn't give up hope, just in case.

Harry sighed. He sincerely doubted that would happen. She had always worked harder than most dancers. Still, he couldn't dash her hopes completely. "If you get the doctor's go-ahead, I'll find you something so quick you'll wish you'd had a longer vacation." He forced himself to look her in the eye. He wanted her to be happy no matter which direction her career took her. He only hoped she was open-minded enough to accept what happened.

Charlie walked slowly around the living room, touching each item of furniture. Harry was right. She didn't have as much money in her savings as she had implied. Then, too, pet food and parrot mix wasn't cheap, and she had to take Donnie to the vet's for a checkup next week. Perhaps if she took this job, made sure to take good care of her knee, and resumed her dance classes as soon as she received the okay, she might be able to return to her dancing in six months or so. It just seemed so long! She cursed herself for that fall. Of course, it wasn't the first and certainly wouldn't be the last. If she hadn't worked herself so hard and been more tired than usual during rehearsal, she wouldn't be where she was now.

"Who do I call?" She sounded resigned to her fate.

"Would you like me to set up the appointment for you?" he asked, sensing her pain. Poor Charlie, all she ever wanted to do was dance, and it looked like it was being taken away from her before her time. True, dancers didn't have long lives in their careers, but hers didn't have to end so traumatically.

She shook her head. "No, thank you, anyway. This is something I guess I should do myself."

Harry reached inside his jacket pocket and withdrew a small address book. Taking a pen and notepad out of another pocket, he wrote down the pertinent information. "The administrator is out of town this week. He was only referred to as James, so I'm afraid I don't have his full name for you," he explained. "Anyway, speak to Mrs. Finch, the secretary, and she'll set up a time." He handed her the slip of paper and reached out to awkwardly pat her shoulder. "You let me know how it turns out," he insisted gently.

She nodded and conjured up a reassuring smile. "I'll call, Harry. I promise."

He left, feeling more helpless than he had in a long time. While Charlie had great talent, she didn't have that special spark to make her a star, but she did have the stamina and love for her craft to keep her in steady work over the past few years. He just prayed she could adjust to her new way of life.

When she was alone again, Charlie wandered out to the kitchen to get something to drink. A director of activities for a retirement home? The idea didn't appeal to her.

What was she supposed to do? Plan shuffleboard and croquet tournaments? Make sure the badminton set was in excellent condition? She was sure she'd go crazy within a month, but it was a job, not too demanding, and Harry said the pay was good. Besides, she did promise Harry she would call for an appointment. It certainly wouldn't hurt to find out more about it, would it? If it wasn't something she'd like, she'd bow out gracefully and breathe a sigh of relief. Then, if necessary, she'd find some kind of work to keep her in L.A.

Four days later, Charlie drove to Santa Barbara to meet with the board of directors of New Eden.

Meeting the seven board members made her feel like Alice stepping through the looking glass. They didn't care that she had no experience as an activities director. They questioned her about the shows she'd been in, and other work she'd done, and discussed the differences between show business in the thirties and the eighties. None actually told her how they had been connected with that magical world, but they certainly knew what they were talking about.

"You certainly have the legs to be a dancer," Maude Springtime, a woman in her late sixties with bright red hair, informed her.

"More like having the stamina." Charlie tried to smile.

"It's a shame an injury had to take you out of the business when you're still young," Lena Summers, a silver-haired woman with traces of her earlier beauty in her eyes and face, said in a melodic voice. "But that is in your favor, too, because you're young enough to look into another career."

Jason Craig, dressed in expensive black slacks and a cream-colored silk shirt, fiddled with a deck of cards as he asked Charlie several questions. She wondered if he had been a card dealer, judging from the way he fanned the cards out and expertly shuffled them.

"It's not being young; it's having the brains and

24

know-how in order to make it in this world," a whip-cord-thin bald man Charlie remembered as being introduced as Sylvester brought up in a voice that could easily grate on one's nerves. "Hollywood is probably just as bad now as it was when I worked there."

"Oh? What did you do?" Charlie asked politely.

Piercing dark eyes gazed at her haughtily. "I was *the* best hairdresser those idiotic studios ever had," he announced with what had to be his usual arrogance. His gaze swept over her hair and face with that same arrogance. "If I were you, I'd *shoot* the person who butchered your hair."

Charlie was stunned. These were the kind of people she'd be working with? If she had an ounce of brains, she'd stand up, apologize for taking up their time, and run like hell.

But before she could do anything of the kind, Jason and Lena, obviously the leaders of the group, told her she had the job if she wanted it and quoted a high salary that sent shock waves through her system. Before she could question her sanity, Charlie accepted the job and agreed to report for work the following week, when the administrator would be back from his business trip.

"James is an easy man to work with, Charlie," Lena informed her. She waved the air with hands studded with diamond rings. "I'm sure the two of you will get along famously."

Charlie didn't feel as confident. She was sure the administrator had to be a no-nonsense man in order to run a community this size, and someone as easygoing as she was would probably end up as an eternal thorn in his side. Well, if he'd keep out of her way, she'd stay out of his, she decided. This job was too good to pass up, even knowing there were probably more like Sylvester, Felix, who she learned was a retired magician, and Maude, an ex-stripper—or exotic dancer, as the older woman stressed.

She would also have the use of a small bungalow, which on inspection was more than large enough to hold her animals. The board explained pets were more than welcome.

At the end of the day, Charlie drove back to Los Angeles, pleased with her good fortune and surprisingly looking forward to her move and new job. She could be stubborn, but she was no fool. She had to make arrangements for her future, and this job at New Eden just might be the stepping stone to a new career.

When she reached her home, she called Harry and told him of her plans. He was happy for her and promised to visit her when he drove up to see his aunt. After that call, Charlie honestly couldn't think of anyone else to contact who would truly care about what happened to her. The one person she had considered a close friend, who had also been a special lover, wasn't there anymore. But she reminded herself that that had happened nine years ago, and she couldn't reflect on the past when there was a brand-new life waiting for her. She only hoped she wouldn't screw this one up.

That evening, New Eden's board of directors was getting together for their bridge game, which they held several times a week.

"I just know Charlie will be a wonderful director of activities," Lena commented. "She seems to have so much energy and vitality."

"And pretty, too," Jason spoke up, studying the cards he held in his hand.

"Do you think James will like her?" Ramona asked in her soft voice.

The others seemed to display the same sly smile at the idea of their administrative director meeting the lively young woman.

"Too bad she isn't a bit flashier in her dress and manner," Maude remarked. "James can be a bit stuffy at times. He needs someone to liven him up. Oh, I'm not complaining. If I thought I had a chance with that hunk, I'd be after him in a second."

"You're talking about fixing him up after that last fiasco of ours?" Sylvester jeered. "Don't you remember how long he yelled at you after he fired Velma?"

"We had no idea she escaped from that sanitarium," Lena defended the group. "She seemed perfectly normal whenever we were around her."

"Well, there was that circus performer who worked in the health club," Ian brought up. "It took the police six months to track her down with the eighty thousand dollars worth of jewelry she stole from the residents. James wasn't too happy about that episode."

"I just think we should lay off the matchmaking and let him make up his own mind," Sylvester said haughtily, getting up to pour himself another glass of wine. "After all, she might not even be his type."

"That's true." Lena sighed. "But we can always dream, can't we? And if it looks like they're the right couple, we'll just add a few incentives if it appears they need a little push." She smiled brightly. "Does that sound fair?"

There was still a little grumbling about the idea of

matchmaking after the last three disasters they'd suffered during their search for the proper partner for their administrative director. In the end, they agreed to keep an eye on Charlie and James. If it looked as though they were interested in each other and needed a gentle push now and then, the residents would be around to do just that. After all, Charlie would be the sixth woman they were setting up with James. One of them had to work out!

CHAPTER TWO

James Patrick Murphy, New Eden's administrative director, had returned from a tiring trip only to learn the board had hired a new director of activities without his knowledge or approval. He also noticed they were all conveniently out of touch when he was given the news by his secretary, Hazel Finch.

He sighed as he looked at the manila folder lying on his desk. He wasn't too eager to look over this woman's background because he sincerely doubted she was right for the job and it would be up to him to get rid of her. Oh, well, he'd played the part of the villain enough in the past. In fact, knowing the board as well as he did, he'd bet everything he owned this was another one of their matchmaking schemes. Why couldn't they just leave well enough alone?

A smile curved his well-shaped lips. He knew why they didn't. Lena had once told him she wanted to see him as happy as she and Jason were. What better way to ensure that than to find a lovely woman for him?

He leaned back in his chair and clasped his hands behind his head. At thirty-five he was in his prime and aware of it without being conceited. Regular workouts kept his body in shape, and playing tennis a couple of times a week gave him a tan no tanning salon could give him. His longish ebony hair, cobalt blue eyes that could freeze or burn a person in seconds, and craggy good looks got him enough acting jobs over the years to keep the creditors from the door. The trouble was, he was always cast as the bad guy and never the hero. The money may have been good, but getting killed in the last act all the time got a little tiresome after a while. He had always hoped he would land a meatier role.

When the realization came five years ago that he couldn't get any farther in his career, he decided it was time to get out of the business while he still had his sanity. A friend had told him about a job opening as assistant administrative director at a community for retired show people. Murphy hadn't wasted any time interviewing for the job. Though he had had serious doubts they would hire him since he had no experience, he soon learned all they were looking for was someone who could work with the director and got along well with people, especially senior citizens. Murphy passed the interview with flying colors. When the director died of a heart attack three years ago, Murphy was promoted to the position.

Coming out of his reverie, he looked down at the folder on his desk. He may as well look at the application form, he decided. Murphy opened the folder, looked down at the form, and noticed a distinctive handwriting that tugged at his memory . . . and his heart.

Charlie. Was this some kind of joke? he wondered. Were there so few jobs between shows that she had to travel this far? No, that couldn't be it. This kind of work wasn't her style. If anyone should know that, he should.

He had met her under unusual circumstances nine years ago and had probably begun falling in love with her from that first meeting. They had lived together for six months, and their loving had been passionate and terrific. There had been only one flaw in their affair: Charlie's obsession with her dancing mixed with Murphy's doubts about his own career. He hadn't talked his fears over with her because he didn't think she would understand. Charlie loved her own career and never doubted her choice. Maybe they should have talked some of the times they had made love, he thought; the ending might not have been so painful. He knew she had loved him back then, but obviously it hadn't been enough. Charlie had abruptly walked out of his life when she got a part in a traveling musical. He had been so hurt he had vowed she wouldn't have a chance to hurt him again. In fact, perhaps she wouldn't stay long after she realized just how time-consuming the job was.

He was still wondering why she had looked for work at New Eden and decided there was only one way to find out the truth. He picked up the phone and dialed a number. The way gossip ran around L.A., Murphy knew it wouldn't take long to find out.

Charlie stopped at the guard shack at the entrance of the New Eden Retirement Community. She received words of welcome from the elderly man dressed in a gray twill uniform, then drove slowly up the winding road that passed a golf course. During her drive, she could see people in golf carts as well as golfers who

31

preferred to walk the lush grassy course. At the top of a gentle hill, she noticed the wire fencing and lights denoting tennis courts. A sense of relaxation seemed to pervade the air around her. Sensing something new was happening, Huggie Bear leaned over the seat and nuzzled her ear.

"Soon, boy," she promised, turning onto what was little more than a paved lane that led to a one-story house. It was smaller than her other house, but it was also in much better condition. She'd just bet the heater worked on cue during the winter, and she even had an air conditioner. She parked her Honda station wagon in front of the bungalow that was to be her new home and slid out from under the steering wheel, stretching her arms over her head to ease the stiffness from her long drive. She let Huggie Bear out and watched him sniff around the front of the tiny house while she inspected the flower-filled border that brightened up the pale blue house.

"Hello."

Charlie spun around to see Ramona, one of the women on the board, walking toward her. "Hello," she returned warmly, frowning when Huggie Bear bounded up to the woman. "I hope dogs don't bother you." She knew big dogs sometimes frightened people, even though Huggie Bear was gentle for such a large dog.

Ramona smiled and held her hand out to Huggie Bear, who sniffed it and licked her palm after deciding he had found a new friend. "No, I love animals," she said in her soft voice. "I thought I'd come over to see if you need any help."

Charlie grinned. "That's very nice of you to offer, but I think I can handle everything."

"I also came by to tell you that James would like to see you as soon as you've settled in," she told her. "He was sorry he wasn't here to meet you last week."

"I'll just let the animals out, and I can walk over to the offices then." Charlie opened the back door and pulled out a carrying cage filled with a frazzled parrot who kept rasping, "Hello, Donnie. Hello."

Ramona reached out to clasp the handle so Charlie could pick up the cage holding an irate cat. With a few soft words, the older woman soothed the parrot's ruffled feelings and did the same with Snickers.

"It usually takes them hours to calm down after a long drive," Charlie marveled at her ease in calming them.

Ramona led the way into the house. "I have a way with animals," she said simply, setting the cage on the floor and opening it. Donnie stepped out cautiously, shook out her feathers, and allowed Ramona to pick her up. Their conversation was unintelligible to Charlie but must have been clear to bird and older woman. "I'll take care of everything here if you'd like to go up now."

Charlie glanced around. It was true she wanted to get her interview with James over with, but she wasn't going to ask Ramona how she knew that. Charlie was sure she would just see her inscrutable smile again.

"I'll just freshen up so I can make a good first impression on my new boss," she decided, gathering up her purse and heading for the bathroom. After a new application of makeup, she'd feel more like her old self. Her jeans and pale pink cotton oxford shirt under a pink and khaki plaid sweater vest didn't look too wrinkled, but she wondered if she should put on a more businesslike outfit.

"You look beautiful." Ramona appeared in the doorway. "Besides, James doesn't worry about what a person looks like on the outside—only what they are on the inside."

Charlie hoped the older woman was right because she didn't feel like rummaging through her suitcases to find something else to wear. If the man insisted on seeing her after her long drive, he would just have to settle for the mussed look.

"You have very lovely eyes," Ramona complimented her, watching Charlie place her hairbrush on the bathroom counter.

"Thank you." She smiled, guessing the woman wanted to become friends. "How long have you been at New Eden?"

"Two years," she replied. "I came here after my sister passed away." She made an effort to smile. "I mustn't keep you from seeing James. If you'd like, I'll fill some pans with water for your animals," she offered, adding, "I won't mind at all."

"Thank you. That would be very nice," Charlie said sincerely, wanting to get her meeting over with so she could come back and collapse. "I'll see you later, then." She dashed out of the bungalow and headed up the path. She made her way to the main buildings that housed the offices, a large recreation center, an indoor pool, and a health club. Even before meeting the board members, she had learned from Harry that the residents of the community were all financially well off. It didn't take her long to reach the administrator's office, where she found Mrs. Finch, a tiny sprite of a woman who was named appropriately.

"Ah, Ms. Wells . . ." The woman even seemed to

34

chirp when she spoke. She pressed an intercom button. "James, Ms. Wells is here." She nodded when she heard an unintelligible reply. "Go right in, my dear."

Charlie smiled and walked over to the door, knocking softly and stepping inside. She faced a large desk piled with papers and the back of a dark brown leather chair. The chair swiveled around and a dark-haired man with bedroom blue eyes and incredibly sexy features met her shocked gaze.

"Hiya, Legs." His husky, intimate voice matched the searing intensity of his eyes.

"Oh my God," she mumbled, hanging on to the doorknob in case her knees decided to give out on her. No, it had to be a hallucination after her long day. That was it—a fabrication of a tired mind. She closed her eyes and opened them. Nope, he was still there.

"Sit down, Charlie, before you fall down," he suggested with the barest hint of a smile on his lips.

Somehow she managed to make it to a nearby chair without falling flat on her face. After all those years of dance lessons, she couldn't even walk gracefully. "Why . . ." she croaked. She paused, licked her lips, and began again. "Why do I feel as if I've been set up?"

"I don't know. Why do you?" He had always irritated her by answering her questions with another question.

"Dammit, Murphy, why did you let me come up here to be humiliated?" Charlie demanded angrily, gripping the chair arms.

"Is that what I'm doing?" James Patrick Murphy was trying very hard not to laugh. Charlie hadn't changed one bit; he could still goad her with a minimum of words. And she never looked more beautiful than when her eyes were flashing and her face was flushed with temper. "I don't recall saying anything that would humiliate you."

She shot him a scathing look. "All right, you've had your joke. Now, if you don't mind, I have to repack a few animals and drive back to Los Angeles, where I'm going to kill my agent by chopping him up into little pieces. Then I'll bake him in a cake and send it to you!"

Murphy shook his head. "This is no joke, love. The board hired you as director of activities, I signed the paperwork, and you'll find your name painted on a door and a nameplate sitting on a desk two doors down the hall. In other words, you're hired. Usually I'm not too pleased when the board does the hiring because they invariably screw things up, but this was their absolute best."

Charlie took a deep breath. It had been more years than she cared to count since she had seen Murphy. Correction, it had only been five since she had *seen* him, and that was at a party attended by at least fifty people. He had been with a redhead who looked as if her bust size exceeded her I.Q., but he never really had to bother talking with a woman, had he? Deep down, she knew she wasn't being fair. She and Murphy had certainly talked a lot when they lived together. But it was his lovemaking she remembered the most, and she didn't dare recall it now if she was going to keep calm. "I don't think working here would be a good idea," she said finally.

"Scared?"

His low-voiced taunt sent strange tingles down her spine. He knew very well she never backed down from a challenge. Wasn't she the one to climb in and swim

36

around that fountain in the park? Wasn't she the one who used her acting ability to talk the police officer out of giving her a speeding ticket?

"That isn't it at all." She was better off giving him a taste of very cold medicine. Over the years, he had been in the back of her mind, and there were many times when she missed him dearly, but she knew she couldn't expect him to welcome her with open arms after the horrible way she had left him. "I just don't believe in dredging up dead relationships."

"Good, neither do I."

Charlie ground her teeth in agitation. Yet she also felt relief. At least he wasn't looking to resume something that had ended a long time ago. She had ended their relationship, and to this day, she felt she had done the right thing. Men and her career just didn't mix. She had decided from the time she was ten her dancing mattered more than anything else in the world, and she never regretted her decision.

"Judging from your résumé, I'd say you've been a very busy lady over the years," Murphy commented, leaning back in his chair and looking much too relaxed. "You should be proud of yourself."

"I am." She raised her chin defiantly.

His eyes softened. "I'm sorry about your knee giving out on you."

Charlie shrugged, unable to reveal how deeply she hurt. She didn't question where he learned about her injury. She knew he probably made a few calls the moment he found out she was coming up here. "It's just one of those things."

"Did you leave anyone special behind in L.A.?" Murphy's question was altogether too casual, but his gaze was sharp with curiosity. "Because I'm afraid you won't be able to have the kind of active social life here you were used to in L.A."

"No one important. You know me."

"Yes, I do. You forget how well I know you. I wonder if you shouldn't have been the one to write the song on fifty ways to leave your lover."

Her face reddened. "Our parting was very civilized, Murphy. You certainly didn't seem too broken up the times we ran into each other after we parted."

"I'm a man, Charlie, not a fool," he reminded her unnecessarily. "But I didn't ask you in here to rehash an old affair. I thought if you weren't too tired from your drive, I'd give you a guided tour of the place and introduce you to the rest of the staff. Of course, you're not expected to start until Monday, but it might help if you were more familiar with the area before you started work."

"Yes, that sounds good," Charlie agreed, standing up and watching Murphy do likewise. She hadn't remembered how tall he was. Did men over thirty still grow? Perhaps he just looked taller because she was wearing loafers instead of heels. Sure, and maybe she could land the lead in the next hot musical on Broadway.

Murphy smiled and shook his head. "Ah, Charlie, still the master of the understatement." He walked around the desk. "Shall we go?"

Charlie's eyes swept over his deep teal crewneck with a white shirt collar peeking out and his neatly creased jeans. "Do all retirement community administrators dress so informally? I thought their uniform of the day would be a dark three-piece suit with a white shirt and rep tie."

38

"The first thing I was told when I was hired was that the day I wore a tie in here was the day my tie would be cut off." He gestured toward the door. "As you can tell by meeting the board, the residents here aren't your average senior citizens. Jason can still wield a mean golf club, and I've refused to play tennis with Lena ever since my third defeat. Maude and Ian swim laps every day, and Sylvester walks two miles every morning."

"What about Ramona?" she asked.

His eyes took on a soft, dreamy look. "Ramona, yes, she's very special. She has a garden and keeps busy tending it. As for Felix, I think he'd be happy if he could just saw ladies in half all day." He opened the door and ushered Charlie outside. Mrs. Finch looked up at her boss with open adoration. "Hazel, I'm going to show Charlie around and doubt I'll be available for calls for a couple hours. Can you hold down the fort for me?"

"Of course, James."

Charlie arched an eyebrow. "Do you command such strong adulation from all your staff?" she asked as they walked down the hallway.

He winked. "Only the pretty ones. Hazel has a soft spot for me because I resemble one of her grandsons." He took her arm and led her through floor-to-ceiling swinging doors. "Our fitness center." He indicated modern equipment including Nautilus machines. "It's open to anyone who cares to use it. Thad and Karen are in charge here and are the most healthy couple on our staff." He motioned them over and introduced Charlie.

Thad was a muscular man in his late forties or early fifties. He was wearing a tank top and nylon athletic shorts. Karen, who could have been his twin, looked cheerful and professional in bright pink shorts and a matching top.

"I hope you'll organize an exercise class for our more energetic ladies," Karen said with a bright smile. "They've missed the ones we used to have."

Charlie showed surprise and mentioned that she thought Karen would have the perfect qualifications for such a job. The woman shook her head.

"No patience for teaching a class," she told Charlie wryly. "I'm fine working out in here and helping the ladies with their circuit program, but I hate all these aerobics and jazz exercises, although many of the women here enjoy them. Our other director led two classes each day."

Charlie wasn't sure if her knee could handle that kind of strain, but she vowed to see what she could do.

"Don't let Karen push you into anything you can't do," Murphy advised her as they left the fitness center and walked the perimeter of the indoor pool with a bubbling spa nearby. "She's a friendly woman, but she tends to come on a bit strong at times."

"No one has ever pushed me into anything," Charlie replied.

"True," he murmured, gesturing with his hand that she should turn to the left.

Charlie had no complaints about Murphy's behavior. She was surprised to see him here. While the board members had called their administrator by his first name only, and Mrs. Finch had done the same, it never occurred to her that "James" would be the same man she had lived with nine years ago.

"This is a far cry from the film studios," she remarked after he showed her the medical center and in-

40

troduced her to the prune-faced Mrs. Page who ran it. "I can't believe that you gave up acting to run an old folk's home."

Murphy's head snapped up. "You repeat that phrase around here and they'll tar and feather you. And when they're through, I'll personally throw you out," he added sharply. "These people are far from old in mind or body. There are days when they have more energy than even you, and I know what a bundle of pep you can be. As for my acting career, I got smart and left the business before I was phased out. I got tired of playing the villain and ending up dead in the last scene of the movie of the week, so when this job came along I took it with a big sigh of relief."

"But you don't know anything about running a retirement community," she pointed out, unable to understand his new love.

"Maybe not, but I was quick to learn, and I have a degree in business administration, which makes me look more official to the more conservative residents. I also understand why these people don't live life the way people their age are expected to, and I accept their idiosyncrasies."

"Idiosyncrasies?" She shook her head, not understanding exactly what he was talking about.

Murphy grinned. "You'll find out soon enough. I wouldn't want to spoil your fun."

Charlie didn't see it that way. To her chagrin, he wasn't about to give her the slightest hint.

For the next hour and a half, Murphy led her through the various buildings and outdoor areas that made up New Eden, including the golf course and tennis courts. He explained to her that while all the bungalows had kitchenettes, a dining room was available to the residents who didn't care to cook their own meals.

During that time, Charlie's preconceived ideas about senior citizens turned around three hundred and sixty degrees. Admittedly, in the course of her lifetime, she hadn't met that many people over the age of sixty, and her memories of her grandparents were of two couples that were happier sitting around the house than getting out and doing things. She couldn't even imagine her grandmother trying to play tennis.

"Something tells me many of these people are in better shape than I am," she murmured, allowing Murphy to guide her back to the dining room for coffee. She had already met many of the residents, and they all looked so energetic to her. She felt as if she had been sheltered all her life and never realized age had nothing to do with fitness or vitality.

"Just don't play tennis with Lena," he advised with a chuckle. "Not unless you're into humiliation."

"What is it with this board?" She noticed the dining room was set up with tables for two, four, or six people with colorful tablecloths and flower centerpieces. She watched Murphy place two cups of coffee on a tray along with a plate of cinnamon rolls that looked good enough to be sinful. He directed her to a table in the corner and set out their snack.

"Lorraine, who's in charge of the baking, makes the rolls. I guarantee they're great," he told her, taking the chair across from her.

"And full of calories," Charlie added, sipping the hot brew. It was delicious, not at all like the murky stuff she made each day. It hadn't taken her long to discover that drinking plenty of coffee kept her appetite level down and her weight the same way. There were days she hated having to watch the scale so carefully, but a dancer's costume hid little. A tiny voice told her one roll was safe, but two would be murder to anyone's diet. She picked up a warm sticky roll and bit into it. Murphy was right. They were too good to be real. "Lorraine must have been a real find for you."

"That she was," he replied, also taking a roll. "She had owned a bakery and after a month of living here was baking like crazy. We asked her if she'd like to occasionally bake for the dining room, and now she comes in every day and whips up something different for dessert."

"The board . . ." she reminded him, taking another bite of her roll. "What do they have to do with this place?"

Murphy leaned back in his chair, an arm looped around the back edge. "Oh, yes, the infamous board. Actually, they're the founding members of New Eden. From what I understand, Lena and Jason had known each other in San Francisco, and Lena mentioned she wanted to find some place quiet to retire to. They both complained that there wasn't a true retirement community that suited them. A lot of their friends were in show business, and while there are homes for actors and such, it still wasn't what they were looking for. So they decided to build their own. They were the core of the group and they searched for others who would be interested. It wasn't difficult to find them. They set it up so that the initial cost to live here is pretty stiff, but that goes into a trust fund to cover staff salaries and such. There is also a monthly homeowner's fee to cover the grounds keeping and another fee for the use of the dining room. But it's all been figured out well enough so that no one goes broke living here."

"What about the staff? Do you have a large turnover?" she asked curiously. They were a distance from Santa Barbara, which made late nights out somewhat difficult unless the person cared to spend the night in town.

"Not really. Oh, there is a higher turnover in the medical center, but that's separate from the rest of us." He sipped his coffee.

"Why?"

Murphy frowned. "Because Winifred Page runs it."

Instead of using a napkin, Charlie licked her sticky fingers, unaware Murphy watched every move she made. "Something tells me you don't like the lady." She had to admit she hadn't been very impressed when she met the woman earlier.

"Something tells me you're right. She's a bitch, pure and simple."

"Then, why keep her?" Charlie asked, taking another roll.

"Because she has an excellent background in running nursing homes." Murphy sighed. "I don't like the woman personally, but I can't fault her qualifications, and nursing home administrators are hard to find. As long as she does her job, I have no complaints. I just wish she had more of a heart." He watched Charlie with an unnerving stare. "But that isn't something you would understand, is it?"

She blinked at his abrupt question. "Would you care to elaborate on that?"

"Someone having a heart?"

Charlie stiffened. "Why don't you come right out

with it, Murphy," she said tersely. "You're still bitter over what happened nine years ago, aren't you? I don't understand why. It wasn't as if we were having the love affair of the century. We met, we made love, we lived together for six months in order to pool our money, which was practically nonexistent. I worked in two shows that barely lasted the first night, and you were told you'd make better money if you would star in porno films." She held up her hand to stop him from interrupting. "I'm not saying you should have made them, because the idea repulsed me just as much as it did you, and I understand why the man who suggested it ended up with a black eye and two broken caps after your so-called discussion. But I'm stating the facts. I got a chance to travel in that musical, and you landed a small part in a daytime soap. Wasn't it better to part the way we did? That way, there was no harm done." She smiled brightly. But even as she spoke the words, something gnawed at her. There had been much more to their relationship than her flippancy indicated. It had meant a great deal to her, but she hadn't let him know that when it counted. Now it was probably too late.

Murphy wrapped his hand around his coffee cup so he wouldn't wrap it around Charlie's neck. Didn't she have any feelings at all? How could she so callously dismiss what they had shared? Well, he vowed, he was going to break down her indifference and never let her resurrect it. No matter what, he was going to show her that emotions were much more important and lasting than any dancing career, even if he had to hit her over her very hard head to do it! But since the odds of her return to dancing were slim, he knew he wouldn't have much trouble getting through to her. After all, he still knew what buttons to push. At the same time, he was going to have to be very careful that she didn't weave her spell around him. He was not going to let her hurt him ever again.

"I better get back to my office." He stood up, deciding he would be better off away from her before he did something disastrous like pulling her into his arms and kissing her senseless.

Charlie looked up, surprised by his sudden change. At first she thought it was because of the topic of their conversation, but she dismissed that right away. After all, their affair ended a long time ago, and there should be no hard feelings left after so much time.

"And I should probably check on the animals," she said, also standing up. "Ramona offered to look after them, but it isn't fair to leave them with her for the rest of the afternoon."

The expression in his eyes softened. "She's a wonderful person and will do anything for her friends. If she's talked more than three words to you, consider yourself adopted into her family."

"She's very nice." Charlie wished he'd look at her that way. "Thank you for giving me a few days to settle in. I have a lot of unpacking to do."

"If most of your money still goes toward your wardrobe and the other bits of junk you buy, you'll need more than a couple days," Murphy teased, back to his old self. In fact, there was a strange light in his eyes that, if construed the right way, could certainly raise her blood pressure!

Charlie wrinkled her nose, an action Murphy remembered well. "I'll have you know I don't spend a fraction on clothes that I used to," she informed him haughtily, then added with a note of triumph, "Not after I had fun discovering the garment district and garage sales."

Murphy laughed loudly. "That's Charlie—always looking for loopholes."

She shot him a suspicious look, unsure what he meant, but she decided to let the remark pass. She was positive there would be more in the months to come. As they walked back to the main offices, she became more aware of the man by her side. It was already obvious that everyone here respected him. The men stopped him to trade a few words or a joke; the women looked at him as if he were the best thing they'd seen since Geritol. And now she was beginning to see him in that same light.

She remembered the man she had first met nine years ago when she was still a novice in the profession. It was Murphy who helped her keep her sanity when she went to more auditions than she could count and none of them panned out. And it was Murphy who—She looked up, realizing they had passed his office.

"Where—" Her question was cut off when he grabbed her hand and pulled her through the next door and closed it after them.

"I thought I'd give you a tour of your office," he stated in a soft, silky voice.

Charlie nodded dumbly. So she wasn't imagining some of those heated signals at the table when Murphy's voice was cool but his expression belonged in the tropics. "Very nice," she finally managed to say. She noticed it had all the standard equipment—a desk, two chairs, a file cabinet, and a lovely painting on one wall.

"What would you think about putting a couch over there?" Murphy gestured toward one empty wall.

hy?"

"In case you care to rest," he suggested, leaning over her until she felt her shoulder blades pressed against the cool wood of the door. "It could come in very handy at times."

"I . . ." She licked suddenly dry lips. Oh, God, he still wore that incredibly sexy after-shave that smelled like a rain forest. If she didn't come up for some fresh air soon, she was certain to fall under his spell.

"Are the memories coming back to you, Legs?" he whispered, keeping his hands on her shoulders in an unbreakable hold. "What do you remember most? The way we met? Or how about when we first made love? It was your first time and you couldn't stop crying because you told me I made it so beautiful for you. Remember?" His breath was fragrant with coffee and cinnamon as it wafted over her.

She moaned softly, not wanting to remember those particular moments of her life. "Stop it, Murphy." Her voice was too breathless to make any impact.

He smiled, one that spelled danger and something else. "Let me give you something to complain about first," he murmured, dipping his head to hers. His lips touched hers as lightly as a spring breeze, and Charlie was powerless to halt him as the tip of his tongue traced the outline of her mouth. "I always did like it better when you didn't wear lipstick," he said. "You have your own very special taste." His tongue teased the corners of her lips, and then he slid the slightly rough tip over her lips.

Charlie clenched her hands at her sides to keep them from lifting and encircling Murphy's neck. He knew she had a sensual nature, and he knew too well how to bring it out.

"You're being unfair, Murphy." She drew in much needed air but by doing so allowed his tongue entrance into her mouth. She almost slid down the length of the door as his tongue thrust leisurely into the sweet caverns and explored every inch as if he had all the time in the world. Indeed, if he continued much longer, she would probably give him more than he bargained for!

He merely chuckled and moved closer until their bodies brushed sweetly against each other. One hand rose and found its way under the hem of her sweater, halted at the obstruction of her shirt, and soon dispensed with it by unfastening several buttons. Very knowledgeable five fingers were now stroking bare flesh under the lace edge of her bra.

Soft sounds escaped Charlie's lips. Her eyes drifted closed, and she floated on the sensation of his mouth making love to hers and his hand cupping her breast and his thumb rubbing seductively over her tight nipple. Surrendering to her needs, she linked her arms around his waist, sliding her hands under the waistband of his jeans and finding the soft cotton of his briefs and, beneath those, skin that tensed under her touch.

If anyone had stumbled in on them, they would have known the couple were once lovers by the sound of their intimate murmurs and the way each one's hands glided expertly over the other's body.

"Keep touching me, Charlie," he ordered huskily, trailing moist kisses from her parted lips to her ear and behind to the sensitive spot he recalled gave her such pleasure. Her whimpers told him he had remembered correctly.

Charlie tipped her head to one side to allow him access to her neck. His touch was a soothing balm to the end of a frazzled day, yet displayed a searing heat that identified with her own earthy nature. She opened her mouth over the rough triangle of skin displayed above the sweater neckline and rubbed it gently with her tongue, savoring the salt and taste that was all his. She could feel the ache beginning with the warm blanket of his hand kneading her breast and streaming down to the center of her femininity.

Long moments passed as they both fell into a world of swirling mists. Groaning, Murphy reached down to cup the front of her jeans and rotate his palm. When that wasn't enough, he lifted her against his pelvis and rocked his rigid proof of arousal insistently against her. She could only moan in response to the heat searing the soft denim, seeking out her femininity.

"I want to make love to you, Charlie," he said thickly. "I want to find out if you're still as velvety soft and welcoming when I'm inside you. I want to hear you crying out my name when you climax. I want to spend the day in—hell, I want to spend the next week in bed with you." A tiny, saner part of his brain tried to remind him that with the pleasure eventually came the pain. Well, he'd think about that later.

Charlie inhaled sharply at the images racing through her mind. Did he realize how tempting he was making it? No matter what problems she and Murphy had had in the past, making love was never on the list. But if she was to work here, she knew she couldn't give in to him.

"No," she sobbed, shaking her head. "It's too late, Murphy. We can't go back the way we were. You said as

50

much yourself. Too many years have passed, and we're not the same people anymore."

He lifted his head. "That's true. We aren't the same people, but that doesn't mean we can act as if what we shared in the past never happened." His voice was still ragged with desire. "This is much too fast. You've only just arrived, and I already want to throw you into bed." He slowly withdrew his hand from her breast and awkwardly patted her sweater into place. He concentrated on plastering a casual smile on his face, not an easy task with a raging inferno still burning inside him. "I guess it's because I haven't dated lately, and you know how I get if I don't get my daily ration of sex." Then he had the audacity to wink at her. If she only knew he had to do that or pull her back into his arms again. He hadn't realized until now that his feelings for her were still strong. That frightened him.

Charlie's eyes widened. "You—you . . ." She found herself at a loss for words. Any name she could think of calling him wasn't horrible enough. In desperation, she finally struck out and punched him in the stomach—hard.

"Oomph!" Murphy's face turned a bright red as he doubled over, cradling his abdomen. He never knew she could hit that hard.

"You listen to me, you pervert," she warned, sliding away from the door and keeping her distance, "if you ever touch me again, I'll hit you even harder. And next time, I might not be so polite about *where* I hit you!"

Murphy winced, at her punishment and at her promise of what could happen, because he knew she never backed down from a threat. "You're a bloodthirsty woman, Charlotte Wells."

"Buddy, you ain't seen nothing yet," she raged, pulling the door open and storming out. She made sure the door slammed loudly behind her.

CHAPTER THREE

Charlie's temper hadn't cooled very much by the time she reached her bungalow. But then, she doubted a ten-minute walk was long enough to take care of the anger brewing inside her, thanks to James Patrick Murphy. She could kill him! She wanted to do worse—as soon as she thought of something horrible enough.

So he hadn't had his daily ration of sex lately, had he? she fumed, slamming around the living room. Well, if he thought she was willing to contribute to the cause, he had another thing coming! She didn't want to think about the frustration she sensed in his kiss. A frustration that wasn't just because he hadn't been with a woman for a while, but something more complex. Right then and there, Charlie decided Murphy would have been happier managing a hotel for women than a senior citizens' residential community.

With a strength born from anger, she carried heavy boxes from her car into the bungalow and rummaged for cans of dog food and the box that held packets of cat food along with parrot mix. After feedings her animals, she unpacked the boxes holding her kitchen utensils. She had been told that major and minor kitchen appliances were provided, so she only needed to worry about personal items. Everything else she had put in storage until she could decide what to do with them.

When the kitchen was in order, Charlie decided to work in the living room and bedroom. By the time she finished, it was late evening, and she was more than ready for bed. Except ready for bed and getting to sleep were two different things. Especially when memories of Murphy's kiss and the feel of his body against hers were overtaking any need for sleep.

In desperation Charlie rolled over, punched her pillow as if it were Murphy's face, and finally settled down to sleep with a snoring Huggie Bear ensconced at her feet and Snickers fighting her for the pillow. She thanked Donnie for having the brains to prefer her cage to sharing a bed with her mistress. She decided to take the weekend to look over the area and prepare herself for her first day of work. And then, watch out James Patrick Murphy! Charlie Wells hadn't let a man get the best of her yet.

The trouble was, the past had a way of creeping up and hitting her over the head. After all, how could she forget the first man to make love to her, the man she probably would have fallen in love with if she had given him and herself a chance? But she had been too caught up in her dancing. Yet, she had loved him back then, in her own way. Funny how she could remember that after so many years. And for some reason, it sort of hurt.

Her first workday, Charlie mused as she sipped a cup of coffee, the extent of her breakfast. She smiled as she looked down at her outfit, a red silky knit V-necked sweater with its sleeves pushed up to her elbows, a black leather short skirt, black sheer hose, and black pumps.

Her one vanity was her long, shapely legs, and she admitted to enjoying showing them off, although she knew she was overdoing it a bit this time. She doubted this was the proper attire for a director of activities of a retirement community, but it was one of her favorites and it would be interesting to see if the administrator would say anything about it. She finger-combed her hair into loose curls, then made sure that Huggie Bear was secure in the small fenced-in backyard and that Snickers wasn't left in the house in case he decided to claw the furniture when he got bored.

"Go bye-bye?" Donnie rasped, pacing back and forth on her perch, her yellow head with the blue fringe just above her eyes fuzzed upward in excitement. "We go bye-bye?" She looked hopeful that Charlie would agree with her. She loved nothing more than to go for a walk.

"Not this time, sweetheart," Charlie told her, offering her a spoon coated with peanut butter, one of her favorite treats. "But I'll see if I can set up a perch in my office for you. I don't think my boss would argue too much." She remembered that Murphy had adored the ladylike parrot and used to spoil her with her favorite foods and walks outside. She was positive that by pointing out that a perch in her office was for Donnie's benefit and not hers, Murphy wouldn't refuse. She walked out of the bungalow and started up the road.

"Good morning," Lena greeted her with a warm smile. "Are you settling in all right?" The older woman carried a sport bag with a special side pocket for a tennis racket. Charlie couldn't help noticing that for a woman Lena's age her body was in excellent condition.

"How often do you play tennis?" Charlie asked as

they walked along. She remembered Murphy telling her how good the older woman was.

"Two or three times a week, although I'm afraid of ruining my skin being out in the sun so much," Lena replied. "Jason got me hooked on the game years ago. Now he complains since I beat him about fifty percent of the time."

"You have beautiful skin," Charlie said truthfully, again seeing her eternal beauty. It was easy for her to visualize a younger Lena as the belle of the ball, flirting lightly with men and never giving her full attention to just one. She wondered if she had ever married, although she was willing to bet that Lena and Jason were more than just tennis partners!

Lena smiled and inclined her head in reply to the compliment. "I'm of the old school that still uses honey and yogurt masks and plain old-fashioned cold cream at night."

Charlie's eyes widened. Lena's skin was that of a woman twenty years younger. "Are you willing to share your secret recipes with someone who's going to be thirty before she's really prepared to be? I'd hate to think I'd wake up one morning looking older than you."

Lena laughed. "My dear, I don't think you have anything to worry about." She stopped and looked Charlie over with a keen eye. "In fact, if we had met not all that many years ago, I would have found a much better position for you than dancing." Her eyes twinkled as if she knew a clever joke. "Ah, there's Jason. Good luck on your first day, Charlie. We all have faith in you." She walked swiftly toward the man waiting at the top of the hill.

Charlie lifted her hand in response to Jason's wave. "Have lunch with us one day!" he shouted.

She smiled and nodded her head. "I'd love to," she called back before finishing her journey to the office building. She found Mrs. Finch waiting for her with a cheerful greeting, an offer to fetch her a cup of coffee, and the ability to explain the contents of the file cabinet and Rolodex. Charlie adored her.

"James said if there's anything you need, to feel free to call on either one of us," Mrs. Finch explained, after bringing Charlie a cup of coffee and a small plate of cinnamon rolls.

The woman hadn't even glanced at Charlie's outfit, so she assumed that hers was nothing unusual.

Charlie spent the first couple of hours looking over the files and what the previous directors had done in the course of their jobs. Obviously the job entailed more than just organizing shuffleboard tournaments and keeping track of badminton equipment. There were parties to plan throughout the year for special events, dances, golf and tennis tournaments, and even a sports meet. The more she studied, the more she thought about running back to Los Angeles and calling up Harry to tell him he was out of his mind to tell her this job was perfect for her. So she could get a better idea of what to do, she sorted through the folders and kept out only those that pertained to that time of year. If the enclosed information told her anything, it was that the next few months were going to be very busy for her.

"You do get a lunch hour, you know." Murphy's amused voice drifted over her lowered head.

Charlie looked up and smiled brightly. "I don't eat lunch."

57

He shook his head. "Don't you know lunch is the most important meal of the day?"

"Isn't that supposed to be breakfast?"

"You don't eat breakfast either."

Another reminder of their times together. In the mornings, Charlie had raced from a warm bed to dress for dance class and then make the endless round of auditions. She claimed she couldn't afford the extra calories breakfast gave her and always promised to eat lunch. She never told Murphy that she rarely did. Somehow, though, he knew.

How long were they together? A little over six months? Then came the chance of a lifetime in a traveling musical. She had rushed back to the small place they shared to pack for the trip, blithely explaining to Murphy that their time together was wonderful, but she couldn't give up this chance. And, oh, by the way, would he take care of Snickers and Donnie for her while she was gone?

"In many ways you're a selfish bitch, Charlie," Murphy had bit out the words that afternoon. "It's a shame I love you because, personally, I feel I deserve better. Hopefully, by the time you return, I'll have found a woman who knows how to share herself with me. I'll take care of the animals only because it wouldn't be fair to board them out and you don't have any close friends to pawn them off on."

When she returned from her travels, the animals were in her house and a dull brass-colored key was placed on the kitchen counter. Except for brief run-ins at a few social gatherings, Charlie hadn't seen Murphy again.

"I guess I could have a cup of coffee," she decided, pushing the folders away and standing up. She didn't miss his eyes moving leisurely over her legs and brief skirt.

"Better not wear that around Walter," he advised, opening her door and ushering her outside.

"Who is Walter and what's wrong with him?"

Murphy grinned. "He's our resident lecher . . . very harmless. Actually he gives a few of the ladies a thrill with his innocently whispered propositions and roving hands. You have to watch out for him—he loves to pinch shapely bottoms." He held out his hand to guide her to the dining room. "Someone said he used to be a juggler in the circus."

"Sounds appropriate for someone with roving hands," Charlie said dryly. "How many residents have unusual occupations?"

"Just about all of them," he replied, glancing up at the printed menu above the cafeteria-style counter. "Um, pot roast. Barbara must have known I'd be in here today. She makes great pot roast. You should try it."

Charlie did, along with freshly baked ranch rolls and a green salad. She looked at the filled plate and groaned that she usually didn't eat that much in two days.

"You're much too thin as it is," Murphy criticized as they walked to a nearby table. During their progression, he stopped at tables, spoke to the occupants, and introduced them to Charlie.

All greeted her with genuine warmth, and she couldn't help noticing there was a special warmth where Murphy was concerned. It was as if he were a member of their family. Then she remembered he had no family and had grown up in a succession of foster homes after his mother abandoned him when he was only a few days old. Charlie wondered if part of the reason he enjoyed his job here was because it gave him a sense of belonging.

"You're very popular," she teased lightly as they seated themselves. "I just bet these dear ladies offer to darn your socks and insist you take your vitamins every morning."

A dark flush colored his cheekbones. "They're all very nice here, Charlie," he said gruffly, adding cream to his coffee. "Some of these people have no other family and take an interest in the staff if they let them. It doesn't hurt anyone, and the residents feel needed, which is very important for their well-being."

"Meaning if someone decides to adopt me, I'm to go along with it?"

Murphy's eyes hardened to dark blue chips. "Don't be a smart ass, Charlie. I can handle that mouth of yours, but you are never, *never* to hurt the feelings of any of the people here. As far as I'm concerned, that's perfect grounds for dismissal. Their mental as well as physical health is very important to all of us who work here."

Charlie was stunned by Murphy's verbal assault. Where was the good-natured, gentle man she had known?

"I'm not kidding, Charlie," he said in a low voice, leaning forward to give emphasis to his words.

"I cannot believe that you think I'd be that callous," she retorted. "I have feelings just like everyone else."

"It's not that you're intentionally callous. It's more that you usually only think of yourself."

"Don't be tactful. Go ahead and say what's on your mind!" she said, stung. Not wanting him to know exactly how much his words hurt her, she looked down at her fork, which was scoring lines in a neat square of pot roast.

Murphy exhaled a deep breath. "This is a different world for you, Charlie," he explained, speaking slowly. "You've been living in the 'think for yourself' world for so long I honestly don't know if you can handle a place where you have to think of others."

"Then why did you hire me if I'm not what's really needed here?" she demanded.

"Because I think New Eden is exactly what you need to get you out of that insulated bubble you've been living in," he answered bluntly.

She was glad when his eyes finally warmed to a darker blue. During the time they had lived together, Charlie had never liked it when Murphy was angry with her because she knew he had a typical Irish temper. While her own was something few men cared to reckon with, she knew her rage could never stand up to his.

"It sounds as if you're trying to save me from myself," she said lightly in hopes of changing the somber mood between them.

But Murphy didn't smile back. "I am."

Charlie didn't pursue the conversation after that. She applied herself to her lunch, thanked Murphy for his company, and mumbled that she had to get back to work, since she still had a lot of paperwork to get through. She silently blessed him for not saying anything more as she made her escape. She needed to return to the solitude of her office and mull over his words.

And mull over them she did.

Charlie wasn't used to anyone criticizing her unless it

61

was a choreographer, director, or dance teacher. Everyone else saw her as a lively, nice person who was fun to be with. But Murphy made her sound like the all-time bitch!

She wasn't a horrible person! she asserted, banging file drawers closed. Oh, sure, there was jealousy among the close-knit groups of dancers she knew, and she hadn't been friends with everyone. She never meant to be. It was natural that all dancers couldn't become close friends. Not when a hundred dancers might audition for two openings in a show. The competition was fierce, but she never let it bother her. Charlie couldn't afford to let insecurities enter her mind because if she did she wouldn't be able to concentrate on her dancing, and that had been all that mattered to her. Now it was past tense where she was concerned.

She spun around and collapsed in her chair. Why was Murphy doing this to her? Why was he raising questions she had no answers to? She had no idea why she was bothering to worry over what he had said to her at lunch. She hadn't allowed anyone else's comments to bother her before . . . So why *now?*

Charlie was still driving herself crazy trying to figure out why Murphy said the things he had when a gentle knock sounded at her door.

"Come in," she said grumpily, not sure if she really wanted to see anyone. She only knew her visitor better have a good reason for interrupting her.

The door opened a crack. "I hope I'm not disturbing you." Ramona peeked around the door and looked ready to bolt at the slightest sound.

Charlie swallowed a sigh. After Murphy's lunchtime lecture, she knew she better be very careful.

62

"No, I'm not very busy, Ramona." She smiled. "I'm discovering there's a lot of work ahead of me, and I'm not sure if it's my kind of job. I'm not used to a lot of paperwork and planning, I guess."

Ramona looked horrified. "Oh, you mustn't feel that way," she insisted, timidly making her way to the chair and seating herself on the edge. She wore a pale lavender dress of a soft cotton that seemed to float around her. Personally, Charlie thought the dress was too young for a woman who had to be in her seventies, although she doubted Ramona dressed that way to make her look young. Charlie wondered if it was because she didn't know any other way to dress. Why hadn't anyone taken the time to show her?

"How long did you say you've been living here?" Charlie asked, deciding this was a perfect opportunity to get to know at least one of the residents better.

"Two years." Ramona's voice was little more than a whisper. She peered out from her mane of gray-streaked hair like a tiny bird peeking out of a nest. "It's very peaceful here."

Charlie thought that was an odd word to use considering the comings and goings she had seen with the other residents. "Have you always lived in the Santa Barbara area?"

The older woman shook her head. "My sister and I lived in San Francisco."

"Your sister?"

"She died a little over two years ago." She spoke again in that hushed tone.

"You must miss her very much," Charlie said gently.

For the first time, Ramona's fragile nature hardened. *"No."* There were no ifs, ands, or buts about it.

Charlie decided it was time to change the subject. "Do you play any sports?" She cursed herself for not coming up with a brainier question.

Ramona shook her head. "I have an herb garden." She smiled, the action lighting up her face, which was curiously free of lines, though her skin was parchment-thin. "I will bring you some of my teas, if you like. Caffeine is so bad for you." She cast a disapproving eye on the half-filled cup on Charlie's desk. "My teas will keep you calm and in control of yourself."

Charlie chuckled. "I mean no offense, Ramona, but I can't remember the last time I've felt anything close to calm. Perpetual motion is my middle name."

Ramona shook her head sadly. "That isn't at all good for you," she remonstrated. "Tension is very bad for your body." Then, as if feeling she might have said too much, she looked nervously around and stood up. "I should go." Before Charlie could say a word, the woman slipped out of the office.

Charlie looked at the closing door with astonishment. What had happened to send Ramona off that way? Shrugging her shoulders, she returned to her work and soon forgot her earlier visitor. Until another knock was heard at her door and a bald head popped inside.

"Good afternoon," Sylvester trilled, wandering into the office without waiting for an invitation. He settled himself in the chair without asking Charlie if she was busy or if she wanted company. He looked around the room. "This is really a very dreary place, my dear. If I were you, I would bring in some plants and pictures to add some color."

"I just have to look at a plant to kill it," she informed him.

He tsked. "You surely must have *some* talent."

Charlie stared him straight in the eye. "I've been told I'm good in bed."

Sylvester didn't react at all. "If you're trying to shock me, it won't work. I've seen and heard things that would curl your hair, which might not be a bad idea. That cut really isn't very flattering for your face."

She sat up straight. First she had been told to allow the residents to mother her, then that she needed to cut out caffeine, and now her haircut was all wrong! It wouldn't take much more for her to blow as long and hard as Mount St. Helens.

"I give a small fortune to a man in Beverly Hills to cut my hair," she gritted. "And I certainly haven't had any complaints before. Besides, where do you get off telling me about haircuts?" She looked pointedly at his bald pate.

Sylvester smiled and rattled off a list of movie studios and stars he worked with, clearly enjoying Charlie's surprise. "Little girl, I was cutting hair before your mother knew about sex, and one thing I know is what looks good on a woman and what doesn't. You need more length in the back and height at the top. A bit more curl wouldn't hurt either."

Charlie counted to ten. "I realize you have a great deal of experience, but I like my hair cut this way."

"Only if you're a boy, which you aren't, or have an angular face, which you don't. Yours is more round." Sylvester tipped his head to one side. "I'd also lay off that particular shade of blue eye shadow. It makes you look as if you have heavy circles under your eyes. A smoked turquoise would be much more flattering. You have beautiful eyes, and you really should show them off more." He stood up, quivering with energy. "I'm available to cut hair on Tuesdays and Thursdays." With that, he seemed to sweep out of the office.

"Now I'm positive I came to the wrong place," she murmured.

After her crazy day, the last thing Charlie wanted to do was eat in the dining room that evening. She chose to fix a large salad and relax in her living room with a book. She fed Snickers and Huggie Bear, put them outside for a while, and ate her salad in blessed solitude.

When she was done, she settled in an easy chair with a book and a stack of records on the turntable. Charlie was engrossed in her novel, the bouncy tunes from *A Chorus Line* floating through the room. She idly thought about taking her small tape recorder into work so she could listen to music while she worked. Also in the back of her head were plans for several new exercise classes. Without realizing it, she was already becoming engrossed in her work. She had just stood up to refill her glass with ice water when someone knocked on her front door.

"Who is it?" She knew the community had its own security system, but caution was a way of life with her.

"The big bad wolf. And if you don't let me in, I'll huff and I'll puff and I'll blow your door down."

Charlie scratched the skin just above her eyebrow. "What do you want, Murphy?"

"To hear a polite lady ask me inside to talk."

"You've come to the wrong place for that."

"Charlie, I just want to talk to you. Please?"

She sighed. It was the "please" that undid her. Murphy always knew her weak points, she grumbled silently as she walked to the door and pulled it open.

"What do you want?" she asked as ungraciously as she could.

His smile was just as disarming. "I came to see how you were doing. And to find out if you needed anything." He slipped around her and entered the small living room, looking around as he walked. He screamed when a blur of golden brown jumped onto his back. "Son of a—!"

"None of that, now!" Charlie quickly grabbed the cat from his back and rubbed the furry stomach until she heard purrs. "You scared her."

"So, how's my least favorite cat?" Murphy glared at the cat, who used to delight in waking him up just past dawn by jumping onto his chest and digging in her claws. The cat, in turn, looked just as disgusted at the visitor. "Still making people's lives miserable?"

"Don't be nasty," Charlie chided, walking through the kitchen and putting the cat outside. She latched the cat door and returned to the living room.

"Yes, thank you, I'd like a drink." Murphy smiled at her.

She didn't look as happy. "I don't recall offering you one."

"No, but I knew you would," he explained. "Anything nonalcoholic is fine."

Charlie nodded. She went into the kitchen and came back a moment later, handing Murphy a filled glass.

"Water? Very original." He lifted the glass in a toast.

"And nonalcoholic," she retorted. "Now, why are you here?"

Murphy shook his head. "I'm really disappointed in you, Charlie. Here I make a friendly call, and you act as if I've come to steal your silver."

"Murphy, I know you too well. You never do anything without an excellent reason." Another part of her brain was marveling that any man could look so handsome and well put together in jeans.

He inclined his head as he sat in a nearby chair. "We need to talk."

Charlie perched on the edge of the couch. "I thought that was what we did at lunch."

Murphy grimaced. "I was hard on you and I'm sorry. After all, it was your first day, and I came down on you like a ton of bricks without allowing you to settle in first. I guess I wanted you to know what it was like, right off the bat."

"I'm already getting the picture," she said wryly. "Ramona and Sylvester came to visit me this afternoon."

"And?"

"Ramona offered to bring me some of her herb teas since caffeine is bad for me, and Sylvester offered to cut my hair since this style is unflattering to my face. We won't go into what he said about my makeup."

Murphy chuckled. "That's Sylvester. If nothing else, he believes in speaking his mind, no matter who it hurts." He set the glass on the coffee table. "You're looking real good, Charlie."

"I brush my teeth, cleanse my face with all the right products, and use deodorant," she said flippantly. "According to the commercials, I won't fall apart as quickly that way."

He shook his head. "It's not that, and you know it. You've matured very nicely. The body still looks good, and you seem to be mellowing out. At least you've begun to."

"Mellow out?" Charlie laughed. "What does that have to do with my body?" She couldn't stop the warmth flowing through her body at his intense appraisal. She resisted the urge to fidget in her seat because she was certain he was deliberately baiting her.

But Murphy became serious. "You've been on the edge of a burnout, Charlie. You're very lucky your injury wasn't more serious."

"Oh, come off it!" she argued. "The last thing I've been is burned out. After all, I've seen enough people go through it to know all the signs."

"How long have you been living on pure nerves?" he demanded, leaning forward. "Look at you . . . You've got to be at least fifteen pounds underweight."

"I have to be thin with my work and you know it."

"And how many dancers are anorexic and have died because of it? Besides, you're no longer in the business, so you don't need to watch your weight so drastically."

"I'm not anorexic," she stated coldly.

"No, you do eat, but it's barely enough to keep you going," he said quietly. "You'll have to keep up your strength to take care of that knee. It was beginning to weaken when we first met. What was it that doctor said back then? Something about it being hereditary and that you'd always have to be careful with it. That you'd be better off in any other occupation than the one you were in . . ."

Charlie shook her head in amazement that Murphy remembered so much after all these years. If she cared to pursue her thoughts, she would recall the kind of toothpaste he used, that he hated cauliflower, that he insisted on the bedroom window being open every night, no matter how cold it was outside . . .

"If you came to apologize about this afternoon, fine, apology accepted," she said swiftly, not caring to think too much about the past. "Now, if you don't mind, I'm very tired and I have some things to do," she lied.

The twinkle in Murphy's eye told her he knew she was lying. "I was wrong . . . You're still a tough old broad."

"I was wrong when I called you a pervert. An idiot with a stone for a brain is more like it!" she flared, standing up. "You're the same arrogant man you were nine years ago. Why don't you go into town and find someone to give you your daily ration of sex so you'll be in a better mood tomorrow!"

Slowly he rose to his feet. "Who says I'd have to go into town?"

"Don't expect any handouts from me!"

"Honey, it would be more than a handout I'd want from you. But that would be a good start." With a lazy gesture, he easily pulled her into his arms. "To make it easy on you, I'll settle for this right now." Without any effort, he covered her mouth with his and proceeded to explore her mouth with alarming thoroughness.

Charlie was too stunned to do more than respond for the first five seconds—or was it the first five minutes? With Murphy, time never meant anything because he took all the time he wanted. When she finally thought about rejecting him, her blood was roaring in her ears and her body was melting against his. It had been too long since a man left her feeling this aroused, and it felt so good.

Her tongue teased his and darted inside his mouth to taste the warm, musky flavor while her arms slid around his neck. Tiny moans slipped past her throat and into Murphy's mouth. It didn't take long for her to enjoy it immensely. Her eyelids lowered over smoky eyes, her cheeks flushed, and her breasts began to swell in reaction, just as a part of Murphy's body was equally swollen against her belly. She murmured, rubbing her body against his and feeling the thrust of his hips against hers. The way they were going, it wouldn't take much more for Charlie to drag Murphy into her bedroom and not let him out for a month.

In the space of a second, Murphy released Charlie and stepped back. "It's nice to know the fire's still there, Legs." He drew a ragged breath.

Reality began to return. "Oh, no," she breathed with a different kind of fire now, "there is no way I'm going to get hooked into becoming your little midnight vigil just because you're too lazy to drive into town."

His smile was pure danger. He chucked her under the chin. "Sweetheart, the least you can do is wait to be asked before refusing. See you in the morning." He opened the door and left before Charlie could give in to her urge and throttle him.

"It will be a cold day in hell before I give in to you again, James Patrick Murphy!" she yelled after him. He merely waved his hand as he continued his trek up the hill to his own quarters. Charlie slammed the door and felt much better for it.

She had no idea two people were standing at the end of the lane, watching Murphy leave her bungalow.

"They make a perfect couple," Lena said quietly to the man at her side.

Jason smiled. "Yes, but it may take awhile for the young lady to realize it. I never knew Murphy could work so fast." He slid his arm around Lena's waist and

71

dropped a kiss on the top of her head. "Look how long it took me to come around to your way of thinking."

She smiled back. "Yes, but I always loved a challenge, and I suspect Murphy is the same way. They'll both appreciate each other more for their wait." Her eyes caught his. "Let's go home."

Unable to speak, Jason nodded. He read the meaning in Lena's eyes, and he had been taught never to keep a lady waiting.

CHAPTER FOUR

New Eden's board had a demanding schedule of their own. Three evenings a week they met for potluck dinner and several rubbers of bridge, and two mornings a week they met for breakfast and held their own executive conferences. The morning after Charlie threw Murphy out of her house was one of their usual meeting days. During breakfast, Lena and Jason related the events of the previous evening.

"Are we doing the right thing by throwing them together this way?" Maude demanded, her brightly dyed hair swept up in elaborate curls. She pulled her cigarette holder out of her purse, stuck a cigarette in it, and lit up.

"I do," Jason said firmly. Sylvester and Ian nodded in agreement. "James has few opportunities to meet suitable young women up here, and I'm sure the few times he does take a weekend off, it isn't looking for *the* woman."

Lena sat back in her chair, fingering the strand of creamy pearls at her throat. "Our being involved in getting them together is nothing to worry about at this point. From what Jason and I saw and heard last night, the electricity between them is there. We've all worried about James and his sporadic love life since he came here. As Jason said, James has escorted some lovely young women in the past, but he never showed any real interest in one until now, with Charlie."

"What I'm talking about is getting involved in something that isn't our business—and certainly not a subject any of us is conversant in," Maude argued. "What do we know about *true love?*" She showed disdain for the last two words.

Lena smiled enigmatically. "Are you implying none of us understand romance? Of course, my dear, I realize that wasn't one of your better-known attributes, but there are some of us who know what love is and still believe in it." She glanced at Jason.

Maude's eyes narrowed and she looked prepared to battle. "We can't say the same about you, can we?"

"I thought we were talking about Charlie and James," Ramona intervened hastily, dreading any kind of argument and doing anything possible to circumvent one.

"True," Felix Orsini agreed, nodding his head. He smiled, reached inside his black coat pocket, and pulled out three red roses. He handed one to each lady with a dramatic flourish. "What we must decide is our next step."

"Why don't we invite them to a get-together?" Lena suggested. "We can put on a get-acquainted party to properly introduce Charlie to the rest of the community."

"Excellent idea," Ian spoke up in his impeccable British accent. He plucked his pipe and tobacco pouch from his tweed jacket pocket and proceeded to light up.

"And I'm sure it gives you ladies an excuse to dress up, as we gentlemen know you enjoy doing."

"True," Lena said smugly. She looked at the others and noted their smiles. "Do I gather we're all in agreement with this?"

"For once," Sylvester replied, yawning, looking bored with the whole conversation. "But only if Maude doesn't flaunt that hideous pink feather boa she so enjoys wearing." He glared at the woman seated across from him.

"Darling, if you want to borrow it, all you have to do is say so," she cooed.

"Enough," Jason said in the authoritative voice that never failed to diffuse any difficult situation among the group. "Shall we plan what evening to hold the party so we can let Hazel know we want to take over the hall?"

Pretty soon, all petty differences were forgotten as they decided the night the party would be held, what decorations to use, and the easiest way to let all the members know. In a closed community such as theirs, they all enjoyed a party, and anything passed as a good excuse to have one.

When the board told Murphy about the party, he told the group he thought the idea was a wonderful one and said he would help out in any way he could. He also knew he would be able to see Charlie and talk to her without fear of bodily harm in case she got in one of her moods again.

At the same time, Charlie was touched by the idea and laughed when she was told she was an excellent excuse to have a get-together.

The evening of the party, Charlie had no trouble choosing what to wear. After a leisurely bath, she washed and dried her hair and applied her makeup with more than her usual care. In honor of the festive mood, she wore a cobalt-blue sequined silk tunic and a black velvety slim skirt that hovered just above the knee. Sheer black stockings and black high heels drew attention to her long legs, while the brilliant blue brought the viewer back up to her huge eyes. Her only jewelry was a pair of silver and lapis earrings that dangled seductively against her neck. After one last check to make sure her lipstick hadn't smeared and a spray of heady perfume, she walked up to the recreation hall where she could hear music through the open windows.

Inside the hall the board greeted her with warm hellos, and Lena took her around, introducing her to people she hadn't met and reacquainting her with others.

"This is just beautiful," Charlie said sincerely, accepting a glass of wine from Jason. While trying to act very casual about it, she glanced around for a glimpse of her boss, but his familiar dark head wasn't in sight.

"You can compliment the ladies for that," Jason told her. "Ramona provided the flowers, Lena and Maude did the decorating, and the rest of us were here to provide the manual labor." He blessed Lena with a warm smile.

"Have you two known each other a long time?" Charlie asked, unable to miss the intimacy between the two.

Lena nodded. "We met the day Pearl Harbor was attacked. Jason was a Marine captain who couldn't wait to get overseas and win the war."

"Among other things." Jason shared another secret smile with the woman.

"Did you two meet at an officers' dance or just by

chance?" Charlie was convinced she was going to hear one of the all-time great love stories, which her romantic soul enjoyed. And she wondered why they had never married.

Lena sipped her wine, considering Charlie over the rim of her cup, wondering how the younger woman would take the truth. She decided in favor of telling it. "Jason was one of my customers."

Charlie continued smiling, not understanding what Lena meant. "I, ah—I'm afraid I don't understand."

"To be brutally honest, my dear, I worked as a call girl," Lena said gently.

"Call girl, hell," Jason broke in gruffly. "She ran the best house in San Francisco, which said a lot for someone her age."

Charlie's eyes widened, and she hastily gulped down the rest of her wine. She had a pretty good idea Jason didn't mean a guest house. "Why am I not as shocked as I should be?" she mused. "Lena, you don't look like anyone's idea of a pros—hoo—" She laughed as she stumbled over the proper word. "Now I feel very foolish."

Lena shook her head, placing her hand on Charlie's arm. "Please, don't. Admittedly, not everyone knows about my past, but I saw no harm in telling you. All of us have our secrets. Jason indulged in black market dealings during the war and afterward was known as a high roller, a gambler. And Maude worked as an exotic dancer on the Gold Coast."

"A stripper," Charlie clarified.

"I was the best damn dancer on the coast." Maude approached them when she heard her name. "Gypsy Rose Lee was nothing more than an amateur, compared to me. I did things she wouldn't have dreamed of putting into her act."

"That's probably why you were arrested so many times," Lena murmured.

"Ignore the ongoing battle," Jason told Charlie, who was again feeling like Alice standing on the other side of the looking glass. "Those two have been at it for so long I'm sure neither knows how it began."

Lena shot him a dark look. "Don't press your luck, darling."

He sighed and turned back to Charlie. "Would you care to dance?"

"I'd love it." She set her wine glass down and allowed Jason to lead her toward the filled dance floor.

It didn't matter that the band played swing tunes from the forties and fifties. Charlie picked up the new steps quickly and was soon jitterbugging with Jason, who danced with an energy that belied his years. She threw back her head, laughing as she was swept around and around.

It wasn't long before other men were cutting in to dance with Charlie. Ian danced a slow Glenn Miller tune with her and briefly discussed his days as a secret agent for Her Majesty. Felix Orsini presented her with a rose, swept her into his arms, and almost killed her feet with his faltering steps. Surprisingly, it was the dour-faced Sylvester who turned out to be another excellent dancer when it came to complex steps, and it wasn't long before the other dancers had slowed and stepped back to watch the couple swing around the floor. When the music slowed, Charlie decided it was time to find a cold drink to soothe her parched throat, but her next partner had something else in mind.

"You looked good out there, Legs," Murphy complimented her, gathering her into his arms. "You also made a lot of men happy."

"I may have made them happy, but they sure wore me out," she puffed, forgetting that she was still angry with him. "I swear they saved all their energy for the past twenty years and expended it tonight on me."

He slowed his steps to give her a chance to catch her breath. "I was hoping for a chance to dance with you, but maybe you should sit this one out." He steered her toward a corner of the room and, before she could protest, guided her through the door that led to the indoor swimming pool.

Charlie freed herself from his arm and walked away. "I hate to tell you this, but I'm not exactly dressed for swimming," she said dryly, watching Murphy move toward a plant stand and retrieve a bottle and two glasses.

"I know." He filled the glasses and handed one to Charlie while gesturing her to a nearby chair. "I bet your knee is feeling a bit tender right now, and you'd feel much better if you could get off it for a while."

"I hate smart people," she grumbled, heading for the chair and collapsing in the seat with a groan of relief. Using her toes, she nudged her shoes off and wiggled the ten digits.

Murphy slipped off his tweed jacket and bent down before her, taking one of her sore feet in his hands, kneading and carefully bending the tired joints. He rubbed the calluses gently and pressed his thumbs along the sides, listening to her sighs of contentment. "So you're still a hedonist when it comes to having your feet rubbed," he said, carefully flexing her toes back and forth. One hand roamed slowly up her leg until it covered her knee. The heat radiating out from the skin told him it was the injured one. "You've done enough dancing tonight. If I were you, I'd take it easy for the rest of the night."

"But you told me I was to be friendly with everyone tonight—and it seems to include dancing," she argued. Actually, all she wanted to do was sit there and allow him to ease the ache from her feet. She couldn't understand how his touch on her feet made her nerve endings sizzle. With a smile, she gently pushed his hand from her knee before she could find herself experiencing more than a casual foot massage.

"Then talk to them instead of dancing with them," Murphy advised, now taking her other foot in his hand and kneading it carefully. "Charlie, you'll never change. You always have to do everything the hard way." Keeping his hand around her stockinged foot, he looked up at her. "Who's lived with you since me?"

Her eyes narrowed, trying to read more into his question than friendly curiosity. Finding none, she answered readily. "No one."

He tipped his head to one side. "Couldn't find anyone to replace me, huh?"

Her smile spelled pure danger. "Oh, it would have been easy enough to replace you, but I didn't see any reason to have someone around full-time. I didn't want to share the bathroom on a daily basis again. You never left me enough hot water after your morning shower, and you always left your dirty clothes all over the bedroom."

Murphy smiled back. Did she realize he wasn't about to believe anything she said in that airy voice? He knew her too well. "Maybe that was why we tended to share our showers so often," he murmured, pretending to concentrate on the narrow foot she always considered ugly owing to calluses from the demands of her career. He reached behind him for her shoe and slipped it onto her foot. "You're still stubborn and bullheaded . . . But then, I guess I couldn't expect you to change overnight, could I?"

"You're beating that same old dead horse, Murphy," she told him with a decided bite to her words. "And it isn't going to get up after all this time."

Murphy shrugged as he straightened up and took the chair beside her. He stretched his long legs out in front of him and stared at the shimmering water, lighted by the moonlight streaming through the glass dome overhead.

"Do you still wear those little bits of lace to bed?" he asked in a soft voice. "You know, the kind that reveals more than it hides."

Charlie just barely managed to swallow her gasp. How many nights had she gone to bed in a sleep teddy or short nightgown only to have Murphy strip it off without any preliminaries? She told herself her memories were vivid only because no other man could equal him as a lover. Was that what he was doing to her, forcing her to remember what they had shared in hopes she would want him again?

"I'm into celibacy now, Murphy," she informed him coolly. "And from what you've said before, it's not your style."

He chuckled. "I've missed your quick comebacks, Legs. No one else could keep me on my toes the way you could."

"True, most women preferred you in a more horizontal pose, didn't they?" She smiled sweetly. "What was the name of that soap opera star who chased you for a couple of months? Rene . . . something. If I recall, she finally got you, didn't she?"

"Why not?" he answered in a gruff tone. "You certainly didn't want me then."

"Oh, Murphy, we parted as friends. I don't want you to be bitter over it." She leaned over to touch his arm, but his stiff posture told her he wouldn't appreciate any friendly overtures. "Why are you acting this way?"

"You can't tell me that you remained friends with all your other lovers."

Charlie glared at him, although it was too dark to let the full meaning of her expression intimidate him. Finally deciding she had had enough of his light sarcasm with its heavier overtones, she jumped to her feet and almost lost her balance because she still only wore one shoe. She stood in front of Murphy and called him every name in the book; she would have thought up some new ones, but her breath finally gave out. She inhaled but didn't feel the least bit calm. She spun around as gracefully as she could, still wearing only one high heel, and walked away calling him another not-so-polite name over her shoulder. Her anger was refueled by his taunting laughter, and she hurried out of the pool area, taking a side door she hoped led outside.

"Damn, she's turned into quite a woman." Murphy chuckled, reaching down to pick up her other shoe.

Charlie soon learned the door took her into the recreation hall, but by skirting the wall, she was able to slip outside without anyone noticing her. Or so she thought. She was so engrossed in making sure she would make a safe escape that she didn't realize several people were watching her from across the room. Those same people later noticed Murphy come through the same door Charlie had and saw him stuff something that looked suspiciously like a shoe in his jacket pocket—the shoe that matched Charlie's.

"Shades of Cinderella," Jason murmured, smiling at Lena.

"If Prince Charming has any smarts, he'll wait a few days for the lady to calm down. Otherwise he'll be thrown out on his can," Sylvester spoke up in his stinging drawl.

"That's another story, you idiot," Maude told him, mimicking his cynical voice. "Get them straight, will you?"

"Then let's call him Mr. Macho, shall we? That's the kind of man you enjoy, isn't it?" Sylvester glared at her and stalked away.

"Poor Sylvester," Lena said, sighing.

"Poor Sylvester, my ass. That man has had a viper's tongue in his head since I met him," Maude argued, drinking her wine as if it were water. "I'm going to find myself something decent to drink."

Jason swung Lena into his arms and swept her onto the dance floor to the tune "I Could Have Danced All Night." He smiled and whispered that there was much more he cared to do than dance with her.

"A man of seventy shouldn't have such lecherous thoughts," she chided, but smiled warmly as she said it. "Don't you know you're supposed to sit back in your rocking chair and watch the world go by, instead of thinking about sex all the time?"

"Then why do I feel as randy as a sixteen-year-old

kid when I'm around you?" He rubbed his hips suggestively against hers.

Lena tipped back her head and stared up into the face of the man she had loved for more than forty years. "Keep it in your pants for a while longer, and then I'll see what I can do," she said with the suggestive wink and throaty laugh that had been her trademark for so many years.

Charlie was cursing all the way down to her bungalow as she pulled off her shoe and tried to dodge pebbles and tiny burrs on the path near her cottage. She knew her stockings were a lost cause and damned Murphy for that, too. In her state of mind, she was ready to blame even a perfect stranger for the state of affairs she was in at that moment.

"Missing something?"

She turned around, wincing when another pebble dug its way into the ball of her foot. She stared at Murphy, who stood a few steps away, holding up her other shoe.

"I'm trying to remain angry with you," she grated. She reached for her shoe, but he held it easily out of her reach.

"Your temper has always had a short fuse," he commented. "It flares up fast and is just as slow to ebb."

Why did she feel as if he were talking about something a bit more basic and earthy than her temper? "Murphy, you're saying one thing but meaning another. If this strange mood of yours is due to your lack of recent sex, I will gladly loan you my car so you can drive into town and find an amiable woman. We're not the same people we were nine years ago, so don't expect anything else from me."

"I didn't say we were and I wouldn't want us to be,"

he countered, giving her her shoe. "All I ask is that you think long and hard about yourself and what you expect to happen during your time here. Don't turn into a hard-hearted woman who has no use for mankind other than the most obvious use."

Charlie closed her eyes and counted to ten. What was he trying to do to her? She thought about her somewhat sane life before she came to New Eden. It had been so nice and orderly! If she wanted to go out and dance the night away, there was always someone to take her out. If she wanted to spend a quiet evening at home, she merely turned her answering machine on and curled up in bed with a good book. Her life had been run the way she liked it, and she knew that in time she would be able to plan her life here the same way. That is, as long as James Murphy stayed out of her way. She hated to admit it, but he was a reminder of a painful past she didn't care to think about.

"I still remember that skinny kid who approached me near Sunset Boulevard, Charlie." He spoke softly.

She turned on him with a fury even she didn't know she possessed. "Don't remind me about that!" she shouted. "Do you realize how dirty I felt that night? I've often asked myself how I could have even *thought* about doing such a thing. As it was, I was running back to my apartment when I met you."

"You hadn't eaten in three days and you had an audition the next day. You knew you needed to get a meal in you so you wouldn't faint while you were dancing—not to mention pay your rent before you were thrown out. It's unfortunate, but many young women have ended up in the same situation."

Charlie spun around. She couldn't face him any longer. She didn't want to remember.

"Good night, Murphy," she bit out, then finished her walk to the bungalow. Unable to resist, she looked back as she unlocked the door and found Murphy still standing on the path, his hands in his pockets. Intending to show him his presence didn't bother her, she took her time entering.

He waited until the light in her bedroom was turned on before he walked away.

Charlie undressed and took her makeup off quickly. It wasn't until she huddled under the bedcovers that Murphy's words came back to haunt her, and she began to remember the events that brought her to him.

From the age of six, when she saw her first musical, Charlie had been determined to become a famous dancer. She attended every dance class she could, and nothing else in her life mattered but her studies. When she turned eighteen, she pulled her savings out of the bank and took a bus to Los Angeles. She was sure the competition wouldn't be as fierce as it was in New York, and she hated cold weather. After six months of fruitless auditions, she learned how many dancers hated the cold weather just as much as she did. But she wasn't about to give up. Pretty soon she got jobs in new shows, some of which didn't last long, and worked as a waitress or file clerk between jobs. But the time came when there were more show people looking for work than jobs available.

She didn't like to remember the defiant nineteen-year-old who soon couldn't find any kind of job to hold her over until something better came along. Her rent had been due in less than a week, her savings was just about gone, and she had had no idea where the money was going to come from. One fellow dancer told her there were ways of getting easy money if she didn't have much of a conscience. But Charlie did have a conscience—until her stomach reminded her of all the missed meals and she feared losing her room. And she knew she couldn't—and wouldn't—contact her family for money.

In the end, Charlie dressed in a tight sweater and miniskirt and struck out for Sunset Boulevard. She was scared, and only the thought of getting money for a meal so she would be strong enough for an important audition the next day kept her walking down the street with the other women looking for that same easy money.

She stood around, watched women approach men and vice versa, and suddenly knew she couldn't go through with it. Feeling dirty even though she hadn't done anything, she almost ran down the boulevard to safety. During her escape, she ran into a man who assumed she was trying to proposition him. He kindly told her she was in the wrong business, took her to a nearby coffee shop for a hamburger and coffee, and listened to her predicament. He gave her several suggestions for a few jobs and teased her out of her morbid mood. It wasn't until months later that he told her how horrified he had been at the idea of what could have happened if she had gotten picked up by one of the weirdos that cruised the Strip looking for a good time.

With some of her worries off her mind, Charlie breezed through her audition the next day, then called her new friend and invited him over for a meal. It was over a tuna and noodle casserole that she told James

Murphy that if it hadn't been for him, she wouldn't have won the part. From that day on, they were fast friends, and when neither was auditioning for a part, they spent time together, finding cheap ways to explore the city and learning about each other.

Charlie also recalled the night they had stayed up drinking wine and talking about every subject in the world. She wasn't sure who started the first kiss, but it wasn't long before just kisses between them weren't enough. That was the night she lost her virginity, and no matter what horrible thoughts she had about Murphy now, she never regretted the beautiful night he had given her.

She rolled over and punched her pillow. Why did he have to bring the past up? The night after she had first met him, she sat down and thought with horror about the events of the previous day. That was when she knew she could stand an empty stomach much better than she could handle the loss of the morals she had been taught from birth.

These past couple of weeks had shown her the Murphy she hadn't dared remember. He had always cared about someone, whether it was her or a friend down on his luck. Charlie had enjoyed Murphy as a lover and a friend because he understood her. The trouble was, the time had come when she feared he might understand her too well and press for a commitment. On the outside, Charlie was happy-go-lucky and had a smile for everyone. Inside, she had fears like everyone else. She had already thought of breaking up with Murphy when an important part in a musical came up. Charlie did the only thing she could. She told Murphy it was time for her to move on. What she didn't tell him was that she was beginning to feel too emotional toward him, and she felt she had no time or energy for a meaningful relationship. To this day, she was convinced she did the right thing.

After Murphy left Charlie's bungalow, he went home instead of returning to the party, which, by the sounds coming from the recreation hall, was still going full swing. He entered by way of the back door, stopped in the kitchen long enough to pour himself a drink, and wandered through the darkened living room to his bedroom. He set his glass on the bedside table and went into the bathroom for a quick shower.

Ten minutes later, he lay between the cool sheets, sipping his drink and thinking about Charlie. How many nights had he come back to the apartment they shared fed up with the whole business of film making only to have her tease him out of his bad mood? How many times had she managed to make him laugh when he hadn't felt like it? It was because of her loving and generous nature that he had begun to fall in love with her. And because she had the dedication to her craft he had felt himself losing.

Of course, working as a character actor kept his bank account healthy, but after a while, he grew dissatisfied with the roles. Murphy wasn't stupid; he admitted the money was good and it paid for life's necessities and his acting lessons, but he always dreamed of becoming a star once he left his home in Colorado and traveled to Hollywood the way so many other hopefuls had. Oh, he wasn't vain; he didn't expect to become a sex symbol or world famous star, just someone who people readily recognized, someone who had the producers coming to him. Except it didn't work that way. When he'd audition for a leading or supporting role, he'd hear every rejection in the book. But then they'd mention a role as a serial killer coming up in a television movie, and they were sure he'd have the part if he'd just say yes. In the beginning, he gave in because the money was more than decent. After a while he began to refuse some of the parts because he was tired of being typecast. It become a never-ending story for him.

When Charlie waltzed out of his life, he figured it was time to make some changes. He dated other women and even felt something more than casual affection for some of them. Then, years later, he'd caught a glimpse of Charlie at a party, and he decided the past couldn't stay in the past when a woman like Charlie was involved. He had wanted nothing more than to get out of the life he had and find a new one.

Luckily he found just that at New Eden. He never regretted moving up to Santa Barbara, even if it did put a bit of a curb on his social life. He'd made that barb about a daily ration of sex only to get a rise out of her, which it certainly had. He wondered if it meant Charlie cared for him more than she thought she did. He finished his drink and snapped off the lamp. With his arms crossed behind his head, he lay in the dark and decided it wouldn't hurt to find out if she could consider him more than a past lover and present friend. So long as he ensured his heart wasn't part of the deal.

The next day, Charlie was up bright and early with plans to choreograph the new exercise class. The previous week she had asked Mrs. Finch to type up and distribute a questionnaire she had drafted to find out what kind of exercise class the women were looking for. She learned, much to her surprise, that many were used to a strenuous class but were bored with the same old exercises. That was when she decided to come up with different movements and alternate steps each day to make their workouts more enjoyable.

She dressed in leotards and tights, then pulled on a pair of jeans over them and looked through her large supply of records. After walking up to the studio adjoining the gym, Charlie sat in the middle of the large mirror-walled room and sorted through records, deciding which songs could be used in the class. Then she pulled off her jeans, slipped on a pair of leather ballet exercise shoes, and stood up. Humming to herself, she began with simple warm-up exercises for about twenty minutes, then stepped up the tempo. She faltered over a few steps when her knee protested, but she soon got back in the swing of it.

"What the hell are you doing?" She swore softly and stumbled when the angry male voice rang out in the room.

"Shall I be sarcastic and explain that I was doing a bit of needlepoint?" Charlie spun around and faced Murphy. "I was choreographing steps for the exercise classes I'll be running. Now, why don't you tell me why you had to go and scare me half to death?" She sank down on the floor and rubbed the bottom of her feet. Her knee could have used a little comfort, too, but she didn't want him to see any weakness on her part. She hated the idea that she was sweaty and bedraggled from her efforts while he was bright-eyed and gorgeous in a pair of designer jeans and a charcoal gray and silver wool sweater. Even his black leather boots were polished to a high shine.

But Murphy saw her in a different light. Her navy leotard clung to her slim figure, and the red tights outlined the best pair of legs he had ever seen. A T-shirt with the title of a well-known musical printed on the front covered the upper part of her body, the hem tied in a knot just above her waist. He was sorely tempted to have her for breakfast instead of the bacon and eggs he'd been thinking about.

"And to what do I owe the honor of your presence?" Charlie asked, unaware of his thoughts.

He shrugged. "I heard the music and thought I'd look in. Of course, I didn't expect to find you trying to turn yourself into a cripple."

"I was taking great care with my knee," she argued.

Murphy looked down, remembering the many times he had seen her dressed just this way, looking tired when the day had barely begun.

"You need some breakfast to pep you up," he said.

Charlie shook her head. "I'm not hungry."

"Cinnamon rolls fresh out of the oven," Murphy tempted her. "Fluffy scrambled eggs, sizzling bacon, buttered toast, jam."

She moaned, her taste buds running riotous. "All right, I give up!" She accepted his helping hand as she stood up. "But I want a shower first."

He nodded. "I'll give you ten minutes, and then I'll come in after you."

Charlie raised an eyebrow. "I'm sure the ladies in the women's dressing room wouldn't appreciate that."

"Are you kidding? They'd love it!" He chuckled. "Ten minutes."

She grinned. "Start counting because I intend to show you I can make your deadline."

Charlie returned to Murphy in nine minutes and thirty-six seconds. For once, Murphy didn't speak of their shared past. Perhaps they could make a fresh start, after all.

CHAPTER FIVE

When the first exercise class ended, Charlie felt like a wet noodle. She was glad she had wrapped her bad knee before class and favored that leg so there wouldn't be undue stress put on it.

"That was wonderful," Maude enthused, her brightly colored hair frizzy from her exertions. In a bright orange and yellow striped leotard and yellow tights she resembled a gaudy daisy. "There is nothing like a professional to give a person an excellent workout."

"Thank you." She managed a faint smile.

"Honey, you would have made a great exotic," Maude told her, mopping her damp face with a hand towel. "You sure have the body and the moves for it." She shot Lena a glare. "And it's legal, not like some people's profession I know."

Lena smiled. "That's not what Captain Mahoney of the San Francisco Police Department said that time he busted you in 1943."

"All right, ladies," Charlie hastily intervened, "shall we adjourn to the showers? Perhaps a nice cool one?"

She was relieved Maude didn't say anything further along the caustic vein as the ten women in the class showered and relaxed in the whirlpool.

Charlie would have enjoyed joining them, but she knew she should return to her office and see what was waiting for her. Mrs. Finch had mentioned something about walking tours and bird-watching parties, but Charlie wasn't sure how to set them up. She was beginning to see why the exact description of her job wasn't given to her until after she had accepted the position. It appeared she did a bit of everything. She washed her hair in the shower and blew it dry, then dressed in blush pink wool slacks and a matching boat-necked sweater. She dug into her small duffel bag for her silver earrings with pink coral centers and her watch. After she finished putting her makeup on, she said good-bye to the women and walked out of the dressing room and down the hallway to the main offices. She made one stop to say hello to Karen in the gym and found herself agreeing to go in for a workout while silently wondering when she would have the free time.

For the next week, Charlie had to increase her schedule to include a morning class three times a week and an afternoon class twice a week. Murphy had allowed her to set up a portable perch for the parrot in her office, and Donnie was now happily ensconced in the small room during working hours.

The following week was easier on her since she felt more at ease about making decisions, and she set up a boating trip for a group of twenty-five. One afternoon she sat in her office listening to Donnie murmuring to herself as she stuck her head in her seed cup searching for another peanut.

"Apple?" Donnie asked hopefully. "Want an apple?"

Since that was one of her favorite requests, Charlie

ignored her as she glanced through brochures offering a photography tour at Yosemite.

"Depriving your bird of food, are you?" Murphy teased, walking in the door just as Donnie again asked for some apple.

"Kiss, kiss?" Donnie crooned, stretching her head out to Murphy. A parrot purr escaped her throat as he dropped a kiss on her beak, then proceeded to scratch the top of her head. "Apple?" She obviously figured she may as well go for the gold.

Murphy chuckled. "You haven't changed, have you, sweetheart? Your stomach comes ahead of everything else," he murmured to Donnie. "I'll have to see what I can do about that. Maybe I'll bring you some peanut butter smeared on a spoon." The parrot immediately called out her gratitude at the prospect of receiving her favorite treat.

"She's spoiled enough," Charlie informed him, unable to keep her eyes off the black nylon athletic shorts clinging to his muscular legs and his thin tank top. She was beginning to think her heart rate would be better off if he'd wear a three-piece suit. "I can understand why the ladies insist you don't wear a tie," she said dryly. "I bet when you walk by, they run for the oxygen masks."

He reached out and tweaked her nose. "Cute, Legs, real cute. I just thought I'd stop by to see how you were doing."

"I'm managing much better," she replied, settling back in her chair as he perched himself on the edge of her desk. "At least I feel as if I'm beginning to know what I'm doing. I set up that evening cruise for a week from Friday. So far twenty-five people have signed up."

"Including our lovely director of activities?"

Charlie shook her head. "I just plan them; I'm not a chaperon."

"Haven't you learned that's the last thing these people want?" he questioned. "They don't want us to know just how wild they are."

She laughed, shifting her legs under the desk. "I guess I should be glad this isn't a nudist colony. When I was told that most of the residents had a show business background, I didn't realize that meant retired call girls, ex-strippers, gamblers, magicians, not to mention a very nice gentleman who used to act like James Bond. We won't go into retired persnickety hairdressers and a very eccentric woman who claims she was a gofer for Bette Davis. These are definitely not your run-of-the-mill senior citizens, Murphy. They don't believe in sitting in the sun in their rocking chairs; they prefer swimming laps in the pool or playing a couple sets of tennis every morning. They also enjoy backpacking and wearing me out in exercise class."

"Gives you faith for when you hit those golden years, doesn't it?" He grinned, leaning toward the perch and taking Donnie on his arm. He sat there gently scratching every inch of the parrot's head while she crooned in appreciation.

"Ha! At the rate they're going I'll be a wreck by the time I'm thirty-five!" she protested.

"I'm still in one piece," Murphy told her, "and I hit thirty-five almost a year ago. Personally, I think they keep feeling young because they don't worry about their age, kidneys, or liver problems, and they certainly don't have time to mourn if they don't have any relatives because this place is just one large family."

"Like Ramona," Charlie said softly, thinking of the

woman who had shyly asked if she could walk Huggie Bear every day. The large dog and soft-voiced woman seemed to commune in a way most humans couldn't, and the dog loved her dearly. Even Snickers wasn't as arrogant around the older woman. "Although she gives the impression she doesn't have a friend in the world, I've noticed that so many people look out for her. Or maybe it's an act so people will fawn all over her."

Murphy's face darkened. "The last thing Ramona would ever do is put on an act about anything," he bit out. "Maybe you should know a few things about her. She lived under her father's thumb until he died. It seems he hated Ramona since her mother died giving birth to her. He enjoyed telling her how worthless she was and that she would have to make up the loss of his wife to him by waiting on him hand and foot. I guess the old man was a regular tyrant. He made sure she had no chance to make friends—and certainly no opportunity to meet a man who could love and cherish her. When he died she was left with a trust fund, with her older sister as executor. She wasn't much better and took the same kind of enjoyment in telling Ramona she wasn't much good for anything. She had no chance to make a life of her own until her sister died and she moved here," he concluded harshly.

"No wonder she doesn't miss her sister," Charlie said softly in understanding. The woman probably found it difficult to believe someone would want to be her friend. "It's amazing she didn't grow into a bitter old woman after what her family did to her." She thought of Ramona's gentleness toward the animals and her shy nature around people. "No one deserves to have lived that kind of life. She's very lucky to be where she is now."

Murphy nodded in agreement. "I told you you can't take any of these people at face value, Charlie. Maybe next time you'll think twice." He straightened up, set Donnie carefully on her perch, and walked out of the office. "It might not hurt you to think about going along on that evening cruise either," he said over his shoulder. "You still have a lot to learn about compassion, love."

Charlie stared at the closing door. "I know about compassion," she whispered, hating the idea that he thought so little of her at times. Charlie began to wonder what she would have to do to prove Murphy wrong. What she didn't realize was that she should have known what to do in the first place.

Charlie couldn't remember experiencing a more painful afternoon. She had forgotten to wrap her knee before her afternoon exercise class and was now paying for her carelessness with an aching, swollen knee. In an effort to relieve her discomfort, she applied a heat ointment to her knee and pulled her leg warmer up to keep the heat in.

She finished preparations for a weekend outing to Yosemite and by late afternoon thought loudly about cutting off the offending leg. Once, she gazed out her window and saw Ramona strolling across the grass, Huggie Bear walking sedately beside her. Charlie smiled at the incongruous picture of the shy, nondescript woman and the large black dog. Wishing she were outside enjoying the fall sun, she returned to her work.

"Charlie, I'm leaving now," Hazel announced, poking her head around the door.

"Oh?" She looked up. "Is it that late?" She glanced down at her watch.

"Almost five thirty," the older woman confirmed. "James left ten minutes ago, and you should be leaving, too."

"Apple?" Donnie piped up hopefully.

Charlie chuckled. "Okay, I get the hint. Kiddo, the alarm clock in your stomach went off again, and you're convinced you'll starve to death if you aren't fed in the next five minutes." She grabbed her purse from her desk drawer and picked up the parrot. She waited until Donnie balanced herself on her shoulder before she walked out behind Hazel.

Crossing the lawn, she passed Winifred Page, the medical center director. The tall, strong-boned woman gave her a barely civil nod.

"Pets aren't allowed in this area," she informed Charlie in her deep voice.

"Mr. Murphy gave me permission to bring Donnie up here," Charlie said stiffly, feeling the parrot's nails dig into her shoulder and the tension radiating from her small feathered body.

The woman sniffed, obviously seeing another, more intimate reason for Murphy to give Charlie permission.

"I wouldn't be so high and mighty with me, miss," Winifred rasped, her bony face filled with dislike. "I've seen your kind before, and they don't last long." With that, she stalked off.

"I bet she's popular at Halloween parties," Charlie muttered, making her way to her bungalow.

With a hungry Snickers and Huggie Bear greeting her, she fed the animals before fixing a large salad for herself.

An hour later the kitchen was sparkling clean, and Charlie stretched out on the living room carpet to watch television and try to forget her aching knee. It wasn't long before she decided she would be better off if she walked back up to the fitness center and soaked in the Jacuzzi for a while—something she should have taken the time to do that afternoon as a preventive measure, instead of suffering all these hours.

The pool room was deserted, and she was glad to have the Jacuzzi to herself and not have to worry about making conversation when she wasn't in the mood to talk to anyone.

Charlie lowered herself in the hot bubbling water and rested her nape against the tile edge. Closing her eyes, she willed her body to relax and allowed her mind to float.

From the time she had learned the meaning of the word, she decided she was a hedonist. She enjoyed the feel of soft, silky fabrics against her bare skin, lounging in a Jacuzzi, and thought nothing of spending hours in a bubble-filled bathtub or standing under a steaming shower, which added an erotic touch to life. She just plain enjoyed life itself.

As she lay in the water, her thoughts skipped over bits and pieces of her past, mainly those having to do with Murphy. It was too bad she had left him all those years ago, but at the time, she felt she was doing the right thing. But she doubted he saw the situation the same way. Her career had just begun and the musical had been a large stepping stone for her.

"No one can ever mean as much to you as your dancing," her mother had once told her. "That must always come first in your life."

As a frustrated dancer herself, she did everything possible to help her daughter achieve her goal. When

Charlie turned eighteen, her mother had urged her to try for the big stage. Charlie was grateful for her mother's help, but deep down she wished her mother could have cared more about her and less about her talent.

Charlie shifted uneasily in the bubbling water. A disquieting thought suddenly skittered across her brain. Had she been too narrow-minded with her purpose and lost out on something much more tangible?

Shrugging the idea off, she climbed out of the Jacuzzi and wrapped a towel around her wet body. As she walked back to the dressing room, she heard sounds of heavy metal clanking in the weight room.

Wondering who could be working out during the usually quiet hour, she peeked around the corner and took a deep breath at the lusty sight before her.

Murphy was seated at the leg press, his bare upper body drenched with sweat, his nylon shorts sticking to his lower body. He exhaled loudly with each exertion as he performed repetitions in a smooth, seemingly effortless motion. As if sensing he had a visitor, he turned his head.

"Hi." Murphy stretched his legs out, pressing the weights upward, his thigh muscles standing out like thick ropes from his efforts. "Taking a swim?"

"Just relaxing in the Jacuzzi." She was relieved her voice could sound normal when she was confronted with such blatant masculinity.

"Your knee?" he guessed.

Charlie nodded. "I forgot to wrap it before class this afternoon," she admitted, taking a tiny step inside the weight room as if loath to leave but also unsure whether it was wise to stay.

Murphy frowned. "How is it feeling now?"

"Much better."

Murphy took the towel hanging around his neck and mopped his perspiring face. "Feel up to a swim?" He cocked an eyebrow.

"It sounds fine as long as I don't have to swim any laps."

He looked down at his sweaty clothing. "Give me a few minutes to shower, and I'll join you in the pool."

Charlie nodded and edged her way out of the brightly lighted room. When she reached the pool, she was just beginning to regain her breath. It was amazing what a pair of nylon shorts could do for the male body. Especially when the damp fabric cupped his . . . *No!* She shook her head to clear her wandering mind. She mustn't think about Murphy as a man. Well, she didn't want to think of him as . . . especially not as . . .

Charlie laughed softly as she retrieved a dry towel. Until now, she didn't realize a person's thoughts could stammer. She sat down on the top step to the shallow end of the pool, allowing herself to become accustomed to the cool temperature. Her legs floated in front of her as she sat there with her elbows braced behind her.

"Why isn't the water baby making the most of it?" Murphy's voice came from behind, echoing against the dome ceiling.

She didn't bother to turn around. "Too lazy and the water isn't warm enough," she muttered, watching him circle around to the deep end and dive cleanly into the water. He swam several laps before halting nearby.

"What's happening to the Charlie who never says die?" he teased, making his way toward her.

Charlie shrugged. "I prefer my water about thirty degrees warmer."

103

"You've got to toughen up, Legs," he retorted, flicking a shower of water across her bare stomach.

"Tell me about it. I'm finally realizing I'm not twenty years old any longer." She sighed, glancing over his well-muscled body. The dark hair on his chest was sparkling with water droplets. She experienced a sudden urge to touch her tongue to each and every droplet.

Murphy's eyes were riveted on Charlie's face. There was no disguising the intensity of her gaze.

"Charlie," he groaned, "don't, unless you mean it."

The tip of her tongue slipped out to slowly moisten her lower lip, then her upper one. Murphy groaned again, remembering how she tasted, how she always responded to his touch. Without any preliminaries, he reached out and pulled her into his arms. His mouth covered hers with a force that would have threatened to snap her head back if she hadn't met it just as strongly.

Charlie wasn't frightened. She was too busy melting against him and feeling his body heat warm the cool water on her skin. Her mouth opened under his searching tongue, accepting the possession. Her own tongue curled around his in a passionate duel and darted into his mouth to find his secrets. She could feel the male bulge against her belly, the strength of his arms around her bare back, the sensual abrasion of his chest hairs rubbing against her sensitive skin. His evening beard was slightly rough against her face but no less welcome. Murphy's beard felt sexy against her skin. She could have stayed like that forever.

Charlie reveled in the feel of Murphy holding her, the way his hand cupped her swollen breast and teased the peaked nipple. She moaned, feeling the flames snake their way down to the throbbing center of her body.

"I didn't intend to make love to you here, Charlie," he said roughly, nuzzling her earlobe.

"No?" she asked, pouting just a bit at the idea of his walking away from her after what they had just shared. "Then where do you intend to make love to me?"

"As soon as I dry us off, I'm going to spirit you off to my place for a night of debauchery," he promised her, rubbing his thumb over her jutting lower lip, still moist from his possession.

"Why can't we start right now?" She clamped her teeth on his probing thumb and ran her tongue over the slightly callused pad while keeping her eyes on his.

His answering smile sent her stomach into somersaults. "You know, that sounds like an excellent idea, but I wouldn't want us to get caught with our pants down—pardon my pun." He guided her out of the pool and grabbed two towels, handing one to Charlie. "I'd dry you myself, but I doubt I could and hold off until we get back to my place." He dried himself off with an economy of movements.

Charlie didn't believe in hurrying, even when anticipation was so sweet. She leisurely dried each leg, beginning with her toes and ending at her upper thighs. Her bare midriff was treated just as kindly, as was her upper chest and arms. Murphy watched her with dark eyes.

"If you're not careful, you may find yourself tossed onto one of those loungers over there—and the hell with getting caught," he rasped.

Charlie shook her head. "I like my comfort too much," she said softly, wrapping the towel around her hips and tucking the end in.

"Right about now, I bet I could change your mind." She glanced at the bulging masculinity straining his

105

swimsuit. "Yes, I believe there would be no problem there at all." She walked toward the women's dressing room. "I'll meet you out front."

Murphy showered and dressed swiftly, gritting his teeth as he zipped up his jeans. He couldn't remember the last time he had been so painfully aroused. But then, Charlie had always been able to do that to him. Just one look from her big blue gray eyes and he'd want to tumble her into the nearest bed. There had always been more than just sex involved where she'd been concerned. She had been easy to talk to, a fun companion, and more optimistic than most people in her career. If she had cared to take the time, she could have had more friends than she would have known what to do with. The trouble was, she devoted all her time to her dancing, losing out on friendships and relationships because of it.

Instead of using the hair dryer, he settled on combing his damp hair into order. Why couldn't he have hated her for walking out on him so cavalierly years ago? Probably because no one could really hate her, especially not him. He threw his other clothing into his gym bag and headed for the door. Visions of Charlie in his bed tantalized him as he approached her. She was waiting for him and greeted him with a broad smile.

"James, Charlie!" Jason's voice rang down the hallway. "So there you are."

Murphy cursed under his breath. "Evening, Jason, Lena. Are you two going to work out?" There was a hopeful note to his question.

The older man shook his head. "Don't tell me you've forgotten our plans," he chided.

"Plans?" Murphy echoed weakly.

"To come by the house," Jason reminded him. "You were supposed to be there half an hour ago."

Was he? Murphy couldn't remember, but then, erotic thoughts about Charlie could have chased the most important details from his mind. Wait, he did talk to Jason at lunch and something was said about his stopping by. But had it been for tonight? How was he going to get out of this gracefully?

"Charlie, you must come, too," Lena said warmly. "We really haven't had a chance to sit down for a nice long chat."

"Well," she hesitated. Wasn't Murphy going to say anything about the plans they had made? Then she remembered his words about the residents taking precedent. Did that mean even when they hoped to spend the rest of the evening in bed? "Well, maybe for a little while," she replied, directing a look fit to kill at Murphy. Couldn't he say no, just this once?

For the next few hours Murphy silently gnashed his teeth and cursed his bad luck in running into Jason outside the weight room. He should have just bundled Charlie off to his place without talking about it beforehand. But then, he figured, if the older man hadn't tracked him down there, he might have shown up at Murphy's cottage. The director of activities caught in bed with the administrator certainly would have given the gossips food for thought for months! Maude and Ian were already at the house, and Ramona later appeared with Sylvester in tow.

Charlie was just as agitated because she wasn't much for sitting around and just talking. When she went to parties, she was always on the dance floor. She would only sit down long enough to catch her breath, then jump up and start dancing again. But perhaps because the conversation didn't center around the new shows coming up and who made the latest chorus and who didn't, she found she was enjoying herself. She glanced at Murphy, who stood across the living room talking to Jason. If they hadn't been found they would have been making love by now. She began to wonder if they weren't meant to be together again. As an artist, she was superstitious and began to wonder if this was Fate telling her the time wasn't right. Or the man wasn't. She hated to believe the latter could be the case.

Finally, after two beers and listening to a lot of small talk that left Murphy with a roaring headache, he made his excuses and escorted Charlie out of the house.

As they walked down the lane Charlie looked up at Murphy. "I guess you could say the mood is gone," she said wryly, twining her fingers through his.

"I'm sorry I didn't get us out of that," he apologized. "But I did say I'd drop by, and I didn't know if I could get out of it gracefully without tipping them off to the real reason why I forgot about his invitation."

"I understand," she assured him sincerely. "But it wasn't bad. In fact, it was kind of fun."

They halted in front of Charlie's door. Murphy edged her against the door panels, his elbows braced against the wood.

"You could invite me in," he said, rubbing his hips suggestively against hers.

Charlie shook her head. "I don't think it would be a good idea, Murphy," she murmured, just before his lips skimmed over hers.

"Nothing's changed, Charlie," he whispered, exploring her earlobe with his tongue. He smiled when she shuddered from his touch. "I still want you; you still want me."

"But the timing is off," she said softly, almost sadly.

He couldn't help but notice her labored breathing and sensed he was the reason for it. He doubted it would take much to persuade her to allow him in, but he knew he couldn't do it that way. Charlie's decision had to be all on her own.

"I won't wait much longer for you, Charlie," he told her, bracing his hands against her waist.

"You're much too sure of yourself," she grumbled, but the faint light revealed the teasing sparkle in her eyes.

"Not as sure as I'd like to be." He brushed his lips over hers. "I'll see you in the morning. Believe me, the next time we won't let Jason and Lena hijack us."

"Good night, Murphy," she murmured, feathering her fingers over his cheek before turning to open her door.

He waited until she slipped inside and heard the door lock behind her before he walked away. All the way back to his bungalow, Murphy cursed himself for making the move on Charlie so quickly. Why couldn't he be more of a man and put distance between the two of them before he did something foolish—such as fall in love all over again? If he'd had his brains working instead of his glands he'd have made sure Charlie hadn't come to work there. The trouble was, she was in his blood and he doubted even a complete transfusion would cure him.

Charlie stood under the shower, allowing the hot water to stream down over her body. She stretched her arms over her head, her eyes closed against the water flowing over her face. Usually she would spend close to half an hour in the shower, but the erotic streams of water reminded her of the swimming pool and Murphy's heated touch on her bare skin. She could feel her nipples harden at the memory and the heat settle between her legs. Realizing how aroused she was becoming, she merely allowed herself to flow with the tide. Before too long she knew memories weren't enough, and she abruptly turned the cold tap on full force. When she felt close to turning into an icicle, she turned off the water and grabbed a towel. She quickly dried off, pulled on a nightshirt, and crawled into bed after pushing Huggie Bear and Snickers off the covers.

Charlie forced herself not to think about Murphy for fear she'd leap out of bed and run up to his bungalow to finish what they had started earlier. Just as she dropped off to sleep she found herself hugging something close to her, not realizing the large dog had sneaked back up on the bed. In her sleepy state, she only knew he was warm and comforting.

"Do you believe we did the right thing?" Lena accepted a glass of wine from Jason. In an effort to get comfortable she had slipped her shoes off and curled up on the rose brocade love seat. Jason sat down beside her, stretching his legs in front of him. "We should have let James off the hook since it was obvious he and Charlie wanted to be alone." She smiled at the thought of *why* the younger couple wanted to be alone.

"Ah, young lust," Ian said, chuckling, sipping his whiskey.

"Why she'd be willing to spend an evening with us

instead of a lusty man like him is beyond me." Maude sighed, inspecting her long, bloodred nails.

"The love isn't there yet," Ramona spoke up in her soft voice. The other five people looked at her with silent questions in their eyes. "Charlie is physically attracted to James, but that's all it is right now. And James seems afraid. You can see by the way he looks at her that he's afraid to give in, for fear of being hurt, although I don't understand why he should fear such a thing happening. And if they—" she dropped her head, blushing furiously—"if they make love too soon, it won't mean what it should to them."

"Ramona, you are a very perceptive woman," Jason complimented her. "All we're trying to do is guide them along the course of true love."

Maude shot him a look filled with disbelief. "You're getting soft in your old age, Jason. They're just two young people who have an itch to scratch. That's it, pure and simple. So let them get on with the scratching and get it out of their systems."

"Maybe she's right. Perhaps we should just let them discover true love for themselves," Lena spoke up with a wicked smile. "Of course, if it appears one of them needs a little push, there's no reason why one of us can't act like Cupid, is there?"

"It all sounds dreary to me." Sylvester gave an exaggerated yawn, standing up. He glanced at Ramona. "If you'd like, I'll walk you back to your cottage."

She nodded. "Yes, thank you."

The party soon broke up and left Lena and Jason alone. They carried the dirty glasses and dishes into the kitchen, rinsed them off, and stacked them in the dishwasher. Once finished, Jason slipped his arms around Lena's waist.

"Why don't we just stand proxy for James and Charlie tonight?" he suggested.

"Jason, don't you realize you're too old to be so insatiable?" She laughed, hugging him tightly.

"Never." He kissed her soundly.

CHAPTER SIX

"Charlie, you have a visitor," Hazel announced the next morning.

"Hell, it's not as if royalty's come to call," a man's voice grumbled.

"Harry!" Charlie jumped out of her chair and threw her arms around her agent's shoulders. "What are you doing here?"

"I come up once a month or so to visit my Aunt Bernice," he explained, looking embarrassed by her enthusiastic greeting. "And I figured I'd stop by to see if I'm on your hate list for recommending this job to you. If you're still talking to me, maybe you'd like to meet my aunt and go out to lunch with us."

She narrowed her eyes as he stood uncertainly before her. Harry had never looked unsure in his life. Something was up. She could feel it in her bones. She just wasn't sure what it was. Unless . . . "You lied to me. You knew Murphy was here, didn't you?" She pounced on the betraying red creeping up his neck. "You're a horrible man, Harry Simms," she accused. "You meddled in areas you know nothing about."

He shrugged, trying to look nonchalant but failing

miserably. "You don't seem as mad as I thought you'd be." He looked into her eyes. "How's the knee doing?"

Charlie grimaced. "To be honest, it was a great deal better five years ago, but it's improving and I've been taking it easy. I'm not up to trying any complex turns or jumps, but I'll be back executing those high kicks again, never fear." She managed a bright smile. "After all, doctors have been wrong before, haven't they?" She felt she had to keep up a positive attitude. She could still hope for the best, couldn't she?

"Yeah, well . . ." Harry shifted his feet, uncomfortable with the turn of the conversation even if he had initiated it. "So, what do you say to having lunch with me and my aunt?"

"You buying?"

"Of course I'm buying." He appeared affronted she would assume otherwise.

"No hamburger joints." She remembered some of the greasy spoons he had taken her to in the past where the bill rarely amounted to more than three dollars for two meals.

"Charlie . . ." he warned.

"Just checking. Lunch sounds great." She reached for her navy and wine plaid blazer and pulled it on over a wine-colored silky tailored shirt.

"Uh, Charlie?" He scratched the top of his head. "Maybe I should warn you that Aunt Bernice is a bit eccentric."

She threw back her head and laughed. "Don't worry, Harry." She placed her hand on his arm. "After some of the residents I've met here, one more odd old lady won't make any difference."

"Okay, if you say so." He sighed, following her out of the office. "Just don't say I didn't warn you."

Charlie stopped by Hazel's desk to inform her she was going to lunch. The older woman greeted Harry with a smile and asked him to give her best to dear Bernice and Emery.

"So how's business?" Charlie asked as they walked up a gently sloping hill to a small cottage flanked by climbing rose bushes.

"Not too bad," he replied, huffing and puffing even on the low incline. He tried not to say too much for fear she would become depressed at not being in the thick of things any longer.

"Your aunt isn't going to mind my coming along, is she?" she questioned as Harry rapped on the white door.

"No, in fact, she's looking forward to meeting you," he assured her. When the door opened to reveal a tiny silver-haired woman, he bent down to place a kiss on her paper-thin wrinkled cheek. "Here's my favorite girl."

"Go on with you!" she scolded, blushing furiously. She turned to Charlie and looked her up and down with dark eyes. "And you're our new director of activities. My dear, you're as pretty as Hazel said you were. Please, come in."

Charlie entered the tiny living room filled with antique furniture. She was urged to sit on a deep red velvet sofa that felt every bit as uncomfortable as it looked.

"Emery would love your eyes," Bernice told her in her fluttery voice. "They're such a lovely shade, so vulnerable."

Charlie's lips curved in an unnatural smile. It was

115

such an odd compliment that she wasn't sure how to respond to it. "Is Emery your husband?" she ventured to ask.

"Oh, yes." She gave an airy wave of the hand toward the mantel that housed a fake fireplace. "Such a dear, warm-hearted man. No woman could wish for a kinder husband."

"Is he lunching with us?" Charlie asked, confused when Harry violently shook his head behind Bernice.

"Oh, no, my dear. Emery has been gone these past six years." Bernice's bright face dimmed for a moment. "But I haven't truly lost him." She gestured to an ornate vase standing in the center of the mantel. "He's still with me."

Charlie gulped, guessing Bernice's answer before she heard it. "Emery?" she asked in a hushed voice that choked on the last syllable.

"Yes." Bernice smiled, turning to Harry. "Is it very chilly outside?"

"You should wear your coat," he advised her.

"Harry, she has her husband's ashes on the mantel!" Charlie whispered fiercely when Bernice went into her bedroom for a coat.

"Yeah, he's been there since the memorial service," he replied. "She says she enjoys talking to him every evening. Oh, she's perfectly aware he's dead, but she feels better if she can talk over the day's activities with him."

"And I thought Sylvester and Ramona were strange," she muttered, summoning a smile when Bernice returned to the living room wearing a pale gray wool coat.

Charlie gave Harry credit. For lunch, he chose a

116

homey restaurant filled with hanging green plants that exuded a quiet, relaxed atmosphere. It wasn't at all like some of the dives he had taken her to in the past.

"Oh, it all looks so good. I just don't know what to choose," Bernice said, studying the menu. She finally decided on a seafood quiche and a small salad.

Charlie ordered the same, whereas Harry asked for a steak sandwich and french fries.

"No wonder you look ten months pregnant, when you eat like that all the time," Charlie chided with a grin. "Hmm, I bet Bernice has some interesting stories about you as a boy."

"He was such a darling baby." Bernice beamed. "He hardly ever cried or fussed."

A strangled sound came from Harry's throat.

"I named him," she went on, unaware of her nephew's red face. She displayed a moue of disappointment. "I just wish he would use his full name. It's such a lovely name. You see, he was named after a film star," she confided.

"Aunt Bernice," he muttered, shifting in his chair.

"Don't tell me, Harold, as in Harold Lloyd," Charlie guessed with a wicked chuckle, leaning back as the waitress set her plate in front of her.

"Don't I wish?" he groaned, burying his face in his hands.

"No, he was named Harrison, for Harrison Ford," Bernice said proudly.

Charlie choked. She turned her head to study a man in his late fifties with a receding hairline and obvious paunch who stared down at his sandwich as if it held all the secrets of the world. "There's something wrong

117

here. If I remember correctly, Mr. Ford is a great deal younger than you are, Harry."

"Not that one. I'm talking about a very dear man I knew years ago," Bernice explained. "I worked as a script girl in one of the films he costarred in. Oh, dear, what was the title? My memory just isn't what it used to be. I had a bit of a crush on him and vowed I would name my first son after him. But Emery and I had two daughters. When Clara asked me to name Harry, I knew I had my chance."

Charlie glanced sideways at Harry. "Cheer up, old boy. You could have been named for Bela Lugosi," she teased.

"That's a secret you better keep," he ordered gruffly, gesturing with his fork. "If it gets out, I'll know who squealed."

She tried to look properly innocent but failed. "Squealed? Harry, now you're trying to sound like Edward G. Robinson. Besides, who would I tell? And even if I did, no one would believe me."

"With that quirky sense of humor of yours I could see you taking out an ad in *Variety* to announce my full name," he muttered.

"He's only been truly touchy about his name in the last few years," Bernice explained. "I never could understand why."

But Charlie did, and it was all due to an actor who had the same name but certainly didn't look like her agent. She smiled at Harry, silently assuring him his secret was safe with her.

After lunch Harry drove them back to Bernice's house, then offered to walk Charlie back to her office. She declined, told Bernice she enjoyed meeting her, and promised to visit soon. After hugging Harry and requesting he keep in touch, she made her way back to her office.

"Have a good lunch?"

Charlie looked up at Murphy's scowling face. "Yes, I did," she replied. "Obviously, yours wasn't as relaxing." She wondered what put him in a bad mood.

"Hazel said a good-looking man took you out to lunch," he bit out.

"Good-looking man?" she parroted, picturing the balding man with a paunch. "Yes, I guess you could say he does have a certain bohemian charm about him."

Murphy's scowl darkened. "One of your old lovers?"

"Just an old friend." She had to put him out of his misery before he said something he'd later regret, she realized. "The man was Harry Simms, and his aunt accompanied us. Does that sound safe enough?" She walked into her office and sat in her chair.

He groaned, thrusting his fingers through his hair. "I should beat you for leading me on like that," he grumbled, taking the chair across from her.

"I kind of liked it—you sounding jealous," Charlie admitted in a soft voice, her eyes looking like blue gray pools. She wanted to tell him more, that she also liked the idea of someone caring about her. It had been a long time since that had happened.

"I wasn't jealous," Murphy muttered, glaring at her.

"No, of course you weren't," she agreed in an all-too-amiable voice.

"Actually, I came to see if you'd like to go out to dinner tonight." He ducked his head when Donnie flew from her perch and landed on his shoulder. "This sweater has to be dry-cleaned, so be careful," he advised the bird.

Murphy was asking her out! Charlie hastily lowered her eyes to hide her happy expression. Come to think of it, she couldn't remember his ever asking her for a date. In the beginning of their relationship, they just ended up going out together, and when two people lived together, dating wasn't part of the ritual.

"That sounds very nice." She lifted her eyes when she could be sure there was nothing for him to read in them. "What time?"

He shrugged. He had been afraid she'd turn him down and hadn't thought any further than asking her. "How about seven? If you'd like, we could take in a movie or go dancing." He winced. Good going, Murphy. Wrong choice of words. The last thing she should do is put more pressure on that weak knee.

Charlie smiled wryly. "I'm afraid I'm still not up to a full evening of dancing," she told him. "Why don't we play it by ear?"

He nodded as he pushed himself out of his chair and put Donnie back on her perch. "I'll see you at seven, then." Accomplishing what he had come to do, he left her office.

Charlie leaned back in her chair, her fingertips touching her smiling lips. This could turn out to be a very interesting evening.

She left her office at five o'clock sharp and hurried home to shower and change into something dressier. The only problem was she didn't know where Murphy intended to take her. Wanting to look her best but not too dressed up, she chose turquoise silk slacks and a matching loose jacket with a black camisole top. Since her knee didn't appreciate high heels for any length of time, she decided on medium-heeled strappy sandals. She hurriedly fed the animals, checked her makeup, freshened her rose lip gloss—and wondered if she wasn't turning overly paranoid since this wasn't her first date. She doubted Murphy was feeling this nervous. Little did she know.

During the time it took him to shower and dress, Murphy changed his shirt twice and told himself he was acting like a perfect idiot. It wasn't as if he hadn't gone out with Charlie before. After all, how many men knew about that cute little birthmark just above her left buttock? Nope, wrong question to ask. That made him wonder just how many men, over the years, had discovered that birthmark. He did order himself that he wasn't going to try to charm his way into her bed—not yet anyway. This time, he was going to take it slow and easy.

Murphy wondered if Charlie realized how much she had changed in the short time she had been at New Eden. She was already beginning to think of others ahead of herself, and that was very rare for her. He saw the proof the night they went to Lena and Jason's house when she very easily could have come up with an excuse for them to go off by themselves. But she sensed it was important for them to be with the older couple, and she gave in without an argument. Maybe there was hope for her after all. He pulled on a navy blazer and left the house before he decided to change his clothes again.

Charlie had finally relaxed enough to sit down and read a magazine when a knock sounded at her door.

121

Huggie Bear began barking and running to the door, reaching it before she did.

"Just a minute," she called out, dragging the dog away from the door and opening it. She kept hold of Huggie Bear's collar and managed a weak smile at Murphy. In gray slacks, a navy pin-striped shirt, and navy blazer he looked devastating. "Let me put him outside before he gets fur all over your clothes." She pulled the protesting dog to the patio door and pushed him outside. "Would you like a drink?"

"No thanks. I made reservations . . . So if you're ready?" He left the question hanging. Charlie was known for forgetting to do something until the last minute. This proved to be no exception.

"I'm all ready," she assured him, then panicked when she couldn't find her purse. It took five minutes of searching before Murphy found it under her magazine. "Now I'm all ready. I promise." She eyed his dark sedan with surprise. "What happened to the Corvette?"

"It got totaled two years ago, and I decided I needed more car around me," he replied, helping her into the passenger seat.

Charlie's eyes widened. "You were in an accident?" she whispered, reaching out to touch his shoulder when he slid behind the steering wheel. "Oh, Murphy."

He smiled reassuringly. "I was lucky. I only ended up with some scrapes and cuts from broken glass."

Charlie shuddered at the idea of what had happened and what could have happened. "I never knew."

"There was no reason for you to." His reply came out harsher than he expected.

"You're right . . . There was no reason." She withdrew her hand and remained on her side of the car.

Murphy cursed softly as he switched on the engine and put the car in gear. "I'm sorry, Charlie. It's just that it's still a sore point with me. Some kid had been drinking too much and ran a red light. His father tried to explain to me that boys will be boys while I was sitting there waiting to be stitched up. It really burned me up."

"I don't blame you." She accepted his apology. "I'm sure if the position had been reversed, the father would have been after your blood."

"Every pint and more," he agreed, reaching out for her hand and clasping it warmly. "So let's forget it and concentrate on enjoying our evening out."

The restaurant Murphy took Charlie to was on the pier, and their table gave them an excellent view of the small bay. She could look out the window and see the twinkling lights of the boats anchored nearby. They both rejected the idea of a drink before dinner and ordered a bottle of wine to accompany their meal.

"So what do you think of New Eden so far?" he asked after the waiter brought their wine and uncorked the bottle so Murphy could taste and approve it.

"It's been quite an experience," she told him. "You were right when you said I wouldn't find run-of-the-mill senior citizens here. Even meeting Bernice was a surprise. Well, maybe I should say that meeting Emery was the surprise."

He chuckled. "Yes, that can be a bit unsettling if you're not expecting it. But you realize there isn't one incoherent thought in Bernice's head. Unfortunately, her daughters live out of state, and her only sister is dead. I give Harry credit that he comes up once a month or so, takes her out, and spends time with her. She also has a great many friends in the community."

"Did you know ahead of time that Harry recommended me for this job?"

Murphy shook his head. "I was away on business when you were interviewed and didn't know your name until after the fact."

"Then why didn't you turn me down?" she asked. "I should think you'd have the right to do so."

He shrugged. "I saw no reason to. I was sure you could do the job, and you certainly needed to get away from L.A."

"Are you saying you did this out of sympathy?" Charlie was appalled at the idea.

"Far from it. We're not in the business to offer charity to anyone. Everyone is expected to pull his own weight, and you've certainly done more than your share. You're perfect for the job because you've always liked to arrange parties and outings, and there's a lot of that done here. In fact, your next big job will be planning the Halloween party."

"Costumes and all?" Her eyes brightened.

"Especially the costumes," he replied. "In fact, we have a few people who worked wardrobe for the studios and enjoy fixing up unusual costumes for people. In the past years, we've even come up with a theme for the party and costumes, such as famous couples, heroes and heroines of the past—whatever sounds good at the time."

Charlie thought for a moment. "Film titles would be appropriate with this group," she suggested.

Murphy thought it over. "Sounds fine with me," he

agreed. "I'd say give it a try. Lena and Maude will help you."

Charlie knew Murphy was right. She loved to plan parties and had thrown some pretty crazy bashes in the past. This could prove to be a lot of fun. Imagine planning parties and getting paid for it!

"Do you ever miss Hollywood?" She selected one of her scallops and dipped it in cocktail sauce.

"No." There was no hesitation in his answer. "I've finally found my niche, and I wouldn't trade it for anything."

Not even for marriage? she wondered, but wasn't about to ask aloud. Would a wife be willing to live in a retirement community since Murphy seemed perfectly happy living on the grounds? Charlie knew it wasn't a prerequisite of the job since she didn't have to live there either, but she had accepted the cottage because it was convenient and cheaper.

"I'm glad you've found yourself," she said sincerely, leaning across the table to grasp his hand. "I knew you were unhappy with the way your work was going, but I guess I didn't realize how truly unhappy you were with your life. Maybe it would have helped if I hadn't been so wrapped up with my work that I didn't realize you had problems."

"You were still too young to understand that there were people beyond your own little world of dance," he said, not unkindly. "And it wasn't necessarily your fault. You were immature then and we split up not long after."

No matter how nicely he said it, it still stung, she discovered. It was enough she had bad habits then, but to have them vocalized made them sound even worse.

"If I was so bad, why did you put up with me?" she demanded, withdrawing her hand.

"Because you had the best pair of legs in town and the sexiest smile," he replied without a pause. "Not to mention that you were great in bed, once I taught you the basics." He smiled.

But Charlie wasn't easily mollified. She finished her meal in silence except to smile and nod her head at the waiter when he asked if she wanted more wine. She ignored her conscience and decided chocolate mint cheesecake was the perfect ending to the meal. Murphy asked for brandy with his coffee.

"Don't pout, Charlie," he chided, watching her slice the cheesecake with the edge of her fork. "It will only cause wrinkles."

"I am not pouting," she said, feeling perfectly calm. "I just couldn't think of anything nice to say, so I didn't say anything at all."

Murphy saw his idea of a beautiful evening falling down around his ears. Why did he have to get started on her past attitude? She wasn't the young woman she had been then, so why did he bring it up? Probably because he was the worst kind of fool where she was concerned. She smiled wistfully and looked across the table at him.

"We're not doing very well, are we?"

He sighed. "We've done better. What happened? Aside from my big mouth, that is."

Charlie shook her head. "I have a feeling that we're not used to going out together."

"What do you mean? The time we were together we went out to eat and to parties lots of times," he protested, then remembered his earlier thoughts. "But no honest-to-God dates, right?"

She nodded. "We've never truly gotten to know each other," she explained. "Oh, I know what brand of toothpaste you use, that you hate cauliflower, what side of the bed you sleep on, and how you despise to go grocery shopping, but that isn't knowing the real person inside. If we weren't involved in our work, we were partying. I confess, I don't know the real Murphy at all."

Murphy hid the smile welling up from deep inside him. Did Charlie realize what she was saying? Before, she hadn't cared enough to find out about the man behind the face. It was true, he also had been involved in his work. While he hadn't enjoyed acting one type of role all the time, he still believed in giving the director everything he had. Charlie was always engrossed in her dancing, so the only time they saw each other was late in the evening. And rather than talk about their day's activities or what was going on in their minds, they allowed their bodies to carry on a more intimate conversation.

"We didn't bother talking very much in those days," she said softly, echoing his thoughts.

Murphy looked down at his wine glass, his fingers twirling the delicate stem. "Are you willing to give it a try? To see if we can really talk—really *learn* to know each other?" He lifted his head slowly. There was that nasty reminder in the back of his mind that she might leave him again, but he knew he had to take a chance.

Charlie hesitated. If they decided to get to know each other better, she knew they would eventually end up in bed. It wasn't that she didn't want Murphy to make love to her, but she feared something else. She feared this time there would be pain on her side when they parted, and she would suffer more than she ever had during all her hours of dance practice.

"Are you sure you can handle it?" she retorted, mustering up a teasing grin.

He didn't smile back. "Can you?"

She sensed he meant something else. "I'd like to be your friend, Murphy. I've always admired you and the way you handled the problems that came your way. You were always calm and down to earth, whereas I used to fly around scared to death over the most trivial matter."

"You know, of course, that everyone will think we're having a torrid affair," he teased, pleased at her compliment and relieved that she was willing to give his idea a try.

"I have noticed that their minds seem to be primarily preoccupied with sex," she said dryly, lifting the last bit of cheesecake and steering it toward her lips. "It's amazing that they haven't slowed down the least bit."

Murphy reached across and stopped its progress by grasping her wrist and guiding her fork to his mouth. Keeping his eyes on her stunned features, he closed his lips over the rich minty confection and slid it off the fork.

"That"—she licked her dry lips—"that isn't fair."

He grinned. "No, but I figured you wouldn't refuse me one little taste."

Charlie swallowed, feeling a heat build up inside her. "Since you've finished your coffee, there's no reason why you can't ask for the check, is there?" Her voice came out huskier than usual.

He inclined his head and looked around for their waiter. Within five minutes, they were walking out of the restaurant and along the wharf.

Charlie hugged her coat closer in an effort to stave off the cool ocean breeze. Seeing her shivering, Murphy moved closer to drape an arm around her shoulders and pull her closer.

"Still get cold easily, do you?"

She nodded. "And I have the high utility bills to prove it."

"I never knew anyone else who thought nothing of taking hour-long baths and continually replenishing the hot water in the tub," he commented as they walked slowly down the boardwalk.

Charlie grimaced at a reminder of one of her worst habits. She could still remember Murphy's roar of outrage when he had seen the first water bill after they had begun living together. He told her he couldn't believe anyone could use so much water in two months' time. His next shock came when the gas bill arrived. She recalled his relief to know Charlie was more than willing to pay her share of the bill, which they figured out to be a little over eighty percent of the balance.

"At least I never left wet towels all over the bathroom," she said with a touch of a smirk on her lips, "like some people I know."

"I've got a great idea," Murphy said with more enthusiasm than usual after hearing her comment about a bad habit he never considered all that bad. "Why don't we start from the beginning?" He stopped and turned to face her, his hand outstretched. "Hi, I'm James Murphy, and I answer to either name—and a few others not as respectable. I'm thirty-five and an ex-actor who now works as an administrator for a retirement community. I'm housebroken, have very few bad habits, and have been told I'm an all-around nice guy."

Charlie chuckled, shaking his hand. "I'm Charlotte Wells, but I prefer to go by Charlie. I'm twenty-nine and an ex-dancer who now works at a retirement community, and I've been told I have one of the best pairs of legs in Los Angeles."

Murphy looked down, remembering what the slacks hid. "I'd say they're the best in the world," he said huskily, then took her arm. "Well, now that we've been properly introduced, what do you say we find a club and listen to some music?"

"That sounds like a wonderful idea," she agreed, glad they were able to salvage their evening.

The club Murphy took her to had a band that played soft music that urged people to dance if they chose. Charlie assured him slow dancing wouldn't bother her knee, and after they ordered their drinks they merged with the other couples on the dance floor.

"When I'm dancing like this I dream about wearing a long, frothy dress while the band plays a Viennese waltz." She sighed against his shirt front.

"Your romantic streak is coming out," he teased, resting his chin against the fragrant cloud of her hair.

"Maybe so, but I don't care because it still sounds like a wonderful dream." Charlie linked her arms around his neck and tipped her head back so she could see the craggy planes of his face. "Too bad we can't go back one hundred years when they held formal balls."

Murphy shook his head. "I don't think you would like that time period very much. For one thing, there was no central heating, and I don't think everyone had indoor plumbing, not to mention all the other little luxuries you appreciate that weren't around."

Charlie wrinkled her nose. "Stop taking all the fun out of my dream."

"I'm not, love," he murmured, brushing the top of her head with his lips. "I'm merely pointing out the practical aspects."

They remained at the club another two hours dancing and talking. For the first time, they really sat down and talked, and it wasn't all that difficult for them to find many subjects to cover. Before they knew it the club was ready to close, and they reluctantly made their way back to New Eden.

"I don't suppose you'd ask me in?" Murphy asked on a hopeful note as he stood at Charlie's front door, waiting for her to find her key.

She smiled and shook her head. "It *is* pretty late."

After she opened her door, Murphy stepped forward to take her into his arms. Before he could accomplish his objective, Charlie stepped back.

"I'm afraid I don't believe in kissing on the first date." She lowered her eyes in a demure gesture to hide the dancing lights in the blue gray depths.

Murphy sighed. "Perhaps this will change your mind." He pulled her into his arms and set about to kiss her as thoroughly as possible.

Fireworks shot off behind her closed eyelids as she allowed his tongue to plunder her mouth. When she was positive her legs would buckle from under her he released her.

"Now I'll be saying good night to you." Murphy's ragged voice sounded just the way she felt. He turned away and walked to his car without a backward glance.

Charlie stood just inside the door, lifting her fingers to touch her slightly bruised lips. "Wow!" was all she could say before blindly entering the cottage and stumbling into bed.

CHAPTER SEVEN

It was Saturday morning, the sun was shining brightly, and the air was cool but not chilly. Charlie didn't care what it was like outside because she was too busy inside the house pampering herself. After she cleaned the small rooms and baked a large pan of cornbread, she went into the bathroom to try out a new beauty treatment she had bought before she left Los Angeles. The process consisted of applying one mud pack to her hair and another type to her face. When she'd finished the applications, she took a look in the mirror and burst out laughing. Her hair was plastered against her head, thanks to a deep gray mud treatment, and a grayish green mask covered her face, save for circles around her eyes and mouth.

"This is the best I've looked in years," she said aloud, chuckling as she left the bathroom. She began laughing again when Donnie saw her and began shrieking in fright, her wings flapping wildly. "Donnie, it's all right. It's just me," she soothed, walking over to the bird. Realizing she was only agitating the parrot more, Charlie left the bedroom and wandered out to the kitchen. She poured herself a glass of iced tea and carried her drink into the living room. She collapsed in a chair and picked up the book she had started the previous evening. But something else held her back from her reading.

She hadn't seen or heard from Murphy since their dinner out several days before. If she wanted to believe the worst, she would have convinced herself he was avoiding her for some reason. She probably could have brought Murphy's name casually into a conversation with Hazel, but her pride wouldn't allow it. If he didn't want to talk to her or see her, then so be it. She turned in the easy chair until her back snuggled firmly against one cushioned arm and her legs dangled over the other. She cradled the heavy book in her lap, but the printed words still couldn't hold her interest. She wondered what Murphy was doing today.

Had he driven into Santa Barbara to find a woman who kissed on the first date? For Pete's sake, didn't he realize she'd been teasing? She had only wanted to see if she could get a rise out of him, and she certainly had! Oh, the frustration of it all! It was tempting to cry, but she knew she would ruin the drying mask.

From the beginning, Charlie's free Saturdays were always spent the same way. First she cleaned house, then she gave herself an all-over beauty treatment. Since she generally had a date or plans for Saturday night, her preparations never went to waste. Since coming to New Eden, her weekends were solitary, and while it was great in the beginning, now all the peace and quiet was beginning to pall. It wasn't that she wanted to go out and party. She just wanted to know that her gorgeous shining hair and clear skin would be appreciated by someone other than herself.

Finally forcing herself to empty her mind to all but

the book in front of her, she resumed her reading, sipping her tea at odd intervals. She eventually got involved in the intricate plot when a knock at the door disturbed her.

"Oh, good, company," she murmured, untangling herself from the chair and walking to the door. Forgetting about the beauty treatment still covering her hair and face, she threw the door open.

Murphy stared at Charlie, unable to believe what he saw. "Charlie?" he ventured.

"Of course." She scowled, wondering what was wrong, and the protesting skin under the dry mud reminded her of the mask. She swore under her breath.

"I always thought green was your color," he choked, quickly stepping inside before she had a chance to slam the door in his face.

"You weren't invited in." Charlie discovered she couldn't glare at him either. "If you'll excuse me." She ran into the bathroom to wash off the two masks, then wrapped her wet hair up in a towel. Deciding not to improve her appearance by changing out of her old sweatpants and sweatshirt—after all, he'd seen her at her worst before—she returned to the living room.

Murphy was seated on the couch, sipping a cup of coffee. "I fixed instant since I couldn't find anything else."

"I never have the patience to brew any," she replied, settling back in her chair. "And to what do I owe this honor?"

"What do you put all that gunk on for?" he asked curiously.

"Because I'll be thirty before I know it, and I'd like to remain as wrinkle-free as possible until it's acceptable for a woman to look a little shopworn," Charlie retorted, picking up her glass of tea.

"A few wrinkles never hurt anyone, man or woman," he argued, wondering why they were bickering over such a trivial thing as her beauty treatments.

Apparently Charlie didn't see it that way. "That's where you're wrong, and I'm sure many of the women around here would agree with me," she said, a hard edge in her voice. "When a man has lines around his eyes and mouth, they're called character lines or laugh lines. When it's a woman, they're referred to as crow's-feet or just plain old-fashioned wrinkles." She took a deep breath, warming up to one of her favorite arguments. While she never worried about growing older, it always bothered her that the world took different views regarding women and men's ages.

"Whoa!" He held up his hands in surrender. "Hey, honey, I didn't come to fight with you over some thoughtless people's ideas."

"Then why did you come?"

He sighed, silently deciding this wasn't one of her better days. "Since I had to be in L.A. on business for a few days, I thought I'd stop by to see how you were doing."

So that's where he had been!

"Oh, were you gone?" Charlie asked in an all-too-careless voice.

Murphy's lips stretched into a broad grin. The little witch had known very well he'd been gone; he could tell by her attitude. He hadn't wanted to leave so soon after their dinner date, but it appeared to have done some good. He doubted she'd admit it, but he'd bet everything she had missed him, too.

"What's so funny?" she demanded, wondering what put him in such good humor.

"The memory of you answering the door wearing all that fancy mud," he lied smoothly.

Charlie blushed. "Next time I won't answer the door," she muttered.

"Why don't you just have your facials at the beauty spa?"

"Because I enjoy doing it myself." She curled one leg under her body. "You still haven't said why you came."

"A group is getting together to drive over to Solvang for dinner tonight," Murphy told her. "Would you like to come?"

"As a couple?" Charlie asked suspiciously, still not happy he'd seen her wearing that horrible face mask.

"Not really. I played golf with Ian and Jason this morning, and they mentioned it. They asked if I'd find out if you'd like to go along. Does that make you feel better about it?"

It was certainly better than spending the evening at home, she thought, especially since she'd planned to heat up a frozen dinner. "Sounds fine with me."

Murphy nodded. "We're meeting in front of the rec center at five thirty." He drained his cup and stood up, taking the cup into the kitchen before leaving. As he opened the door, he turned around. "I guess it's a good thing you decided to indulge in your beauty treatments at home, isn't it?" A large throw pillow hit the door just after it closed.

Prepared for a cold evening, Charlie dressed accordingly in gray wool slacks and an intarsia print sweater with primary colors of raspberry, gray, and cream.

When she reached the recreation hall, she found Lena, Jason, Ramona, and Ian already there.

"We're glad you could come along," Lena greeted her. "James offered to pick up Ramona since her cottage is the farthest. He should be along in a few minutes."

"Who else is going?" Charlie asked.

"Felix, Maude, and Henrietta and Fred Thompson." She went on to mention four other people Charlie didn't know except as residents of the community.

"Aren't you afraid Murphy and I will cramp your style?" she teased.

Jason shook his head. "He promised the two of you would behave as long as the rest of us did," he told her with a twinkle in his eyes.

Charlie had a pretty good idea what kind of behavior Jason meant and was sorely tempted to reply that there would be no problem as far as she was concerned. Not that it wasn't tempting, but she didn't think this was the time to indulge in a hot and heavy affair. She turned when Lena called her and smiled through introductions to the two other couples who had just arrived.

Five minutes later, Murphy drove up with Ramona, and the other couple appeared soon after. Charlie stood back as the group figured out who would ride with whom so the least number of cars would be used. She learned silence wasn't always the best bet, as she found herself riding with Lena, Jason, and Murphy in Jason's roomy Seville.

"You can drive during the return trip, old man," Jason informed Murphy with a wicked wink. "Lena and I have so few opportunities to neck in the backseat of a car that we take advantage of every chance we get."

"That certainly hasn't stopped you before," Lena retorted as Charlie climbed into the backseat. She, in turn, settled herself in the front. She half turned in the seat to speak to Charlie. "If you don't listen to him you'll be much better off."

"I would advise the same where Murphy is concerned."

"I resent that," the wounded party argued.

"However did you come up with calling him Murphy?" Lena asked once the car rolled silently down the sloping road.

"Actually, we knew each other years ago when he was acting in L.A.," Charlie said, carefully choosing her words much to Murphy's amusement. "He usually wore really old jeans and had a beard then, so I told him he didn't look like a James or even a Jim but a Murphy. Pretty soon everyone was calling him that." She looked him over. "I guess it doesn't fit as well, now but it's hard to break old habits."

Murphy looked her over just as carefully. "Yes, old habits are definitely hard to break. I always called her Legs because she had the damnedest long legs I'd ever seen." But Charlie knew he meant something entirely different.

"Where did you two meet?" Jason asked curiously.

Charlie's breath stopped. There was no way she would confess to the truth behind their first meeting.

"We met at a party," Murphy intervened.

Charlie shot him a look of silent gratitude that Lena noticed easily. It made her wonder what the true circumstances of their first meeting were. She would have bet anything it had to have been very interesting! Especially when she heard Murphy's next words.

"You know what I mean, lust at first sight." He leered at a frowning Charlie.

"It's amazing how a man views a situation differently than a woman," she said dryly, earning a chuckle from the older couple. "We spent most of the evening in a diner drinking coffee until we floated out the door."

"Why do I feel there's more to the story?" Lena murmured, turning around.

Charlie wasn't about to pursue the older woman's comment, especially when she felt Murphy's hand on her knee. She turned to him with a sweet smile. "Murphy, gentlemen do not grope," she told him, adding in anticipation of his retort, "And please don't tell me you're not a gentleman because you can act the part when you want to."

When they reached the Danish town of Solvang, the caravan of several cars parked in a public lot, and its members got out with tiny groans of relief. Jason had phoned in their reservation ahead of time, and they had only a short wait before being seated at a long table in a side dining room.

Charlie looked at the menu, unable to choose among the many Danish dishes.

"If you figure out how many pounds you gain from just looking at the food, you'll go crazy." Murphy leaned over to murmur in her ear.

She wrinkled her nose, not liking the fact that he could still read her mind. "Old habits die hard. And I'll have you know I wasn't calculating calories."

"A few extra pounds won't hurt."

"Once upon a time, they did," she argued softly.

"A director of activities doesn't have to worry about

her weight. Her exercise classes should take it off," he returned just as quietly.

Charlie's head snapped up. She wanted to remind him that there was a chance she just might dance again, but she was superstitious and afraid she might jinx it.

Murphy could read her mind and flashed her a small smile. He also knew if he said too much, it wouldn't faze Charlie at all to get up and walk out. And he didn't want that to happen until he was able to find out how much she had changed over the years. In working with her these past weeks, he'd already noticed new maturity she had gained over the years. He was beginning to wonder if it was just a facade she wore to impress the residents or if she had finally grown up.

"Tell you what, if the meal puts any extra pounds on, I'll help you work them off," he promised with a wicked glint in his eyes.

Her smile was guaranteed to freeze the noblest of men. "I know of excellent ways to work them off without the assistance of a second party."

Murphy grimaced. "But I'm sure it's not as fun." Then he turned away when someone called out his name.

Deciding she only lived once and Murphy was right —she didn't have to bother counting calories just now —Charlie finally settled on duck with small potatoes. She soon became immersed in the many conversations circling the table until a sock-covered foot toyed with her toes. Her head turned and she noticed Murphy's all-too-innocent gaze. He *would* do something like this when there were people around. A wicked smile curved her lips. Well, two could play at this game. She picked up her wine glass, sipping the tart liquid as she slid her foot out of her shoe and reached for the leather loafer across from her. She slid her foot over the polished leather and up to his ankle.

Murphy's head snapped up and caught her bland expression. He leaned back in his chair and waited to see what would happen. Her stocking-covered foot skimmed up his leg under his trouser hem, caressed the skin, and slid back down. His other foot found its way back to her leg. When she tickled his calf, he tickled hers. When he brushed her knee, she snaked around to the back of his. And when her toes found his fly, almost making him jump out of his chair, his foot surveyed the soft wool of her slacks covering the apex of her thighs. Charlie's smile froze. She picked up her glass and held it out as a silent toast before swallowing the contents. Murphy did the same with his wine. It was mutually decided they were better off stopping now before going too far.

When their dinner arrived, Jason rose to his feet and held up his wine glass. "To good friends," he announced.

Around the table they all murmured his toast and sipped their wine.

Charlie was kept amused all through dinner by the different stories. If she expected a sedate affair with middle-aged diners, she soon learned differently. Felix shared his experiences from his years working in popular night clubs, including the times some of his tricks went awry because of inept assistants, a full moon, or whatever excuse sounded good to him for that incident. The more wine he drank, the more outrageous his stories became. From there Jason shared some of his "war stories" from travels around the gambling capitals of the world. Henrietta and Fred Thompson also spoke about their singing with a popular swing band that had gigs all over the country during the Second World War. Everyone had at least one story to relate.

"What about you, Charlie?" Ramona spoke up in her quiet voice that still managed to be heard above the others. "Certainly you've had some interesting experiences in your work."

She shrugged. "Well, there was the time I tried out for the L.A. cast of *CATS*, but I learned I was allergic to the fur they used for part of the costumes. They were very polite when they explained that they weren't performing *Snow White and the Seven Dwarfs* and wouldn't need a Sneezy."

"She forgot about her performance in *Best Little Whorehouse in Texas*," Murphy explained. "She happened to do an interesting little tumble one night."

Charlie groaned. "The heel of my shoe broke and I did a very ungraceful tumble," she explained. "Luckily my partner was great at ad libbing, and the audience didn't know it wasn't part of the show. The choreographer almost had a coronary but quieted down when he realized I wasn't trying to sabotage his work."

"Tell them where you landed," Murphy prodded with a broad grin.

She rolled her eyes. "Right where it would hurt the most," was all she would say, but it was enough to get the idea across.

Dinner ended with small glasses of Cherry Kijafa, a Danish liqueur that was pleasing to the senses and very potent. Owing to the wine drunk during dinner and the after-dinner drinks, Charlie was very pliable when Murphy draped an arm around her shoulders and pulled her close as they left the restaurant.

"I think the lady is a bit smashed," he said to the others as they walked down the sidewalk.

"I am not," Charlie denied, carefully enunciating each word. "There's not one part of my body that's broken."

Lena chuckled. "That's certainly a new way of describing it," she said, tucking her arm through Jason's.

"Hopefully the cold air will sober her up." Murphy found it difficult to keep his grin hidden. He wasn't sure if Charlie would appreciate being described as delightful in this condition—not to mention extremely amiable! He could get to enjoy this in a big hurry.

"We should go dancing," Charlie announced suddenly and to no one in particular. "Murphy is a very good dancer," she confided. "And naturally, I'm excellent, owing to years of intensive training."

"No offense, sweetheart, but I have a horrible feeling you'd trip over your feet tonight," Murphy told her gently.

"I never trip over my feet." Her lower lip jutted out in a pout.

The short walk around the sleepy town helped settle overly full stomachs and clear everyone's head but Charlie's. She continued walking, involved in her own little world, humming snatches of popular songs under her breath.

"She's something else when she's had a few too many," Jason commented when they returned to his car. He assisted Lena into the backseat and slid in behind her. "I've never seen such a happy drunk before."

"I have to admit I've never seen her like this," Murphy replied, ensuring Charlie's seat belt was buckled after she botched her first three tries. "She rarely drinks more than one glass of wine in an evening, so this is new for her."

"It must be broken," she said, looking up at him with wide-eyed innocence.

"I don't think that's the problem, Charlie," he answered dryly before closing the passenger door.

During the drive back, Murphy learned just how amiable Charlie could be when she was tipsy. She slid across the seat as far as the restraining belt would allow her and laid her head on his shoulder.

"Just remember you're driving, old boy," Jason sang out from the backseat.

Murphy gulped when Charlie's hand floated over his thigh. "It can be mighty hard to do," he muttered.

"Oh, honey, it isn't that just yet," she said with demure logic.

Jason roared with laughter while Lena put her hand against her mouth to keep back her own chuckles.

"Perhaps we should change places," Jason offered.

"Uh—no," Murphy managed to say even as Charlie's hand danced its way up his thigh. "I think I might be safer up here. Charlie, cut it out!" he hissed, taking his hand from the steering wheel to grab her erring fingers.

"You never used to mind before," she reminded him.

He rolled his eyes and prayed they wouldn't get pulled over by the police. In her inebriated state Charlie had no conception of doing anything wrong. She continued to stroke the hard muscles of Murphy's thigh and delighted in the feel of the warm flesh under her fingertips. She made a moue of disappointment when he grabbed her hand and squeezed it in warning. The moment he released it she returned to what appeared to be her favorite occupation.

By the time they reached the recreation hall, Murphy was ready to call the men in white coats to cart him away to a very cold shower. He assisted Charlie out of the car and led her in the general direction of his car.

"I think you better get her home in record time, James," Jason advised as he helped Lena out of the backseat.

"And try something other than a cold shower," Lena gave as her own suggestion.

"I don't understand what they find so funny," Charlie mused as Murphy bundled her into his car.

"It must have been something that was said," he muttered, walking around to the driver's side.

Within minutes, he parked his car in front of Charlie's cottage. He plucked her purse out of her hands and rummaged through the contents, looking for her keys.

"I beg your pardon. A woman's purse is private," she informed him haughtily.

"I doubt I'd find anything I haven't seen before. I just wish you wouldn't carry everything but the kitchen sink in here." He found the large key ring and hunted for the door key. He guided her out of the car and to the door, leaning her against the wall as he unlocked the door and ushered her inside.

"Would you like a drink?" She spun around and faced him with a wide smile.

"I think coffee would be more in order." Murphy pushed her into a chair and walked to the kitchen. He barely turned on the light when he yelped. "Damn cat!" he grumbled.

"You probably woke Snickers up." Charlie yawned, pulling off her boots before deciding to lay her head back and close her eyes for a moment. "You know how the cat hates surprises."

Murphy muttered a graphic idea of how to take care of a finicky cat while he poured water into two mugs and placed them in the microwave. For all the times he and Charlie had hosted parties, he couldn't remember her ever acting like this. Of course, he didn't recall her drinking more than one drink either. So why did she indulge more than usual tonight? He stirred instant coffee into the mugs and added some powdered cream to Charlie's.

"Here, this should wake you up. I made it strong enough," he said, walking back into the living room. He stopped short when he found her curled up in the chair fast asleep. He set the mugs down and shook her shoulder gently. "Charlie, come on, wake up," he insisted. She muttered a protest and turned away. Murphy stood back, his hands resting on his hips. Half of him was tempted to leave her where she was, but he knew she'd wake up with more than an aching head. He picked her up and carried her into the bedroom, placing her on the bed. When he switched on a bedside lamp, Donnie fluffed her feathers in protest at having her rest disturbed.

"An invitation like this could give a guy a complex," he muttered. Rolling Charlie to one side, he whipped the covers back before rolling her to the other side. He explored the dresser to find a nightgown and finally came up with a batiste lace-trimmed nightshirt. He couldn't remember ever having so much willpower as when he stripped off her sweater and slacks and found her wearing only a tiny pair of bright red panties. Murphy groaned.

"Just remember, fella, it's nothing you haven't seen before," he told himself, lifting her up with shaky hands and dropping the nightshirt over her head. But he forgot that memory hadn't allowed for the lush beauty before him or the warmth of her skin under his hands. He gritted his teeth and carefully adjusted the covers around her. He went into the bathroom and dampened a washcloth, then ran it over her face to remove as much of her makeup as possible. Her eyelids opened to narrow slits.

"It's late, Murphy. Come to bed," she murmured, reaching up to twine her arms around his neck and pull him down with surprising strength, considering her condition. She fastened her lips on his and teased his mouth open with her daring tongue. Murphy groaned, feeling every last bit of strength leave his body under her seduction. Just as he began to take her into his arms and finish what she had started, she sighed, fell back, and rolled over, tucking her legs up.

He sat down on the edge of the bed and laughed softly, although he doubted anything would wake her up now. "Woman, if I were a less sane man, I'd take you up on your kind offer, but I think I'll pass this time." He stood up and turned to speak gently to Donnie, who hissed at him with her own reminder to let her go back to sleep. "All I seem to run into tonight are bossy women." He turned out the light and left the bedroom, then walked out of the cottage, making sure the door shut securely behind him. He always knew Charlie had the power to drive him crazy, and the events of the past couple of hours were perfect proof.

148

Charlie rolled over and groaned. She opened one eye, closed it, and opened it again. Then she tried the other eye. Well, they worked. She ran her fur-covered tongue around her mouth and grimaced at the bad taste. At least she didn't have a headache. Unless her head was too numb to hurt. Why did she drink more than she could handle? Actually, that was easy. She had been sitting near Murphy and drank too much wine to keep up with the party and block out the sensual web he wove around her. The trouble was, it hadn't accomplished much. She groaned, recalling what had happened after dinner in vivid technicolor. Had she really said all those things to him? Had she honestly acted so brazen? Her memory said yes with a loud shout. She hadn't realized a drunk's memory could be so explicit.

She stumbled into the kitchen and poured herself a large glass of orange juice, drinking thirstily before setting herself to the task of fixing breakfast for Huggie Bear and Snickers. Thank goodness it didn't involve any ability other than pouring dry kibble into one bowl and tearing open a foil-lined envelope, then pouring the contents into another bowl. Once the animals were taken care of, she went into the bathroom for a shower and change of clothes.

As she stood under the hot spray, she wondered why Murphy had impersonally undressed her and left her to her solitary bed instead of joining her. In the back recesses of her mind, she had this faint thought that she might have given him a motive to stay with her, but it was so faint she wasn't sure if it was the truth or merely a dream. Why couldn't her memory be clear on that? What had been his reason for acting like a gentleman?

Come to think of it, had she ever been able to figure him out? Deciding that thinking was too taxing on a tender brain, she rubbed shampoo into her hair and massaged her scalp, then stepped back under the shower spray to rinse it off.

Charlie mentally chastised herself for even wondering why Murphy hadn't taken advantage of her. That had never been his style. Pretty soon a heat not associated with the warm water ran over her skin. She mustn't think about Murphy and his lovemaking abilities! Quickly switching the water to cold, Charlie squealed under the icy flow before stepping out and wrapping a towel around her chilled body. She blew her hair dry and dressed in jeans and a bright blue pullover sweater in record time. Then she decided to take Huggie Bear for a walk. While she might have preferred driving into Santa Barbara or even down to one of the shopping malls near Ventura, she knew she hadn't spent much time with her animals lately. She was grateful that Ramona enjoyed walking Huggie Bear during the week, and the dog obviously adored the older woman.

Huggie Bear barked with delight when he saw his mistress take the leash off the hook in the kitchen. The large black dog danced around her feet as she hooked the leash to his collar and led him out the front door.

Their walk took them past the tennis courts where Charlie saw several people she knew and waved to them, shaking her head to their good-natured invitations to play. The outdoor swimming pool was empty, but she was sure the indoor pool was being used. When Charlie reached the large grassy area to one side of the medical center, she noticed several patients in wheel chairs sitting on the lawn and enjoying the sun. She halted for a moment, stunned by the look of desolation on some of their faces. After being around the more active residents, she tended to forget that not all the members were in excellent health. She walked slowly toward one woman whose gray hair was pinned back in a bun. As Charlie approached her her face betrayed no emotion. It was as if the light in her soul had been switched off.

"Hello," Charlie greeted cautiously. Faded blue eyes looked through her instead of at her. Charlie felt sad that a human being could be so shut off from life. "Are you feeling all right? Would you like me to call a nurse for you?" She wondered if she should get one of the nurses. She looked around but didn't see a nurse or aide in earshot. Charlie frowned. What if one of the patients needed help? Shouldn't there be someone with them at all times? She walked slowly to another person, this time a man who—with gnarled, arthritic hands explaining part of his condition—likewise didn't acknowledge her shy greeting.

"What is wrong with all of you?" she demanded, looking at the five other patients sitting in a semicircle. "Surely you can talk."

"I suggest you get that dog away from here right now."

Charlie looked up to see Winifred Page striding toward her. For a moment she visualized the stocky woman wearing the armor of a female Viking warrior. She bit down on her lip to keep from laughing because she knew that would surely seal her doom with the older woman.

"I was only walking by. And you don't have to worry

about Huggie Bear—he wouldn't harm a flea," she explained stiffly.

"Which he is probably filled with. I want that *thing* out of here right now," the older woman ordered, looking at the large dog with a wary eye.

"Who died and put you in charge?" Charlie snapped, her hands braced on her hips.

"I want you to leave before that animal bites someone," Winifred said more forcefully.

Charlie couldn't believe her ears. She knew only too well that Huggie Bear wouldn't hurt anyone because he was one of the biggest cowards around. And listening to her beloved dog's reputation being maligned only made her angry. She leaned forward and whispered her taunt. "What are you going to do, Winifred? Have somebody rub me out?"

Charlie turned when Huggie Bear whined happily, his large tail thumping. One woman, her parchment-thin skin wrinkled with time and her eyes dimmed from the years, stretched out a tentative hand to the dog.

"Dog," she whispered in a voice rusty from disuse.

"Myrna!" Winifred's voice cracked like a whip, and the woman shrank back under the tone that also carried a trace of fear if Charlie cared to listen for it. "That dog could be dangerous. I don't want you to be hurt."

"Hold on a minute." Charlie was growing angrier by the moment, not bothering to listen to the older woman's fear. "These are people, not animals for you to order around any way you please."

"You just worry about planning your parties and weekend jaunts, little girl, and leave my domain to me," Winifred snapped.

Charlie narrowed her eyes. "This isn't over by far,

Winnie." She stressed the woman's nickname, knowing how much she abhorred it. "That building over there may be your private little kingdom, but out here it's the free world. You better step carefully, because I'm not someone you'd like to have as an enemy."

She looped the end of Huggie Bear's leash around her wrist and stalked off. The idea of a pleasant walk had lost its appeal. She was determined to corner Murphy and find out just what Winifred Page was up to. Charlie was beginning to wonder if the woman truly had her patients' welfare at heart. And once Charlie was on the warpath, there was nothing that was going to stop her.

CHAPTER EIGHT

Murphy couldn't believe so many sledgehammers could fit themselves inside his head. He winced, pulling the pillow over his head to drown out the army marching through his brain.

"Column, halt," he muttered. Even that was too loud for his tender head. Why couldn't he have gone to bed like he planned, instead of sitting up half the night working on a bottle of scotch while trying to figure out Charlie? The two turned out to be a potent combination. He should have known better than to mix alcohol with Charlie. Hell, he doubted if he could have done any better sober!

But the pounding refused to stop. It took him another minute to figure out that all the drumming wasn't in his head; some of it was on the door. He dragged himself out of bed and groped blindly for his robe. Then he remembered he didn't own one. He was saved by finding a pair of jeans lying on the floor near the closet.

"All right, all right," he said, pulling on the jeans and making his way slowly to the door. "Can't a guy get some sleep around here?" he grumbled, throwing it open.

"That woman is a menace, Murphy, and if you have

any brains, you'll get rid of her right away," Charlie announced, marching through the door. She spun around and faced him. "What have you done to yourself? You look terrible."

"Thank you for that sincere compliment." He sighed, raking his fingers through his hair. "Now, if you don't mind, I'd like to go back to bed and die quietly." He held the door open as a silent hint for her to leave, which she promptly ignored.

"Nonsense! All you need is some breakfast." She shook her head at his groan of dismay. "And some strong coffee." Charlie looked around for the kitchen and headed for it.

"I do not want any breakfast and I don't want any coffee," Murphy informed her, following her into the narrow rectangular room. "All I want is to go back to bed and get some sleep."

She shot him an exasperated look as she rummaged through the cupboards and found a can of coffee. "We have to talk."

"If this is a business talk, it can wait until Monday morning," he told her tiredly, leaning his hip against a counter and watching her measure out the coffee and dump the grounds into the percolator basket.

Charlie turned around and looked at him sharply. "You didn't drink enough last night to have a hangover this morning."

"I did, after I got back home."

She turned back to hunt for a skillet in the cabinets, then found eggs in the refrigerator. "I should think someone your age would know better than to drink alone."

"I mean it, Charlie. I don't want any breakfast,"

Murphy insisted, placing a hand over his upset stomach.

"It will help more than going back to sleep. You'll only wake up again with the same headache." She cracked eggs into the pan and began to scramble them. In no time, she had eggs and toast on the small table adjoining the kitchen.

"You've turned bossy in your old age, Charlie," he grumbled, finding himself hungrier than he thought.

"I just want you in a good mood when I tell you my news." She grinned impishly and poured herself a cup of coffee.

Murphy groaned. "That's right . . . You talked about firing someone when you barged in here."

Charlie's grin disappeared. She reached across the table and grasped his hand. "That woman is horrible, Murphy," she said with an intensity that wasn't lost on him. "She's a witch."

He had a feeling he was going to regret asking. "Who's a witch?"

"Winifred Page."

Murphy closed his eyes. From the beginning, he had an idea the free-spirited Charlie and the grim-faced Winifred wouldn't get along. It seemed the first battle had already begun. He wouldn't be surprised if he heard from the medical center director in the morning. Luckily she didn't have the nerve to barge in on him so early in the morning. He glanced at the clock. Make that afternoon. "What happened?"

"She's so mean to her patients!" Charlie went on to describe her run-in with the older woman. During her story, Murphy deleted many of the more colorful adjectives, toned down the story, and figured he had the truth left. He poured himself another cup of coffee and sipped it as he listened to her tale.

"First off, she isn't mean to her patients," he said quietly, setting his cup down. "She's brusque and may not have the compassion we would have wished for, but she is a good director. And considering her personality, we don't have a large turnover at the center."

"But those people are so *lifeless!*" she exclaimed, pounding the table and drawing a wince from him. "Just because they're sick doesn't mean they have to be hidden away from the rest of the world."

"Charlie . . ." He paused, searching for words that wouldn't sound condescending. "Sometimes older people aren't as outgoing as Lena, Jason, and the others. When they grow ill they lose interest in themselves and the world around them. At least they aren't forgotten here and spend an hour or so outside when the days are warm. And even the residents go up there to visit."

"But one lady tried to touch Huggie Bear," she insisted. "She showed interest in him, and if she's sick the way you say she is, she wouldn't care one whit about him, would she?"

Murphy shrugged. "Who knows?"

"All I want to know is if I can take the animals up there occasionally and visit the patients. I'll only do it when they're outside," she added.

"That has to be okayed by Mrs. Page."

"You know very well she'll say no!" Charlie wailed. She got that stubborn look on her face. "You're in total charge of this place, so why can't you overrule her when she denies me? The woman hates me!"

"Because I can't do that!" he shouted back. "The medical center is under her jurisdiction. Besides, I'm not all that sure your idea is a good one. Charlie, I have an idea you're overreacting to this. Winifred may appear to be a harsh woman, but she really isn't. She doesn't talk about her past much, but I suspect she hasn't had a very easy life. So, give us all a break, okay?"

Charlie stood up and gathered the dirty dishes, clanking them carelessly as she deposited them in the sink. Murphy kept expecting something to break. She washed them swiftly and put everything away before she left the kitchen.

"There is nothing wrong with my idea," she said with quiet determination. "Small children are soothed by the presence of a favorite stuffed animal or a pet lying close to them, and I'm sure the same would be true for these people. Having access to a dog or cat wouldn't hurt them."

"I understand what you're saying, Charlie," Murphy replied. "I'm just asking you to have some patience and use a little tact when you deal with her."

Charlie sighed. When she bothered to think about it she had to admit she had overreacted with Mrs. Page. But she wasn't sure she wanted to acknowledge she was wrong. At least, not yet. She knew she should go home and think over what Murphy told her, and perhaps she could figure out a more tactful way of approaching Winifred Page.

"I'll try," she said quietly before she left the house.

Murphy remained at the table, still recovering from the dark blond whirlwind who had gotten him out of bed less than an hour ago. He wanted to dance and shout with joy that Charlie was thinking of other people, but another part wanted to sigh because he knew she would have a fight on her hands if she didn't try compromising with Winifred Page. This was one battle he intended to observe from the safety zone of the sidelines. He had to admit that it could turn out to be the battle of the century. If anyone else at New Eden heard about Charlie's idea and the identity of her opponent, he was certain he could sell tickets to the bout.

Charlie began thinking over new ideas as she walked back to her bungalow. She may have been jumping into a situation she couldn't handle, but she wouldn't know until she tried. She thought about the woman who had reached out to touch Huggie Bear and knew she couldn't give up before she even tried. She prayed she'd find a way to work with the formidable Mrs. Page.

Before the week was out, Charlie learned just how difficult Winifred Page could be. Once Mrs. Page learned Murphy wasn't going to interfere, she refused to have anything to do with Charlie. The older woman had visited Murphy first thing Monday morning to complain about Charlie's high-handed manner. Murphy soothed her indignation, hating himself for having to go against Charlie but knowing this was one time he couldn't back her up. He wondered if Charlie wanted to do this badly enough to show the stamina to go the distance.

As the days passed, Charlie continued teaching her exercise classes and swam in the indoor pool twice a week. In addition, most of her work hours were spent planning the upcoming Halloween party, and the idea of using famous films as the theme was greeted enthusiastically. Charlie also visited a seamstress who had worked for several major film studios as a costume designer to see if she would help her with a costume. Between the two of them they came up with a clever outfit that would be a cute play on words for the movie title Charlie chose. She was curious about Murphy's costume, but he was secretive about its identity every time she asked him.

"It must be X-rated," she told Lena one day during lunch. "I don't see why he has to act as if telling me would undermine the freedom of the world."

Lena smiled and shook her head at the disgruntled expression on Charlie's face. "Give him a break, Charlie. For some reason, he wants to surprise you, so let him."

Charlie nodded, knowing she had no choice anyway. She would just have to wait until the party to see what his secrecy was all about.

Halloween: The night when witches, ghosts, and goblins come out to prey on the unsuspecting—unless they were holding a party at New Eden's recreation center.

Orange and black crepe paper twisted a trail along the ceiling while the band, dressed in traditional funeral black, played rock and swing tunes interspersed with appropriate dirges.

When Charlie entered the hall, she left her long black wool cape in the cloakroom and went in to join the revelers. She stood in the doorway for a moment, unable to hold back her surprise at the energy level of these people.

"Catchy costume, Charlie," Sylvester told her. "One of Joan Crawford's, right?"

She looked down at the brief black leather outfit, black fishnet hose, and spike heels. "I doubt it, Sylvester. You know how she liked padded shoulders in her clothing." She studied his toga and gold leaf crown resting over his brow. "Don't tell me . . . Julius Caesar."

He preened. "Naturally."

Charlie smiled. " 'Appropriate' is more like it." She moved away, greeting people right and left while noticing the usual Cleopatras, western figures, a few Draculas and Frankensteins, and even a Pink Panther. She craned her neck, searching the crowd for a glimpse of Murphy but couldn't find a sign of his familiar figure. She danced several times, drank an alcoholic punch that had the kick of a mule, and continued looking for Murphy. When she had called him earlier to see if he'd like to escort her to the party, he told her thanks, but he'd made other plans. She was surprised but didn't have the nerve to question him further, in case he said something she didn't want to hear—such as he was bringing a date to the party.

"Very sexy," Jason approved, twirling Charlie around. "What movie?"

She grinned wickedly and leaned closer to whisper in his ear. Jason chuckled.

"A great play on words." He grinned back. "James will certainly enjoy the view."

"If he sees it," Charlie muttered, deciding his other plans must have meant he wasn't coming to the party.

She had just accepted a dance with Ian when the band played a drum roll and a dark figure seemed to fly out over the bandstand.

All eyes flew upward to watch Murphy swing from a rope over the stage. Dressed in high black leather boots, skintight tan breeches, a full-sleeved shirt, and a brown leather vest, he looked every inch a marauding pirate.

He dropped onto the stage and ran toward the wings, reappearing with a large chest. After setting it on the floor, he opened the contents and began throwing out large gems, gaudy necklaces, and bracelets to his audience.

"The ship we captured was a rich one, mates, and I wish to share my booty with ye!" Murphy shouted, flashing a pirate's rakish grin. He continued throwing the jewels until the chest was empty. When finished, he dragged the chest back to the wings and jumped down onto the dance floor.

He plowed his way through the clapping crowd, smiling and accepting greetings from friends but never hesitating during his search for a lady dressed in black. When he asked Florence what Charlie's costume was, she would only smirk and tell him the color.

"I thought Tarzan only wore a loincloth," Charlie said when Murphy halted in front of her, his intense gaze taking in every inch of exposed skin. He leaned forward to drape a large chain with a rubylike pendant hanging from it around her neck.

"Tarzan?" He looked properly affronted. "I'll have you know I'm Captain Blood. So beware, my beauty." He leered, stepping back to get the full effect of her scanty costume.

Charlie tipped her head to one side, a red-tipped finger tapping her equally red lips. "Errol Flynn, you ain't."

Murphy drew himself up to his full height. "Milady, you doth slander me," he boomed in a deep voice. "And for that, ye shall be punished." He moved forward another step and, before Charlie could utter a word of protest, picked her up and slung her over his shoulder.

"Go on with your merrymaking, mates," he proclaimed loudly. "This winsome maid and I have other things to do."

"Murphy!" Charlie shrieked, pounding her fists against his back as he carried her out of the hall amid cheers and catcalls. "Help me!" she demanded, but it was clear everyone was on Murphy's side when Jason draped her cloak over her. "I don't find this funny," she warned.

"Now, now." Murphy nonchalantly patted her squirming buttocks. "Settle down or you'll get dizzy." He continued through the people-lined pathway toward the double doors.

"Murphy, you're embarrassing me," she insisted wrathfully, knowing she was going to murder him as soon as she was right side up again.

"You see, mates, just use a firm hand on your wenches and they'll never give you trouble." Even with his fidgeting burden, he easily managed a theatrical bow before sweeping out of the room.

"Let me *down!*" she ordered after they left the hall.

"Oh, no, milady, me thinks you'd run from me before I can have my way with you."

Charlie's skin tingled, and it wasn't because she was hanging upside down. Did he mean what he had just said—or was it part of his charade as a pirate? With the period clothing and gold ring winking from his left earlobe, he certainly looked the part.

"Okay, Murphy, fun is fun, but right now I'm not in a very humorous mood." She strove to keep the semblance of normalcy in her voice. "Put me down and let's return to the party."

"Oh, no, my beauty." His voice fairly boomed. "I'm

saving you from the licentious duke who means to marry you against your wishes."

Charlie choked back her laughter. Did he realize how he sounded?

"Where are you taking me?" she demanded, twisting her head to look around but unable to see very much. "Are you drunk?"

"We're going to me quarters, my beauty." He uttered what had to be a pirate's growl. "And I've not had a drop of grog this evening."

"So help me, Murphy, when you put me down I'm going to murder you!" she threatened, pounding his back with her fists. She yelped when a heavy hand descended on her thinly clad buttocks. "Sadist!" she hissed, vainly trying to lift her head enough to see where they were going.

All too soon, Murphy unlocked a door and entered his bungalow. He stalked through the living room and continued into another room.

"What are you—Augh!" Charlie shrieked when she found herself tipped over and dumped onto a soft surface. She scrambled onto her knees, looking up at the man facing her with his hands braced on his hips. His teeth gleamed white in the dim light, and the gold ring in his ear winked mockingly. She lifted her chin a fraction higher.

"What film does that little bit of nothing represent?" He gestured toward her outfit.

Her smile was pure sex. *Of Human Bondage.* If she had been a cat, she would have purred the words.

Murphy threw back his head and laughed. "Obviously your own definition of the term." He unbuckled the wide leather belt and pulled his shirt from the waistband of the tight breeches.

Charlie's eyes widened. "Wait a minute here." She held up her hands, palms outward as if they alone could hold him off, while she scrambled backward. Her breath caught in her throat when his broad chest with its inviting curly black hair was revealed. "Murphy, I think we need to talk this over," she suggested to his back while he sat down on the bed and pulled his boots off. *"Murphy!"*

"We've done too much talking already, Legs," he replied in a level tone. "Now it's time for some action. Are you still on the pill?"

Charlie nodded automatically. Watching him, she almost moaned when he stood up and the breeches slipped to the floor beside the boots; he wore no underwear.

He stretched out on the bed beside her and began tracing odd circles along her ankle, slowly moving up her leg. His eyes remained trained on hers, noticing the angry blue pupils turn into a soft smoky gray. He masked his feelings of triumph, knowing any type of smug expression would be his death sentence.

Charlie made certain not to look anywhere but Murphy's face for fear even one glance of his gorgeous body would turn her into a quivering mess.

"Everyone at the party will know what's supposed to be going on here," she said in a small voice.

"Supposed to be?"

She sighed under his touch behind her knee. "I guess you could say it's going to happen."

His hand reached her thigh and his face leaned closer

to hers, his lips feathering over her brow. "Do you care?"

"Yes . . . No . . . I don't know." She closed her eyes as his butterfly kisses covered each eyelid, then trailed down along her nose. One hand lifted tentatively to his chest, her palm resting against his warm skin.

Murphy kissed every inch of Charlie's face but the area she wanted him to—her lips. They tingled with awareness of his action and unconsciously pouted in silent invitation. It had been nine years, but she hadn't forgotten how his lovemaking had once made her feel. She wanted that euphoria again; she wanted to feel him inside her, feel him lifting her to heights she hadn't felt since they had parted. She burrowed her face against his shoulder and raked her teeth over the taut skin. Her thighs relaxed under his questing touch, and she sighed in delicious abandon when his fingers probed her warmth.

"Snaps," he breathed, feeling the three metal circles. "They make it much easier." He deftly released each one so he could slide his fingers under the supple fabric to the waistband of her fishnet hose. "Look at this . . . No underwear." He smiled as he proceeded to remove her clothing. "Lady, you went to that party loaded for bear. It's a good thing I carried you off when I did. An outfit like this could cause cardiac arrest."

"You should talk," she murmured. "Those tight pants of yours could end up cutting off blood circulation and ultimately make many women unhappy." She drew her tongue across his lips and delved inside for the taste that could only be labeled as Murphy's.

He shuddered at her intimate gesture. "The only one I worry about taking care of is you."

"Then I guess you got out of those pants just in time." Charlie was rapidly getting into the act. Her brain may have argued that it was still too soon, but her hormones urged her to go for it. "I just hope you're up to the job."

"I eat my Wheaties." He gasped as her hand covered his burgeoning arousal and began a stroking motion guaranteed to blow away any last vestige of sanity.

"Good, because at the rate we're going, you're going to need all your strength." She bit down on his lower lip just enough to gain his attention.

Murphy chuckled. Past experience reminded him it wouldn't take much to arouse Charlie. Then a horrible thought occurred to him. Surely no other man could have the same effect on her? Tightening his jaw, he vowed to give her a night she would never forget. He lay on his side and pulled her body against his.

Charlie felt the soft hair on his chest brush the aching tips of her breasts and his swollen masculinity seek out her feminine warmth. The individual scents of their bodies rose to blend into an erotic perfume.

"You're still beautiful, Legs," Murphy said hoarsely, covering her firm breast with his hand and kneading the swollen flesh.

"Older is more like it," she said wryly.

He shook his head. He hadn't missed the mature fullness of her breasts and the womanly swell of her hips. He remembered the young man and woman who had reveled in the passion of two healthy, young bodies. Although they didn't know it, the same man and woman would now revel in love.

Charlie's eyes closed with the sheer pleasure Murphy's mouth gave her as his lips and teeth paid

167

homage to her breast. She could feel the pulling action all the way to her womb. Her veins sang and every nerve ending sizzled at the contact of his body against hers. As to what his hands were doing—such a touch was probably illegal in many states.

She linked her arms around his neck and brought him closer. Her mouth opened under his plundering tongue and absorbed his taste. She wanted him. All of him. Her legs shifted apart for his knee even as her hips arched upward for the loving intrusion. She reached down to find him more than ready for her. The years fell away as she guided him into her waiting portal. Their eyes caught and remained fixed on each other as the possession slowly took place.

Murphy smiled as her moist warmth surrounded him. He had come home. He chased away his first inclination to thrust deeply and remained still to allow them the wonder of their joining.

"I've never been ravished by a pirate before," Charlie whispered, the merest hint of a smile curving her lips. She wrapped her legs around his hips to deepen his possession. "In fact, I feel sort of kinky."

"I'll leave my cutlass on the floor if you promise not to bring out the whips," he teased, beginning the slow but sure movements guaranteed to bring her pleasure.

She flashed him a wicked smile as her hand snaked down between their bodies to touch him. "Honey, if you dare to take your cutlass away, I *will* bring out the whips."

Murphy laughed, gazing into Charlie's blue-gray eyes. Her face was flushed with love and her lips . . . Oh, that sweet, delicious mouth. He could feast on her from now until doomsday. While he doubted she had been celibate all these years—after all, he knew the depth of her sensuality—he sensed arrogantly that no man had given her the pleasure he knew he could give her. He slid his hands under her tight buttocks as her long legs wrapped around his hips. Murphy breathed deeply, then covered her mouth with his, tasting her essence. While he wanted nothing more than to thrust fast and deep until they soared the heavens, he also wanted their lovemaking to last as long as possible. But the way his body was reacting, he knew he might not have as much control as he wanted. He gritted his teeth and ordered his brain to control the urges his libido was trying to take charge of.

A faint sheen of perspiration lent an unearthly glow to Charlie's face and body, and her high breasts with their cherry pink tips tempted Murphy for another taste as his hips set a rhythm he knew she would follow. His veins were molten rivers of lava, his skin sensitive to the heat radiating from her. He wanted to cry, to laugh, to just reach out and fully embrace all she could give him. He felt her teeth fasten on the ear graced by the gold earring. He was the privateer, in from many months at sea, who needed a woman's body; she, the young maiden abducted for his pleasure. His teeth bared as he felt the pressure building up until his entire body was consumed by the flames and he was forced to give in to the dictates of his body. Murphy thrust faster, watching Charlie fall into the fire before he followed her.

Drawing ragged breaths into tortured lungs, Murphy braced himself on his elbows to take his weight off Charlie.

"Talk about fanning the sparks of an old love." He

chuckled, rubbing his nose against hers. "Honey, we just went through a raging forest fire!"

Charlie's eyelids flickered shut. She hadn't felt so sleepy and content in a long time as she curled around Murphy the way Snickers wound himself around his favorite pillow.

"It was beautiful, Legs," Murphy said softly, unwilling to disturb the mood. "Better than nine years ago." He nuzzled the dark blond hair on her head. The sound of deep breathing alerted him. He lifted his head and looked down. Charlie's eyes were closed, her mouth open slightly. "Well, I'll be damned. She fell asleep on me." Laughing quietly, he pulled the covers over them, tucked Charlie closer to him, and settled down to a good night's sleep.

It was morning. Charlie sensed it by the bright light trying to sneak past her tightly closed eyelids, but she was having none of that.

"Give it up, Charlie," a whispered voice taunted. "It's way past dawn and you have to wake up whether you want to or not."

"Ha!" Her usual caustic reply was muffled by the pillow she drew over her face. "Wake me up in time for lunch."

Warm masculine laughter washed over her like a down comforter. "Darlin', it's already one o'clock—in the *afternoon.*"

"What?" The pillow was pushed unceremoniously to the floor as she bolted upright. "Oh, my God, the animals. They need to be fed and let out!"

"Already done." Murphy handed her a cup of steaming coffee. He smiled appreciatively at the sight of her pert breasts peeking out above the pale blue sheet. "Although that damn cat tried to take my leg off."

"Snickers? You didn't hurt him, did you?" She sipped her coffee.

Murphy scowled. "Hey, what about *me?* Cat scratches can give a person pretty nasty infections, you know." He settled on the edge of the bed near her hip. "Did you sleep all right?" His voice took on a new husky note. He brushed his knuckles across her cheek, then wrapped the same hand around her nape and drew her to him for a thoroughly satisfying good-morning kiss that rapidly escalated to a let's-make-love kiss.

Charlie blindly set her coffee cup down on the nightstand and wound her arms around his neck, preferring to give her all when it was requested so beautifully. It was two hours before either resurfaced to the land of the living.

For a very late lunch, Murphy grilled two steaks while Charlie fixed a large green salad.

It went without saying that she would be spending the night with him.

"This should keep up our strength," he told her during their meal.

Her eyes swept over the more-than-adequate feast. "Oh, yes, that should hold us for at least a few hours," she said dryly, carefully slicing her meat after rolling several inches of cotton sleeves above her wrists.

Murphy buttered a piece of warm french bread and held it over the table so Charlie could take a bite out of the crisp crust and soft insides.

"Mmm, great." She rolled her eyes in appreciation.

"Of course I am."

She shot him a pained expression. "A real man doesn't act like a peacock," she intoned.

Murphy reached under the table and pinched her thigh, his hand lingering to stroke the well-toned flesh.

Charlie continued eating as she plucked his hand from her leg. "Please, no groping during dinner."

He ignored her wisecrack and decided to dine on her instead of the remainder of his steak. It wasn't long before Charlie's blood began to warm.

"If"—she licked her lips at the heavy feeling settling between her thighs—"if we don't eat now, we probably won't have anything until tomorrow."

"True." His tongue slipped out to stroke her throat. Then he abruptly moved away and began to eat his steak with great gusto.

Charlie was stunned Murphy would give up so easily. She silently admitted she was disappointed, because she was on the verge of kissing her steak good-bye even though her stomach reminded her that her last meal had been the previous day.

Refusing to meet each other's eyes, their movements quickened as they dispatched their food and by silent agreement retired to the bedroom where they didn't surface until the next morning.

CHAPTER NINE

Charlie braced her elbows on her desk and rested her chin on her folded hands. It would be so easy for her to fall asleep right now. If she got more than two hours sleep over the entire weekend, she would be surprised. She stifled another healthy yawn. It was too bad she couldn't have called in sick this morning, she thought. She had toyed with the idea but sensed her boss would decide to do the same thing, and there would go any idea of catching up on lost sleep. But there was another reason she had wanted to return to her cottage, one that bothered her the most.

Charlie had realized over the weekend that she wanted more than a lighthearted affair from Murphy. She was surprising herself with the idea of a commitment, with the whole nine yards including the vine-covered cottage with the white picket fence. Hey, kids might even be a nice idea. After working with and talking to people who were in what could be called their twilight years, she saw many who had made provisions for these years and had children who visited them. But so far she had put nothing away for the future. She had only worried about the present. It was due to lack of foresight that she had been forced to take a job while waiting for her knee to heal. But her newly formed practical side reminded her there was a good chance she wouldn't be returning to her dancing. Oh, she could protest to other people that she would be back, but deep down she sensed that wouldn't be happening.

Charlie sighed. One thing that worried her was that she might be using Murphy as a crutch; if she couldn't dance, could she have him again? After all, they were lovers and had lived together in the past. She had loved him in her own way nine years ago. It was just that she hadn't been mature enough to recognize what she had had then, and as a result, she'd lost him. Well, she was determined not to lose him this time!

That morning, she had run into Lena and Jason during her walk to work. They had greeted her with knowing smiles and questions as to how she spent her weekend. In fact, everyone she met looked at her as if knowing exactly where she had spent the last two days. Of course, dark circles under her eyes coupled with flushed cheeks and slightly swollen lips might have something to do with their summation. She yawned again, wishing it were time for lunch, because she was going to meet Murphy in the dining room.

Murphy had escorted Charlie home not long after dawn, where she caught a little precious sleep before it was time to succumb to a cold wake-up shower and dress for work. She ran her hands through her artfully tousled hair and stretched her arms over her head. She didn't want to work; she wanted to spend the week in bed with Murphy, even if it meant no sleep at all. She may be dead tired now, but she wouldn't have missed the past forty-eight hours for anything.

Charlie smiled as she replayed those wonderful two

174

days—Murphy stroking her nude body as if she were a sleek cat; Murphy kissing every inch of her bare skin with a languor that soon turned into passion; and finally, the joy of his body penetrating hers and taking her to heaven again and again. It wasn't long before her breasts began to tingle and swell against the gossamer fabric of her bra, her nipples chafing painfully and an insidious heat creeping along her veins to the insistent throbbing between her thighs. A need that hours of lovemaking hadn't even begun to sate. Charlie's eyes gleamed at the idea of renewing their affair. The ironic twist was that deep down she wondered if she didn't require more than sneaking from her bed to his. But why did that bother her? After all, she was the one well known for not wanting any kind of commitment.

Charlie glanced at the clock again and jumped up, pushing the niggling thoughts from her mind. It was time to meet Murphy for lunch, and she intended to verbally seduce him. And what fun that would be!

Murphy had spent most of the morning at the medical center with Mrs. Page, and he left the meeting in a foul mood. He looked down at his watch and figured he may as well head for the dining room to meet Charlie. Charlie . . . Just thinking of her brought a smile to his face. Especially when he could remember the enthusiastic partner he'd enjoyed over the weekend. His smile began to fade. He was afraid he was falling back into the same trap he had been in nine years before, and he knew he couldn't take that kind of pain again. At the same time, he certainly wasn't going to give her up after the taste he'd already had. Instead, he would just have to set up some ground rules and stick by them.

His new resolution certainly didn't stop him from smiling when he entered the dining room and spied Charlie seated at a corner table set for two. He remained in the doorway, drinking her in while she was still unaware of his presence. She looked great in a black wool skirt with a sexy white blouse and a gray tweed man-tailored jacket. Wait a minute. Yeah, it *was* a man-tailored jacket, all right; it had been originally tailored for *him!* Breathing fire and brimstone, he bore down on her.

"That's my jacket," he announced in clipped tones, skidding to a stop next to her seated figure.

Charlie looked up and smiled. "Good morning," she said in seductive tones. "I've missed you."

"You're wearing my jacket." The accusation was plain and clear.

She glanced over the gray wool and pushed up the sleeves a bit more. "Oh, yes, this was yours, wasn't it?" she said absently.

Murphy's eyes bulged. "Not 'was'—*is*. Take it off, Charlie."

She pretended to look shocked even as a tiny smile tugged at the corners of her lips. "Why, Murphy, we're in a public place. I'm afraid you'll just have to wait until we're alone."

His chest expanded. "I want my jacket back—now. That was my good-luck jacket when I went to important auditions. I was wearing that when I got my first part."

"Your first part was as a corpse in the beginning five minutes of a film," she reminded him, aware that their talk was drawing an interested audience. "The only reason anyone saw your face was because your character was identified in the morgue. Otherwise the viewers would have only seen your big toe."

Murphy ground his teeth. "I want my jacket back, Charlie. There was a time I was convinced the cleaners had lost it, but now I know why it could never be found. It was obviously hanging in your closet. I don't know how you got it, but I want it back."

She glanced up at him coolly. "You abandoned this jacket, along with me, nine years ago, Murphy. You've lost all rights to it."

"I abandoned *you?* Lady, you were the one who walked out on our relationship!" His voice rose with every word, and he was past caring if the entire world overheard their argument. "Where do you come off saying it's *my* fault?"

Charlie looked properly affronted. "I don't care to discuss this any further."

By now, Murphy's temper was raging. He reached down and unceremoniously pulled the jacket off her.

"It's mine!" he told her flatly, but his look of pleasure disappeared as he noticed it didn't fit him as well as it used to. "What did you do to it?" He acted as if she had just torn the wings off a defenseless butterfly.

"I had to have it altered so it would fit me better." Charlie stood up and snatched the jacket away from him. "I don't know what turned you into such a grouch, Murphy, but I don't think I want to eat lunch with Attila the Hun." With her nose held high in the air, she left the dining room.

Sylvester walked by Murphy, who was watching Charlie's dignified exit with incredulous eyes, still not completely sure what had happened.

"That was a wonderful way of displaying how to

177

make a perfect ass of yourself," Sylvester said before moving away.

Murphy's glare switched to the man sauntering to a nearby table where several people, previously engrossed in the dramatic scene played before them, now seemed to be just as interested in their meals.

"Where she's concerned, murder has to be considered legal," he muttered, too disgusted to stay for lunch. He stormed out of the dining room and down to his office to work himself and poor Hazel into a frenzy.

By late afternoon Charlie was able to replay the incident and laugh about it. Especially when Lena was laughing with her.

"It's amazing he could get so upset over his jacket after all these years," Charlie mused.

"I'm surprised you didn't try to return his jacket when you first realized he'd left it behind," Lena murmured.

Charlie took a sudden interest in her rose-tipped nails. "Yes . . . well . . ." She cleared her throat.

Lena's eyes narrowed. She couldn't believe Charlie would ever do something with deliberate malice. "You *did* try to contact him, didn't you?"

Charlie coughed and pretended to look through her desk drawers. "Uh . . . no."

The older woman didn't look at all pleased with her stumbling answer. "Oh, Charlie, it's clear how much that jacket meant, and still means, to him."

No scolding from her mother could hurt as much as Lena's reproof.

"I didn't think he'd care to talk to me after we broke up," Charlie mumbled, then suddenly launched into the story behind her split with Murphy. Over the years, she had come to see that she shouldn't have acted so callously, but by the time it was all over, it was too late to make any kind of amends if she had chosen to.

Lena wasn't surprised by Charlie's story, and she didn't see the younger woman in the bad light Charlie might have expected her to. After all, there had been many times when Lena had allowed her head to overrule her emotions. If anyone could understand the younger Charlie, it would be Lena, because she saw the vulnerable woman beneath the surface.

"I have a pair of red leg warmers that look as if Snickers had slept with them for the past ten years," Charlie said softly, looking down at the clasped hands in her lap. "I wore them to every audition. I cried for hours when they finally fell apart and I couldn't wear them any longer. I keep the pieces in a dresser drawer."

Lena nodded, a tiny smile gracing her lips. "I have a black silk garter."

Charlie leaned forward, her hands clasped on top of her desk and her eyes bright with interest. "Really?"

From there, Lena told her a few anecdotes from her spicier days as a madam. While no names were given, Charlie had an idea Jason was part of many of the stories, judging by the gleam in Lena's eyes. Sometime later when she rose to leave, she glanced sternly at Charlie.

"It wouldn't hurt you to talk to him now and explain why you didn't contact him about the jacket. I wouldn't be surprised if he doesn't think you did it deliberately."

With him anything was possible, Charlie thought, offering a feeble smile. But she knew Lena was right.

179

She'd just have to come up with a legitimate reason to approach him.

She didn't know that Snickers would do it for her.

She had just finished eating her dinner that evening when her phone rang. Hoping her caller was Murphy, she injected gaiety into her hello.

"Get over here." He didn't sound happy at all.

Her previous vow to act all sweetness and light with him flew out the window. "I beg your pardon?"

"Get your damn cat out of here before I shoot him!" The telephone slammed down in her ear.

Charlie looked at the pan of fudge brownies she had just taken out of the oven. She had planned to take them over to Murphy's in the next hour. She decided against it. In his present frame of mind, he'd probably put her face in them!

Ten minutes later she approached the open front door where Murphy stood watching Snickers with a wary eye. It didn't take her long to figure out Murphy's predicament.

"How sweet . . . Snickers brought you a present," Charlie cooed, dropping down to scratch the cat's head.

"Get it out of here," Murphy insisted between clenched teeth.

The cat meowed around the wiggling lizard he held in his mouth. Charlie would have sworn she saw dark amusement gleaming in his yellow eyes as he gazed up at her.

"He knows very well I hate those things." Murphy glared at Charlie as if she had put the cat up to it.

Crooning softly as she crouched down, Charlie finally

edged the helpless lizard away from Snickers and allowed the wiggling creature to go free.

"Most boys think lizards are better than peanut butter and jelly sandwiches," she told him, straightening up. From their first meeting, he had admitted his aversion to any kind of reptile.

"Not this boy."

Charlie patted his cheek. "I wouldn't worry now, Murphy. The big bad lizard is gone."

Muttering darkly, Murphy grabbed her wrist and pulled her inside the cottage, slamming the door behind her. At the same instant, his mouth fastened on hers, then he lifted her up and carried her into the bedroom.

Charlie wasn't allowed a coherent thought until morning. Frankly, she didn't mind one bit.

"It's awfully cold in here."

"The air is usually cold when it's barely five in the morning."

"Don't you think you should turn up the heat?"

"The electric blanket is on high now, and I'm beginning to feel like a piece of toast."

"I meant the central heating, silly."

"I don't seem to feel the cold as much as you, and if you're that cold you can turn up the heat yourself. I don't see a cast on either of your legs."

"But you *know* how I hate the cold. Couldn't you do it just this once?" Charlie rolled onto Murphy's chest and gave him her best imploring expression. He wasn't buying it.

"If you're so afraid of freezing to death, which I sincerely doubt will happen, you're going to have to expose

181

that sexy body to the elements and make your way to the thermostat in the living room."

"It's commonly known that women feel the cold much more than men," she declared.

"And I just bet a woman started that rumor. Personally, I don't see how they can if they have more layers of fat than men."

She pouted. "That is not a nice way to treat your lover."

Murphy hid his wince at her choice of words. Yes, they were certainly lovers, but sometimes he felt it was an inadequate word to describe their relationship. Stifling his conflicting feelings, he ran his hands down her back until they reached her buttocks, then back up to her nape. Finally clasping them against the back of her head, he drew her face down for a searing kiss.

"It might not be nice according to you, but it certainly sounds fine to me," he whispered just before warming her up most effectively.

As the days passed, Charlie forgot she and Murphy had ever been apart. The residents smiled at the young lovers as they spent the majority of their free hours together. Yet something always teased at the back of her mind; while Murphy was the consummate lover, he always seemed to hold a bit of himself back. That bothered her, but otherwise she had no complaints. Not when she had a man who gave her daisies one day and swept her off for a private picnic lunch in his office the next.

Charlie felt happy all the time and even greeted Mrs. Page with a bright smile that made the older woman suspicious. Charlie hadn't forgotten her cause. She still visited the patients, who spent the nice afternoons on the back lawn of the medical center, and was usually accompanied by Huggie Bear or Donnie. And Ramona tagged along more often than not. The shy woman seemed to be coming out of her shell as she spent more time with the gregarious Charlie. Mrs. Page complained to Murphy and threatened Charlie, but the bright-eyed young woman merely smiled and stated that as long as it wasn't against the law and the animals remained outside the medical center, she would visit when she wanted to. Ramona always remained in the background, listening to Charlie's arguments with awe and wishing she had the courage to stand up to people the way the younger woman did.

During this time, one thing Charlie noticed was Ramona's love for Huggie Bear and the affection the dog returned. More often than not, when Charlie arrived home in the evening Ramona was still out walking with the dog and seemed reluctant to part from him. Charlie invited her to dinner a few times and learned more about her life with her father and sister but still felt she didn't truly know the woman. She doubted she ever would.

"I've gained six pounds, thanks to all these heavenly meals," Charlie accused Murphy over lunch one day.

"Hmm, now that you mention it, I do detect some rounding where I shouldn't. Maybe you better have cottage cheese for a while," he teased.

She wrinkled her nose and pointed to the beef stew and dumplings on her plate. "You expect me to pass this up for cottage cheese?"

"Maybe not, but you didn't have to pick up that slice of cheesecake for dessert."

Charlie sipped her diet drink. She felt she had to make some concession to her calorie count, however little it might be.

"Charlie, I adore your dress," a sprightly little woman named Meg said when she stopped by their table. "In fact, I once saw that same dress on *Hawk House.*" She named a popular afternoon soap opera. "Madeline wore it when she killed her lover, who turned out to be her fourth cousin on her mother's side."

Charlie smiled, then leaned forward to deliver a confidence. "It's the same dress. I buy a lot of my clothes from a shop that receives the wardrobes from the soaps. I even have the blouse Halette wore when she found Eric in bed with Serena."

Murphy blinked and shook his head in disbelief at the conversation. "Do you mean to say you still keep up with those shows?"

"That's what my VCR is for," she told him. "I've had a crush on Eric for the past five years."

"I'm surprised you didn't try to get a part on the show in order to be close to him." He glowered at her.

Charlie loved the jealousy Murphy was displaying but didn't dare show how much it pleased her. "I'm a much better dancer than actress. If they had needed a dancer I would have auditioned like a shot. Eric's a real hunk." Meg's head bobbed in agreement, then she left.

Murphy expelled a deep breath and tackled his stew. "Your food is getting cold."

Charlie hid her smile and proceeded to eat her food.

That evening, Charlie prepared dinner for the two of them and watched Murphy fiddle with her VCR and sit down to watch *Hawk House.* When the character playing Eric came on the screen, Murphy's lips tightened, but he said nothing for the next half hour.

"Mmm, you're such a teddy bear," Charlie cooed, rubbing her face over his.

"If you're trying to butter me up, it won't work," he insisted, pulling her onto his lap.

"Hmm, that's what you think." She linked her arms around his neck and cuddled closer to him. "I once had a teddy bear that felt just like it. You're warm and comfortable."

"*Terrific.* I'm being compared to a toy."

She began unbuttoning his shirt and running her fingers through the soft hair on his chest. "Honey, you're far from the image of any little girl's toy unless she happens to be well into puberty." Her lips found his in a light, teasing kiss. Before she could pull away he grasped her arms and kept her there for a harder, more intimate kiss.

"Dinner," she murmured, not very convincingly.

He muttered his idea of what could be done to their meal and stretched out on the couch with her wedged between him and the back. After that, there were only murmurs that said nothing but meant everything to the lovers.

After their late dinner, they sat facing each other on the living room carpet with the intention of talking about what had happened to them over the past years. There was an unspoken edict that there would be no kissing, no hugging, no touching sensitive body parts, just talking. Charlie settled herself Indian fashion, her elbows propped on her knees, watching Murphy sip his wine.

"Did you really go to bed with Adele Palmer?" she

asked in a curious voice that betrayed no traces of jealousy, but she couldn't stop the ache in the pit of her stomach.

Murphy choked and just barely stopped himself from spewing wine all over her. "Where did you hear that?" he demanded once he regained his voice, wondering what brought about that particular subject.

"Murphy, you know very well gossip was one of the major pastimes in the business," she chided. "You'd be surprised how many times you were the prime source." Not to mention how many times a "well-meaning friend" sought her out to tell her the latest scoop. The truth behind their breakup had never been known, and it was somehow assumed that Murphy had walked out on Charlie and that she might be interested in learning what has happening to him.

He decided he didn't like the smile she wore. Probably because he wasn't sure what it meant. "I thought we were going to talk about things in general?" he countered.

"That is a casual subject. So, did you ever make it with her?"

Murphy's jaw set in a rigid line that silently stated that not even torture would get the information out of him. He also cursed Adele for spouting off about something so personal. Sure, he had taken her to bed. He had been drunk, lonely as hell, and she was a warm and more-than-willing body. It wasn't until the next morning when he woke up with a monumental hangover and the realization he had been seduced by an expert who expected to be a semipermanent addition to his bed that he discovered his mistake. He made sure he never erred that badly again.

"If you're that hot for kiss and tell, you can tell me all about Rod Latham," he insisted in a smooth voice. "You know, 'Steel Rod.' " When Charlie's eyes widened he knew he had hit a nerve. He then discovered he didn't really want to know the truth because if he heard the words spoken, he'd be tempted to drive down to L.A. and rearrange Rod's face until it wasn't so pretty anymore.

Charlie turned away to grab her glass and took a gulp of wine. "You're right . . . This isn't such a good idea," she muttered, wondering why she had wanted to know in the first place. What did it matter who Murphy went to bed with after they had split up? Right, it didn't matter; after all, they hadn't been together then. But it did matter, a tiny voice in the back of her mind taunted. She was one stupid lady if she thought it didn't matter.

She forced herself to smile, acting as if nothing was wrong. But she didn't like these conflicting feelings she was experiencing. She, who had always believed in living a carefree life, now wanted a man to tell her she was the only woman in his life and he wanted to spend the rest of his life with her. The trouble was, after the hell she had put Murphy through in the past, did she really believe he was willing to take a chance on getting hurt again? She blinked back the tears threatening to spill. Charlie rarely cried, but right now she wanted to sit down and bawl her eyes out. She never looked good when she cried. She always ended up with red swollen eyes and a pasty face, but at the moment, it would be worth it.

Murphy looked just as unhappy about the situation. "Why don't we just forget about what happened to us in the past, Charlie?" he suggested quietly. "We're not the same people anymore. I'm not the reckless actor who wanted to show the world he could do more than play the villainous psychopath. I'm in charge of a large retirement community and I love my work. There's a slim chance you'll be able to return to your dancing, and if the time comes, you'll be long gone." He leaned across to take her hand between his, warming the cold flesh between his palms. "Let's just take things one day at a time. We've got something good here. Why don't we just enjoy it while we're together?" He hated himself for saying the callous words, but he knew he had to in order to keep himself from being set up for a fall. He was determined he wouldn't end up one of the walking wounded when Charlie found something better and left the way she had before.

Charlie withdrew her hand to pick up her glass and tilt it up for a good long drink. His words sounded very much like her past philosophy. Why did they sound so heartless?

"Yes, I guess you're right," she murmured, setting her glass to one side. She resisted the urge to rub her hands together to keep away the numbing cold in her fingers. "You know, I'm more tired than I thought I was. If you don't mind, I think I'll have an early night."

Murphy inclined his head, understanding her unspoken meaning. He stood up with fluid grace, grasped his glass, and carried it out to the kitchen. "Would you like some help with the dishes?" he asked over his shoulder.

She shook her head. "There aren't that many. I can manage them myself, but thank you for the offer." She got up and walked with him to the door. For the first time in a long while, there was no good-night kiss or seductive entreaties for him to spend the night.

Disdaining the easy way out by using the dishwasher, Charlie washed and dried the dishes, then put them away. When she finished, she turned off the kitchen light and walked to the bedroom, turning off lights along the way. She quickly undressed, creamed off her makeup, and slipped into bed. It was a long time before she got to sleep. Murphy's words kept replaying through her mind.

Charlie woke up in a horrible mood the next morning, but not just because of what happened the night before. Grumbling under her breath, she dressed in black; she wanted to look like her mood. She walked up to the administration building, poured herself a cup of coffee, and holed up in her office after asking Hazel that she not be disturbed.

Charlie cursed softly over the lists of schedules and letters that covered her desk and wondered if they would be missed if she tossed them into the wastebasket. If questioned, she could always claim she didn't know what happened to them.

She drank more coffee than usual during the morning and wandered around the perimeter of her office with no idea of what she really wanted to do. Correction. She knew what she wanted to do, and that was to go home and crawl into bed and hide for the next few days.

"You coming to lunch?" Murphy stuck his head around the open door.

"No."

He started, surprised by her abrupt tone. Taking a chance, he walked inside. "Is something wrong?"

"Not a thing," she bit out, looking up to glare at him.

Murphy nodded in understanding of her mood.

"Hey, honey, I understand what's going on," he soothed, perching his hip on the edge of her desk. "After all, women do go through these periodic moods. It's been happening since the beginning of time."

Charlie reached across the desk and pushed him off. "I am not in some kind of mood."

The sappy look didn't leave his face. "Charlie, we used to live together, and I'm not exactly a stranger to women's problems. You always acted bitchy the first day but snapped right out of it in no time."

She clenched her teeth and counted to ten. "Get out, Murphy."

"Why don't you come to the dining room with me and have a cup of tea? That should fix you right up," he suggested. "You'll be feeling like your old self in no time."

"I'm going to kill you."

"Look, if you're not feeling very well, why don't you go home? Maybe a day in bed with a hot water bottle will help."

Charlie told Murphy in concise terms what he could do with the hot water bottle, but insults didn't seem to penetrate his stubborn hide. In his mind, she wasn't feeling well and wasn't responsible for anything she might say.

"Honey, go on home," he said in a soft voice.

"Don't call me honey."

"Would you like some aspirin?"

"I just want to be left alone!" she shouted.

"I'm just trying to help." He looked at her with soulful eyes.

Charlie rubbed her aching temples. When Murphy walked around behind her chair and began soothing the throb with his knowledgeable fingertips, she could only tip her head back and wallow in his sympathy. She was acting like a bitch, she silently admitted, but her bad moods were beyond her control during this time and all she truly wanted was to be left to her own devices.

"Doesn't that feel better?" he crooned, dropping a kiss on the top of her head.

"Yes." She sighed, finally lifting her head. "Look, Murphy, I appreciate your being so nice, but I'd rather be left alone. Please."

Murphy looked at the violet shadows under her eyes and the tightness around her mouth. She didn't feel well at all, he knew, but she probably thought she would be better off coming into work rather than staying at home feeling sorry for herself.

"Going home isn't a sign of weakness, Legs," he said quietly, moving around to sit on the edge of the desk. This time she didn't push him off. "You can give all the excuses you want, but as your boss, I'm going to order you to go home and take a long nap." He held up his hands in anticipation of her argument. "Don't worry, I'm not going to mention the hot water bottle again. I already have a good idea of what you think of that."

Charlie buried her face in her hands. How could she stay angry with him when he was acting no nice? "Please stop playing Sir Galahad and leave me alone," she pleaded. She glimpsed movement out of the corner of her eye and looked up. "What are you doing?"

Murphy searched through the drawers and dug out her purse. "I'm making sure you go home. From past experience, I know you're going to feel like hell by this afternoon and will probably be swallowing aspirin by the dozen."

"You don't know what I do anymore," she informed him in a hard voice. "And don't act like it's your business what I do." She snatched her purse out of his hand and slammed the drawer shut. "I'm going home." She walked through the door, closing it behind her with a mighty bang.

Murphy slid into Charlie's chair and smiled widely. She did just what he wanted her to do—even if it took more muscle than usual. The smile abruptly disappeared when he recalled her informing him he didn't know what she did anymore. That was true, and while he wasn't going to set himself up for any more pain, it still seemed feasible that he find out exactly how much Charlie had changed over the years. Maybe he could ensure that the past wouldn't repeat itself.

CHAPTER TEN

Charlie hated people who were right; and right now, she hated Murphy with a vengeance. She had gone home, changed into a bright yellow fleece caftan, fixed herself a cup of hot broth, and crawled into bed with her electric blanket turned on high.

"Ooh," Donnie crooned, leaning out over her perch.

"You got it, kiddo," she groaned, curling into a fetal position under the warm covers. She barely got comfortable before she fell into a deep sleep.

Two hours later, Charlie woke from her nap feeling more like her old self. She plucked Donnie from her perch and took her into the living room to her playpen, a large stand filled with climbing bars and perches, set in one corner. She deposited the parrot there, gave her fresh seed, and smiled when the bird promptly picked up a cinnamon stick, demolished it, and went on to search through the pumpkin seeds, dried corn, peanuts, and other parrot goodies. Charlie also fed Snickers and Huggie Bear before trying to decide what to prepare for herself. All she really wanted to do was lie on the couch and pamper herself. She had just decided on warming up a bowl of soup when someone knocked at her door.

"No offense, but I'm not in the mood for company," she said, swinging the door open.

Murphy nodded in agreement. "I don't blame you, but you could be a little more polite about it until you learn the identity of your visitor."

Charlie chewed on her lower lip. "I really hate you right now."

"Why?"

"Because you're always right."

Murphy bit back his grin, knowing if Charlie had an inkling that he was amused, she would hit him. In fact, in the mood she was in she could hit him without any provocation.

"I brought dinner." He held up two familiar red and white bags. "Chicken, mashed potatoes, cole slaw, and buttered biscuits."

Chicken sounded so much better than soup, her hungry stomach informed her. Charlie grabbed the bags out of his hand and walked to the kitchen, investigating the contents. "This is too much for one person." She turned her head, looking at him suspiciously. "I suppose you're hinting for a dinner invitation."

"It wouldn't hurt to share since I brought the food. All you have to provide are plates and drinks."

"What about company?"

"Not unless you improve your mood." He brushed past her to go into the kitchen and search through her refrigerator for something to drink. "Don't you have any beer?"

"I hate beer and there's nothing wrong with my mood," she said slowly, snapping off the last syllable of each word.

Murphy shrugged off her last statement as he pulled

194

out a can of Diet Coke. "What's wrong with having Coke that has sugar in it?"

"The less sugar I have, the better off I am," she said a bit haughtily.

His head disappeared into the refrigerator again. He pulled out a foil-wrapped packet and opened it. "Don't these have sugar in them?" He held the package of brownies in front of her.

"I had baked them for you." She snatched them out of his hand.

"Then why are they in your refrigerator and not mine?"

"Because I made them the night you called about Snickers. I figured with the mood you were in you would have thrown them in my face, so I kept them," she explained.

Murphy studied the thick fudge frosting. "Do they have chocolate and peanut butter chips inside?"

Charlie nodded, knowing they were his favorite. Whenever she had baked a pan of the brownies, they would be gone within an evening's time if Murphy was anywhere near. "Now we have something for dessert."

He looked her up and down in that assessing way of his. "I would plan on something else for that course, but I have an idea you'd throw me out for thinking such a thing. And since I'm starving, I think I'll act the part of polite gentleman tonight."

Charlie couldn't keep back her smile. "You were never a gentleman." She opened a cabinet door and brought down two plates and glasses.

"I said I'd *act* the part." He fixed their drinks and pulled the containers out of the bags, lining them up on the counter.

Charlie got out the silverware next. "Do you miss it?" she asked softly, turning around to face him.

"Miss what?"

"Acting."

Murphy's hands stilled their movement for a fraction of a second. As if nothing happened, he continued his chore, but Charlie didn't miss the hesitation. "Not a bit."

"Oh, I can imagine you don't miss the pain of going through all the cattle calls and cold readings or the hassles with some of the directors you had to work with, but you can't tell me you don't miss it," she persisted, heaping food on her plate and carrying it to the small table in a corner of the kitchen. "You enjoyed the challenge."

"That's right, 'enjoyed' as in past tense. I have other enjoyments now that mean a great deal more to me."

He took the chair to her right and immediately dug into his food. Charlie ate much slower, carefully peeling the skin off the chicken breast and putting it to one side before sinking her teeth into the tender white meat. For the next ten minutes, they ate without conversation, another indication of how hungry they were. Charlie wanted to say more about their previous conversation but decided to wait until after their meal. She had an idea the outcome could turn into a shouting match, and she wanted the chance to enjoy her food first. It wasn't until after Murphy had put the dishes in the dishwasher and steered Charlie out of the kitchen into the living room that she spoke.

"I miss it." Her statement was barely audible.

Murphy gave her a sharp look, knowing exactly what she was talking about. "You miss it because you weren't able to leave dancing voluntarily. Leaving acting was my own choice."

Charlie winced at his blunt statement. "I *will* dance again." But her conviction was too weak. The more she thought about it, the more convinced she was she wouldn't be dancing six months, a year, or even five years from now, no matter how carefully she took care of her knee.

He grasped her hand and held it tight even as she tried to jerk away. "And probably end up a cripple."

Her head shot up, the expression in her eyes chilling him to the bone. "That's a cruel thing to say."

Murphy felt the ice begin to flow through his veins. She was already thinking of leaving. Why had he started up their affair again? He cursed himself for being such a fool when he should have known he'd be the only one hurt when it was all over. He took a deep breath and chose his words carefully. He didn't want her to get upset more than possible, but he had to get his point across to her, make her realize what she lost but that she had a new life if she cared enough to have it.

"Then, dammit, make a new career!" he shouted back, gripping her hand so hard he almost broke the bones. "You're not some moron who can't do anything but dance, Charlie. Look how well you've done here. The people adore you. Your exercise classes are popular, and you've even got Mrs. Page looking over her shoulder for fear you'll win the battle. Six months ago I would have said nothing could upset that woman. Now I know differently. You're doing a lot of good here, Charlie."

"I can't do it the cowardly way you did!" She gasped

and covered her mouth with her hands. "Murphy, I'm sorry. I didn't mean it." She reached out for his hand, but he slowly pulled away.

"Yes, you did." He sighed. "But then, I've always been able to count on your honesty even when it hurt. If you want to think I was a coward, then go ahead. I got out of the business because I wasn't happy there. I needed something more lasting and I found it here. I realize you can't understand that because you've always cared more about your dancing than anyone or anything else. I can't be that single-minded. In the beginning, I thought I could, but it wasn't long before I realized there was more to life than going to a studio every day and playing the part of the latest killer."

Charlie hung her head, mortified by her cruel words. Murphy was the one person she wouldn't dream of hurting, and she had used the sharpest blade possible to wound him. His statement that she couldn't care about anyone else stung because she did care about other people. Wasn't her plan to use animals to bring the medical center patients out of their stupor proof she cared about someone other than herself? Ironically, she then thought about something that had happened two years ago.

Graham had been a dancer in a show she was in then. He had been a solace during some long nights, but she knew when the show was over, their affair would be over. That was the way it usually worked out. She wasn't hurt because while she liked him a great deal, she didn't love him. Graham didn't see it that way even though many affairs began during a run and ended when the show did. He had accused her of having no heart and using him purely as a stud. He had called her horrible names that she ignored purely because she couldn't be hurt by someone she didn't love. After that, Charlie made sure not to audition for the same shows Graham did. She had never been promiscuous, and she could count her lovers' names on one hand. Her dancing had always come first—she loved dancing, and it had been her lifelong dream. But she realized that her intense preoccupation had also filled a void: it had helped to displace her memories of Murphy, memories no other man could equal.

"Murphy, I don't want to fight with you," she murmured, silently cursing herself for the tears in her eyes. She never used to cry. "I'm sorry for what I said. I could blame it on my erratic hormones, but it wouldn't be fair to say it was all that. I guess it's a combination of everything. I hate being sick and I'm not too fond of myself right now."

"And you hate to apologize even more," Murphy said quietly, pulling her into his arms. He braced his back against the side of the couch and put his arms around her, rubbing her abdomen with a gentle hand.

"You have a perfect right to be angry with me," she said, closing her eyes as she relaxed against his chest. The circular motion, along with her full stomach, was making her feel very drowsy. "I wish we didn't fight. I don't like to argue with you, Murphy." Each word became more slurred.

Murphy grinned as he looked down at her relaxed features. "Why is it I always seem to put you to sleep?" he murmured, gently lifting her up enough so he could slide out from under her. He picked her up and carried her into the bedroom. Deciding he didn't want to worry about waking her up if he undressed her, he merely threw back the covers and laid her on the bed, then covered her up again. Charlie murmured several indistinguishable words and curled up on her side. Then Murphy checked on Huggie Bear and Snickers and carried Donnie back into the bedroom.

As he was getting ready to leave, he stopped to check on Charlie. Calling himself a fool for always getting taken in by her, even when she was asleep, he shucked his clothes and slipped into bed next to her. The moment he put his arms around her, she sighed and wrapped herself around him. Murphy switched off the lamp and lay back, staring up at the dark ceiling and wondering if his kind of insanity could ever be cured. Or was he so crazy that he didn't want to be cured?

Over the next few weeks, Murphy was unable to forget Charlie's words from that night. But it certainly didn't stop him from seeing her every chance he had. Jason had even cornered him after one of their tennis games and laughingly asked him if his intentions were honorable. Murphy was sorely tempted to confide in the older man; maybe Jason had a solution. Murphy certainly didn't, but he was too used to solving his own problems. Then, too, how could he explain about Charlie when he didn't know the whole story himself? Oh, he knew he was in love with her, and he knew it could only lead to heartache. He finally decided that that meant he would have to settle this all on his own.

Charlie was doing a little soul-searching of her own. She hadn't forgotten about that night either and regretted her words over and over again. While Murphy acted as if he hadn't given it another thought, she sensed that deep down it still bothered him. She wanted to go out of her way to make it up to him, but she knew that wasn't the answer. She would just have to be a bit more subtle about it.

"Have any plans for the weekend?" Murphy asked her one day during lunch.

Charlie shrugged. "Oh, the usual exciting fare—laundry, cleaning house, grocery shopping. You can't imagine how I'm looking forward to it."

"It sounds like you'd have more fun doing that than driving down to L.A. with me for the weekend," he said casually.

"What time do we leave?" she asked without hesitation.

Murphy laughed. "I guess this means you'd like to go with me. How about leaving after work on Friday? That would give us most of the weekend. I'm sure Ramona wouldn't mind looking after the animals."

"Wouldn't mind? She'd love it," Charlie said honestly. "As it is, Huggie Bear spends more time with her than he does with me. Oh, I don't mind it," she added hastily so he wouldn't think she was complaining. "In fact, Ramona acts a lot more outgoing lately."

"She does seem to be getting out more since she walks with him," Murphy agreed. "I think she feels wanted now."

"But Ramona has so many friends here," she protested. "Why would she feel wanted by a dog when there are so many people who obviously enjoy her company?"

Murphy's smile didn't reach his eyes. "Maybe because Huggie Bear doesn't expect anything from her but her love." He finished the last bite of his stuffed pork chop. "I've got to get back to the office. We'll talk about the weekend later."

Charlie remained at the table finishing her coffee. She thought about Ramona, who was so shy around people but seemed to have no inhibitions when she was with the large dog. While so many of the residents socialized at the drop of a hat, Ramona rarely attended any of the functions, preferring to stay home. Even Lena had commented that Ramona seemed more lighthearted since she had Huggie Bear for company during the day. And Huggie Bear seemed happier when he saw the shy woman. Charlie suddenly felt very guilty for having so much when others seemed to have so little.

There was no problem with Ramona watching the animals for the weekend. She was only too happy to help out. Charlie left the office half an hour early so she could pack and was ready when Murphy stopped by her cottage to pick her up.

"I still can't believe that a woman could cram everything for one weekend into one small bag," he commented, picking up her small weekend case and placing it in the trunk of the car. "Where's all the luggage most women bring along so they'll have something appropriate for every occasion?"

"Traveling so much taught me to pack light," she replied, opening the passenger door. "What prompted the idea of going to L.A.?"

Murphy shrugged. "I just thought it would do us some good to get away. I usually go out of town for the weekend every six to eight weeks. It's a welcome break for me, and I have a chance to recharge my batteries."

Charlie wondered if he always went alone or met someone there, but her new possessive self where Murphy was concerned doubted she wanted to hear the truth. Knowing Murphy's sexual appetite, she didn't think he would go without a woman for long, and going away for the weekend was certainly a good way to keep his affairs discreet.

Curling her feet under her, she-shifted to face him, placing one elbow on the back of the seat.

"You'll never believe what Donnie did tonight," she told him.

"She bit Snickers and he ran away from home, never to return?" he asked hopefully.

Charlie grimaced. "No. She was sitting in her cage and staring at her bell hanging on the other side of the cage and kept telling it to come here. Since the bell didn't move, she got angry and walked over to it, hitting it real hard with her beak. Naturally, it swung back and bopped her in the face." Charlie started giggling. "She stared at the bell, then said very loudly, 'No, don't bite!' "

Murphy joined her in her laughter. "She's a bit crazy at times, isn't she? Obviously she hears those words occasionally."

"Only when she's mad at me and tries to take off part of my hand." She braced her chin in her cupped palm. "Are you going to feed me dinner?"

"I thought you were complaining you were gaining weight," he teased.

"That doesn't mean I go without meals. I just do without dessert," she said airily.

"Can you wait until we get into L.A.?" he asked, turning onto the road that would lead to the highway.

"Sure." She continued to study him.

"Is my nose on crooked?" Amusement laced his voice.

"No, I just like to look at you. Do you mind?"

"Not as long as I can return the favor."

"Anytime." Charlie's husky voice promised him much more than just looking at her. She decided this was her chance to give him a weekend he'd never forget!

She noticed that the closer they got to the hotel, the more uneasy Murphy grew. She was tempted to ask him what the problem was but sensed he would tell her in his own time. Only a few blocks from the hotel, Murphy abruptly pulled over to the curb, sliding the gear into park. He stared straight ahead as if he were afraid to face her.

"I, ah—I made the reservation for one room only," he said hesitantly. "If you want a room of your own, I'll understand and arrange it when we check in." He still refused to look at her.

Charlie smiled, feeling the warmth steal through her body. "A second room would be a waste of good money since I'd be spending all my time in yours," she said softly, reaching across the short distance to place her hand on his arm.

He turned his head and saw the unspoken words in her eyes. "Oh, lady," he said huskily, "do you have any idea what you do to me?"

"Yes. And I hope to do even more when we're alone," she whispered throatily, giving him a flirty wink.

Murphy threw the car into gear and quickly pulled away from the curb. "Give me twenty minutes," he promised, "and you can do with me what you will."

The luxurious hotel lobby Murphy steered Charlie

into was awe inspiring with crystal chandeliers and deep ruby carpeting that seemed to flow around her shoes.

"I hate to think how many months salary this place is going to cost you," she whispered as they rode the elevator to their floor.

"Then just lie back and enjoy it," he murmured, a wicked gleam in his eyes.

Charlie didn't miss the double meaning in his words and privately assured herself she would most certainly enjoy anything he had in store for her.

The room was a dream come true with a bed that looked larger than king-size, a couch, a table, and some chairs. Charlie sincerely doubted they would need the television set.

"The bathroom has a telephone!" she exclaimed, laughing, after oohing and ahing over the sunken tub that could easily accommodate two people.

"You're not going to have time to call a soul if I have anything to say about it," he told her, circling her waist with his arms.

"What will I have time for?" she asked with a coquettish swing of her head.

Murphy bent down to whisper his reply in her ear, which left her skin flushed.

"Mmm, that sounds very physical," she murmured, stepping forward until her breasts just brushed against his chest. The mood would have continued if Murphy's stomach hadn't given off a very unromantic rumble.

"This hotel has three restaurants. Shall we try one of them?" he asked.

Charlie looked up, surprised he would suggest dining out when she was sure he would have preferred room service. Then she realized he wanted to build up the anticipation.

"Just let me take a quick shower and change my clothes," she replied, stepping away from him.

Murphy would have suggested they conserve water and shower together, but he knew that would only mean they wouldn't leave the room for the rest of the evening, and he was determined to give Charlie a special weekend.

Charlie dressed in a black silk halter dress that left her back and shoulders deliciously bare and would undoubtedly give Murphy moments of grief during their prolonged dinner.

The restaurant they chose was dimly lighted and carried the intimate atmosphere appropriate for lovers away on a stolen weekend. They were shown to a corner booth and left alone after being handed menus.

Charlie leaned across the table to whisper, "Do you have a small flashlight to read this with?"

Murphy grinned. "Just go eeny, meeny, miney, moe."

In the end Charlie chose shrimp scampi and Murphy decided on veal Oscar, also asking for a special white wine to accompany their meal.

While they ate, they talked incessantly about everyday activities, books they had read, anything that would give the other further personal information. Charlie couldn't remember when she had enjoyed a meal more. Murphy was more like the fascinating man she had first met nine years ago. They lingered over coffee and brandy, this time conversing in a silent, more intimate language.

After spending more than two hours in the restaurant, they left for the bank of elevators that led to their room. Inside the small compartment, they stood in the back as several other people got on. Murphy placed his hands on Charlie's shoulders as he stood behind and to her left.

As the car moved upward a little devil inside Charlie's head prompted her to drop her left hand and press back against the front of Murphy's navy trousers. She smiled when she heard his soft gasp and a stirring beneath her hand. She drew an erotic design across the taut fabric before slowly removing her teasing fingers. Murphy's hands tightened on her shoulders as he obviously tried to restore himself to normal.

"Little witch," he accused her as they walked down the plush carpeted hallway to their room. "It would have served you right if I had decided to take you right there."

"Why, Murphy, what would all those people have said?" she asked with wide innocent eyes.

He chuckled. "We either would have been thrown out of the hotel or received a standing ovation, depending on how open-minded the other passengers were." He slid a plastic key card into the slot and listened for the click that signified the door was open. He stepped back and waited for Charlie to precede him. "I hope you realize you're going to have to come through with your earlier promises."

"Of course." She sounded perfectly reasonable as she crossed the room, standing on one foot as she slipped off one shoe, then repeated the procedure for the other shoe. She tossed her purse on the dresser and then spun around to face him, her arms wide open. "I'm all yours."

Murphy closed the door behind him and walked over

to her. In a matter of seconds, she wore only black wispy panties and a silk garter belt holding up sheer black stockings.

"Very sexy," he approved in a husky voice, nuzzling her ear with his lips. His teeth fastened on her earlobe, pulled on it, then soothed it with his tongue. Charlie's sigh of pleasure was music to his ears. He held his hand up and lightly touched one pouting nipple. The tiny nub immediately tightened. He watched Charlie's eyelids lower to cover her darkened pupils, and her breathing quickened as his thumb rubbed over one nipple as his mouth covered the other.

"You taste like the sweetest honey," he muttered against her swelling breast. He nibbled the nipple, then laved it with his tongue to soothe the pleasure-tortured skin. "I could feast on you for the next hundred years."

Charlie's eyes half opened and watched the erotic reflection in the dresser mirror; she was wearing so little, whereas Murphy was still completely clothed. It made her feel very naughty and decadent.

"I want you inside me," she whispered, bending her head to caress his nape with her lips. "Now."

"In time." He was determined to take his time. At least as long as he could hold out against her sensual charms. Judging by the way Charlie was caressing him, it wouldn't take long at all. His mouth opened wide over her breast.

In desperation, Charlie tunneled her hands under his suit coat and shirt and ran her hands over his smoothly muscled back. When the fire radiated outward from her breast to the core of her femininity, she dug her nails into his back, scoring his smooth skin. She sobbed when his hand slipped beneath the lace edging of her bikini panties and delved to find her moist secrets. His fingers probed, rotated, and teased, setting off a chain reaction she was powerless to stop. Charlie ran her hands beneath the waistband of his slacks to find the tensing muscles of his buttocks. Her fingers clenched against the taut skin even as she fell into a deep black abyss.

Before she could recover, Murphy placed her on the bed and tore off the rest of her clothes, then disposed of his own in record time. As his lips closed over hers their bodies merged. Her cry of pleasure was swallowed by his mouth as his tongue plunged inward in the same fashion his body plunged into hers.

"I want to bury myself in you so deeply you'll never be one person again," he muttered roughly, grasping her legs and draping them over his hips. "No one will ever give you what I can. No one will ever be to you what I am!"

"Yes, oh, yes!" she sobbed, thrashing her head back and forth against the pillow.

He thrust deeper and deeper until she began the ascension that signaled another climax, this one more intense than the other. Charlie knew Murphy was right: no one could ever do to her what he did. No one ever had. She could only flow with him until she reached the heavens and dropped among the stars. As she gasped out his name, she could hear him calling hers as he shared himself with her before collapsing onto her.

"Wow!" Charlie whispered, curling up against his side.

"Ditto." He rubbed the back of her neck with his fingertips. He had an idea there was a sappy smile on his face, but he was past caring. "You're really hot stuff, lady."

"You're not so bad yourself." She smiled lazily, rubbing her toes over his calf. "Um, I don't think I'll move until it's time to leave Sunday."

"Wrong. I have very important plans tomorrow," he informed her.

Charlie rolled over onto him and nibbled his neck. "More important than me?"

Murphy chuckled. "I get the message." He wrapped his hands around her head and pulled her down for one of his potent kisses, then made love to her once again.

This time Charlie didn't fall asleep. How could she, when Murphy called room service to order a bottle of champagne and chocolate cake, her two favorite treats? He not only helped her drink the champagne but anointed her with it and sipped the bubbly liquid from her breasts and naval. Not to be outdone, Charlie did likewise with chocolate frosting smeared across Murphy's brown nipples. After such a feast, there was no recourse but to take a bubble bath together, which inevitably led to more loving. By the time they finally tumbled into bed they were so sated they could only curl up in each other's arms and fall immediately into a deep sleep.

The next morning, Murphy refused to give in to Charlie's teasing suggestion to call room service for breakfast and swatted her on the bottom as he sent her into the bathroom for her shower . . . alone.

After breakfasting in the coffee shop downstairs, they took the car and drove down to Venice. The narrow canals were nothing like her sister city, and the beach boardwalk was filled with every kind of vendor imaginable. Charlie bought a pair of red heart-shaped sunglasses and immediately slipped them on, affecting a movie starlet's pose. She bought a purple and white scarf to wind around Murphy's neck and insisted he leave it on. He didn't bother worrying that he might look odd. Alongside the many people in bizarre dress, and the roller skaters wearing skimpy bikinis or what could have passed for fifties prom dresses, he looked quite conservative. Since the day was warm, Charlie had worn a red and white striped cotton romper with a wide red belt and red sandals, while Murphy had dressed in gray corduroy shorts and a dark green polo shirt, his well-worn deck shoes on his feet.

Holding hands, the couple walked down the boardwalk, stopping at each booth to investigate the merchandise, buying hot dogs and ice cream cones for lunch, and just enjoying their time together. Charlie teased Murphy by insisting she wanted to watch several men work out with weights, but he refused to succumb to her teasing, since he knew she had never been interested in heavily muscled men before.

"Who says I was looking at their muscles?" She flashed him a saucy wink as her eyes wandered over the weight lifters' barely clad bodies.

"Okay, I get the message," he muttered, grabbing her hand and dragging her away.

"I notice men think nothing of undressing a woman with their eyes, so what's wrong with a woman doing the same?" she complained.

"If you want to mentally undress a man with your eyes, you just concentrate on me." He began to walk very fast, but Charlie dug in her heels and forced him to slow down. He turned around and faced her, his hands braced on his hips. "Now what?"

211

Charlie smiled and slowly allowed her eyes to wander over him, from the top of his tousled head to the tip of his toes. "Such an excellent idea," she said throatily. "And I must say that I certainly like what I see."

Murphy's eyes darkened. He grabbed her hand again and practically dragged her in the direction of his car.

"What are you doing?" she demanded, running to keep up.

"I'm going to make sure that you back your words up," he said roughly.

When they reached the car, he pushed her inside and got in himself. He kept barely within the speed limit the entire drive to the hotel.

During the elevator ride to their room, Charlie had the strangest smile on her face. The smile remained the entire time she showed Murphy she meant every word she said.

CHAPTER ELEVEN

Charlie woke up at an incredibly early hour even though they had tumbled into bed very late after an exciting evening with dinner out, dancing, and sitting in at the Improv to listen to a well-known comedian. Though they had been tired from their busy day and evening, they had still found the energy to make love with delicious abandon. She turned her head to look at the window covered only with sheer curtains. Since their room was high enough to discourage Peeping Toms, they had left the heavy drapes open. A pale early morning light dusted the room and the bed.

She turned back to look at the man sleeping beside her. Sometime during the night he had twisted enough that the sheet had fallen to a little below his waist. But she already knew in great detail what the soft white fabric hid from her eyes. Charlie braced herself up on her elbow in order to feast her eyes on Murphy, from his tousled dark hair to closed eyes with incredibly long lashes to the chest that moved up and down in a slow motion only she would find erotic. He lay on his side now, but she knew if he were sleeping on his back he would emit the cutest soft snoring sounds. At least, they were cute to her. His chest was broad and comfortable enough to cradle a woman's head. He had runner's legs, lean, sinewy, and a sexy pair of buns that belonged on a calendar. She knew if he awakened, he would look at her with those warm eyes and give her a lazy smile before pulling her into his arms for the kind of loving she had become addicted to. In fact, there was nothing she didn't love about him.

Charlie sat up in an abrupt motion. No, she couldn't. That wasn't her style. Her dancing had always come first, and falling in love with Murphy after all that had happened in the past wasn't planned. But then, love wasn't something that could be planned in advance; it just happened, like measles or chicken pox. Holding her breath for fear she would awaken him, she crept out of bed and scurried into the bathroom, closing the door carefully behind her.

Charlie sat on the edge of the tub for long moments exploring the unfamiliar emotions coursing through her. She was in love with Murphy, and she didn't know what to do about it. Oh, she had loved him nine years ago, but the emotion then was nothing like the intense way she felt right now. She could tell that her respiration had increased the more she thought about being in love with him, and her entire body felt as if its internal temperature had risen. She half expected to find red spots popping out on her skin.

In a gesture of defiance to her disturbing feelings, she stood up and reached inside the shower stall, switching on the water. She stepped inside the cubicle and stood under the flowing hot water so she wouldn't know if it was tears covering her face or the water from the shower head hitting her. She figured the running water would always hide the sounds if she became too vocal with her sobbing.

"Hey, why didn't you wake me up?" Murphy had slid open the shower door and stood there in all his naked splendor. When a startled Charlie turned to face him, his expression showed concern. "Honey, are you all right?"

"Oh, I just bumped my funny bone," Charlie fibbed, moving back a pace.

Murphy's face warmed in a smile that weakened her knees. Oh, Lord, she was going to need an injection to immunize her from this new disease!

He grasped her arm. "This one?" he asked softly, running his fingers over her elbow, oblivious that water was spraying out at him and making large puddles on the floor.

She nodded, feeling a lump rise in her throat. She stood still, watching him raise her elbow to his lips, and felt his tongue flutter over the damp skin.

"Better?" he murmured, glancing up at her with those incredibly blue eyes that left her weak in the knees again.

She nodded again, still unable to speak a word.

Murphy stepped into the cubicle and slid the door shut. "Perhaps I should practice some preventive medicine and kiss everything better," he murmured, pulling her into his arms.

It wasn't the first time Charlie had shared a shower with Murphy, and it certainly wasn't the first time they had made love in one, but it was the first time she had done it aware of how much she loved him. It made the experience even more memorable.

* * *

By the time they shared a late morning brunch Charlie felt a bit more like her old self. Well, almost. She found herself looking at Murphy through new eyes. Had his smile always been so sexy? Had his eyes always sparkled so brightly? And his mouth, well, that was definitely an X-rated fantasy to her overactive imagination. She studied him as if she were storing up memories to last her for the next hundred years. Perhaps she was, because she wondered if the time would come when Murphy would decide it was time to move on.

She could have told him she loved him, but she still felt shy about her new feelings. She was afraid to admit them after the way she had treated him so many years ago; it could give him a weapon that would destroy her if he chose to. She just hoped the day would come when he'd realize she wasn't the same thoughtless person she had been nine years before. And if that time came then she would tell him exactly how she felt about him.

She also realized it didn't hurt so much to consider the fact that she might not be able to dance professionally again. Maybe it was because she had something else to focus on. When Murphy looked up from his eggs Benedict, she flashed him a heart-stopping smile.

"Penny for your thoughts," he murmured, reaching across the table to grasp her hand.

She ducked her head, knowing she couldn't reveal them. "I'm just sorry the weekend went by so quickly," she replied softly, shrugging her shoulders.

"So am I," he confessed. "But there's no reason why we can't do this again soon."

Charlie felt warm all over. "I'd like that."

Now Murphy felt a rise in temperature. She sounded

216

so sincere and . . . Something else colored her voice that he couldn't quite identify. There was something different about Charlie today. He first noticed it when he had followed her into the shower. He couldn't quite pinpoint the difference, but whatever it was, it left him feeling a bit hopeful about the future. Be careful, he warned himself. The last time he had felt that kind of hope, he had ended up getting kicked in the teeth.

Charlie floated through the next few days. She hadn't thought such a thing was possible, but she just *felt* different. Everything seemed new and alive. Even Winifred Page wasn't so bad if she was approached with a smile and pleasant words. At first, the older woman was suspicious, but Charlie's warm and sunny manner soon began to thaw her icy exterior.

"Charlie's awfully absentminded lately," Jason commented during lunch. "Do you know she came to me three times about that photography tour to Vancouver?"

"It's allowed," Lena replied, smiling to herself.

"She's in love," Ramona explained in her soft voice. Jason and Felix looked at her with surprise, then smiles broke out on their faces.

"It's amazing what a lost weekend can do," Jason remarked, glancing over at the corner table where the lovers sat looking very intent during their low-voiced discussion. Every so often, one would lean across the table and touch the other. He sighed. "I just hope no one ends up hurt." Each member of the group dreaded to think of which one would end up the victim.

"Want to play lusty pirate and virginal aristocrat

again?" Murphy asked with a raised eyebrow, oblivious to the speculation going on across the room.

Charlie shook her head. "You act as if that costume is your good-luck charm," she teased.

"It certainly didn't win the best costume award." He sighed melodramatically. "In fact, I noticed in the newsletter that while Maude won the contest, the identity of her costume wasn't given."

Charlie giggled. "It seemed better not to print it."

"Why? What was she?"

"Lady Godiva."

Murphy choked. "Horse and all?"

She shook her head. "She carried a toy horse and wore a long wig."

"Please tell me she wore some kind of bodysuit?" He groaned.

"Even if she didn't?"

"You mean . . ."

"The bodysuit was flesh toned, but she was still able to get her point across." Charlie looked longingly at Murphy's beef pot pie and freshly baked apple turnover. Then she looked down at her plate piled with cottage cheese and the small dish of pineapple next to it. When her scales seemed to shout that she had gained six pounds, she knew it was time to watch her food intake. This meager lunch was just the beginning. The sad part was that she hadn't had too much trouble with her weight when she danced full time, although she reminded herself she would probably have resembled a blimp long before this if it hadn't been for the exercise classes she led.

"Want to try a bit of my beef pie?" Murphy tempted

her, well aware of the reason she chose the low-calorie food.

"Want to find this cottage cheese in your lap?" She smiled pleasantly.

"Hey, don't blame me because you put on a few pounds."

"Oh, who *should* I blame? I don't believe I was the one who decided it would be fun to make fudge last night," she accused. "Then there was all that butter brickle ice cream you brought over when you wanted to watch the football game on my television set."

"You have better reception than I do."

"That wasn't the reason you gave when you breezed in the door and headed directly for the bedroom after asking if I could get you a beer."

"Now, wait a minute. I didn't make love to you until after the game was over so you couldn't accuse me of just coming over for sex," he defended himself. "And it isn't my fault your television is in your bedroom."

Charlie didn't want to tell Murphy that was the real reason she had been irked that night. She hadn't realized that men who resemble the Incredible Hulk ramming into one another would mean more to him than her floating around the house in a filmy negligee.

Murphy saw the storm rising in her eyes and hid his smile. He already sensed she was less than happy with him because he had seemed more interested in the game than her. Little did she know his blood pressure had been raised to an all-time high that night while he pretended to watch a game he could have cared less about. For that performance alone he felt he deserved an Academy Award. And to think some critics had claimed he couldn't act his way out of a paper bag. If they could have seen him acting as if a lousy football game were more important than throwing Charlie on the bed beside him and burying himself deep inside her warmth, they'd change their stories fast. He shifted in his chair, realizing his jeans hadn't felt this confining when he had put them on that morning.

Charlie slipped another forkful of cottage cheese into her mouth. Perhaps she should start using the indoor pool in the evenings to burn off extra calories.

"Want to go for a swim tonight after work?" she asked, deciding to nibble on the pineapple rings. She was so hungry she would have devoured a dirty spoon!

"Sure." He eyed her speculatively. "Especially if you wear that skimpy bikini of yours."

"I thought nighttime swimming around here was more along the line of skinny-dipping," she quipped.

"So, you've heard about a few of our crazier midnight parties." He chuckled.

"In great detail." She recalled the stories Lena had once told her and still found it difficult to see these sophisticated senior citizens as the wild party types. She had a feeling that the term *sexy senior citizen* had originated at New Eden.

Murphy finished his meal and looked down at his watch. "I've got to run. I'll meet you at the pool right after work." He smiled down at her with a look that was just as potent as a kiss before leaving the table.

"If the two of you aren't careful, we're going to have to put an X rating on this table," Lena said, slipping into the chair Murphy had vacated.

Charlie shrugged, aware she probably had a silly grin on her face. "*You* should talk," she returned.

220

"True. So, what are you going to do for Murphy's birthday next week? Something exciting, I hope."

Charlie looked blank. Was his birthday coming up? She couldn't remember.

"Next Friday," Lena prompted. "You *did* know his birthday was coming up, didn't you?"

She could feel the blush warming her cheeks. "Murphy and I exchanged birthdates nine years ago, and we weren't together long enough to celebrate either one of our birthdays," she said quietly. "I guess the date just slipped my mind. But I would like to do something special for him."

Lena smiled. "Honey, I think all you'd have to do is be there and that would be special for him. I'll see you in exercise class this afternoon." She stood up and walked back to her table.

For the rest of the afternoon Charlie racked her brain over how to celebrate Murphy's birthday. She could take him out to dinner, but that seemed too, oh, ordinary. She could cook dinner for— Wait a minute. Why not kidnap him for the weekend? She could fix him dinner Friday night, then drive up to that inn on the coast with the huge beds and fireplaces in every room. Perfect. She extracted the phone book out of her desk drawer and searched for the inn's telephone number so she could make the necessary reservations.

That afternoon, they decided not to go swimming but to drive into town for dinner and a movie. So much for Charlie's resolution. As they walked down to Charlie's cottage so she could change out of her dress into slacks, they saw Ramona walking with Huggie Bear.

Charlie felt a strange feeling invade the pit of her stomach as she saw the smiling woman and the large dog walking close beside her. She had noticed lately how excited Huggie Bear was when Ramona took him out for their walks. She also noticed how the older woman always made time to play with the dog, while Charlie was usually too caught up in Murphy to give the animals the attention they deserved. The only one who didn't suffer was probably Donnie, since she spent most days in Charlie's office. She released Murphy's hand and stepped forward.

"Ramona," she called out, making her decision swiftly before she changed her mind.

The woman looked up and waved. "I was just taking Huggie Bear home," she replied, one hand curved around the heavy leather leash.

Charlie attempted a smile she didn't feel inside. "You love Huggie Bear a lot, don't you?" She was so caught up in her own world she didn't sense Murphy walking up to stand behind her.

Ramona's face brightened. "Oh, yes, he's wonderful company when I embroider or go for a walk." Suddenly her face lost its life. "I'm sorry, perhaps you don't want me to take him out so often."

Charlie looked down at the dog sitting calmly at the older woman's side. "Ramona, I'm afraid I don't have the time for Huggie Bear that I used to have. I was wondering if you might like to keep him," she said softly.

Ramona's eyes widened. "Oh, Charlie, you don't mean that," she protested. "You've had him for years. You love him."

"You'd be doing me a big favor," she insisted. "I know how much you love him, and I'd rather see him living with someone who loves him and he loves in return."

Tears filled the older woman's eyes. "I don't know what to say."

"Say nothing. Murphy and I were planning to go out tonight, so if you don't mind I'll bring his dishes and food over tomorrow." Charlie smiled.

Ramona ran over to Charlie and hugged her tightly. "Thank you," she whispered, pausing to kiss her on the cheek. Then stepping back, she hurried away with the large dog at her heels.

"That was a beautiful thing you just did," Murphy murmured, placing his hands on Charlie's shoulders. "He's just what she needs."

She nodded. "I know she'll take good care of him. Come on, I don't want to miss the movie."

Charlie said little during the evening, and Murphy knew the reason. He was surprised she had given Huggie Bear to Ramona. He knew she loved the dog, even though she recognized she no longer had the time to spend with him. It was a completely unselfish act, and he was proud of her for it. When they returned to her cottage, Murphy kissed her good night and left, sensing she would prefer to be alone that night.

Charlie wandered through the house with Snickers winding in and out of her legs. She never thought she could be so grateful for a persnickety cat's company as she was that night. There were so many changes going on inside her that she felt as if she was turning into a brand-new person.

Unable to sleep, she curled up in bed with the television on. Snickers was asleep at the foot of the bed, and Donnie hunkered down on Charlie's pillow, fighting her

223

for her plate of chocolate cookies. This was not a time for her to worry about calories!

"What's happening to my life?" she demanded of the animals, but they had no answers to give her. She didn't have any either. All of a sudden her dancing was taking a backseat to Murphy, and she had just given away a dog she loved dearly; and she did it because she knew someone else could take care of him better than she could. Charlie never used to behave this way.

Why had she softened so much in a matter of months? Was it because she spent her time around so many people who cared deeply about others and she was back with the man who had first taught her about love? She wasn't sure what brought all this about, but she intended to explore it further until she understood why she was changing so much.

Charlie's search for insight into the new her drained her of her normal vitality. Now she was quieter, even more thoughtful, and Murphy wondered what had brought about the change. He would have tried to discover the reason behind it if he hadn't had to go out of town.

"It's only for a week," he assured her after explaining the business trip he had to make.

She made some mental calculations. He should be back in plenty of time for them to celebrate his birthday properly. "Why don't you plan on having dinner at my place next Friday?" she suggested with a seductive smile.

"Sounds fine with me," he agreed. "As long as dessert is included with the meal."

"At my house it's part of the package plan."

"Then I'll be there with bells on."

"Just be there. I'll take care of any bells we need to ring."

Charlie soon discovered it just wasn't any fun when Murphy wasn't in the office down the hall. It wasn't as if she lacked for company. Lena, Maude, or Ramona met her for lunch or invited her over for dinner, and she and Lena drove into Santa Barbara for some shopping on Saturday, but it wasn't the same as when she went exploring with Murphy. She missed him, pure and simple.

She took off from work after lunch the day of his birthday so she would have plenty of time to bake a cake and begin preparations for a very special dinner.

"Murphy ate four pieces of this cake when I made it last summer for our Fourth of July picnic," Lena assured Charlie when the younger woman had asked for suggestions several days earlier.

Charlie had glanced over the typewritten recipe and inwardly groaned. "This takes fourteen candy bars," she protested, looking up.

"Yes, but that's what makes it so good."

"I usually make a sheet cake," Charlie murmured, reading the recipe again. After ascertaining how many steps were involved, she felt this was going to be a long job. But if Murphy loved it so much, the effort would be more than worth it. "I don't own any round cake pans."

"I'll loan you mine," Lena offered.

She had felt as if she were being backed into a corner. "It does sound good." She worked hard to convince herself.

"What else are you making?"

225

"Chicken and dumplings and a green salad," Charlie had replied.

Lena smiled broadly. "He'll love it."

"He better," she muttered, walking away and wondering what she had gotten herself into.

Charlie learned soon enough. After pushing Snickers out of the house, she began the tedious process of cutting up candy bars and melting them over a low flame. It seemed to take forever for them to melt into a smooth consistency before she could blend in the flour, sugar, butter, and eggs. While the cake baked, she began cooking the filling, which required another bunch of candy bars to be melted and mixed in. She kept the recipe in front of her in order to follow each step carefully. But that didn't stop disaster.

"It's supposed to *thicken,*" she declared to the room as she continued to stir the filling, which resembled a chocolate, caramel, and peanut gruel. But no matter how much she beat the mixture, it refused to thicken. By then she knew she would have to start cooking the filling all over again. She was just counting the number of candy bars left when the timer went off, indicating the cake was done. After poking a toothpick in the center to determine it was cooked all the way through, she used pot holders to pick up one of the pans and carry it over to the open bread board. Charlie was just ready to place it on the wooden surface when the bottom of the pan caught the edge of an open drawer. In what seemed like slow motion the pan tipped over to deposit the contents on the floor and inside the open drawer. Charlie stared at the mess, unable to believe her eyes. Then she uttered a few words that used to gain her a mouthful of soap when she was young. She would have cried if she hadn't been so angry over the catastrophe.

Still muttering to herself, she wet several paper towels and worked to get the warm cake off the floor but ended up having to scrape it up with a spatula. Then came the job of emptying the utensil drawer and washing the cake-covered forks and spoons. When she finished she looked up at the clock and was stunned to discover two hours had passed. There was no time to try another recipe now.

After the kitchen had been restored to order, Charlie shoved a pan of chicken in the oven to cook before she would debone it for the chicken and dumplings. Now it was time to treat herself to a long bath and beauty session.

Charlie discarded her jeans and sweatshirt and turned on the water in the bathtub, adding a generous splash of scented bath oil to the running water. She happened to glance in the mirror, did a double take, and looked again.

"No!" she moaned, practically pressing her nose against the glass. But the small red spot on her chin wasn't a figment of her imagination. Charlie slapped a speck of face mask on the offending pimple and slipped into the water. By now she felt she deserved something peaceful!

After her bath, Charlie put on an old robe that was the same as a security blanket to her. She had owned it since high school and it was the worst-looking item in her wardrobe, but it was warm and comfortable and she loved it. She washed her face and was looking for her shampoo when she heard a knock at the door.

Thinking it was Lena stopping by to see how the cake

went, Charlie was all prepared to blast her out of orbit as she pulled the door open.

"Do you realize—" She gaped at Murphy standing before her.

"Hi." He grinned.

"You're early." She slammed the door shut.

"Charlie, what's going on?" he demanded, pounding on the door.

Blinking rapidly to keep the tears back, she opened the door again. Murphy swept past her and spun around.

"Why did you slam the door in my face?" he demanded.

"Because you're early." She sniffed.

"So?"

"So, dinner isn't ready, *I'm* not ready, I have a pimple on my chin, the filling wouldn't thicken, your cake ended up on the floor and in my utensil drawer, and it took forever to clean the mess up." She stopped to take a breath. "Shall I go on?"

Murphy smiled and leaned over to kiss her chin.

"You better be careful," she warned. "It may be like a wart and you might catch one."

"Since you're such a cute little toad, I won't mind," he teased.

"Don't be so *nice* to me!" she wailed.

Murphy draped his arm around her shoulders. "Is that the ratty old robe you used to wear when we lived together?" he asked, steering her toward the couch. "I'm surprised it hasn't fallen apart yet."

She nodded, keeping her head downcast. "Couldn't you go away and come back in about two hours?" she pleaded, hoping she would be put back together by then. This was new to Charlie. She had always been in control until today, and she wanted this dinner to be so special for Murphy.

"Why don't I give you a hand?" he suggested, dropping a kiss on her forehead. "You go in and get dressed."

"What's wrong with what I'm wearing?" she demanded.

"Nothing," he assured her hastily.

"I had a very sexy caftan to wear for tonight," Charlie mourned.

"Then go put it on," Murphy urged her, leaning over to sniff the faint floral scent on her skin. As far as he was concerned, she didn't need to wear a stitch of clothing to look sexy, but he didn't think she would care to hear that just now.

Charlie pushed Murphy down onto the couch. "Stay there," she ordered before moving away to fix him a drink. After assuring herself he was settled, she returned to the kitchen to take the chicken out of the oven and let it cool. The remaining cake pan was set to one side, along with the pan of soupy filling. She made a face at the filling, as if it would thicken automatically under her silent threat.

Charlie again ordered Murphy to stay put and went into the bedroom to dress in the dark blue gauzy caftan she'd bought for the occasion. She applied her makeup, with special attention to her chin, and sprayed on her cologne.

"Pretty," Donnie crooned, lifting one foot in hopes she would be taken into the living room.

"Thank you, and no, you may not come with me," Charlie told her before leaving the room.

"Are you sure I can't help?" Murphy asked, listening to the sounds of pots and pans rattling around in the kitchen.

"No, everything is just fine," she called back, adding under her breath, "Thank heavens."

Luckily the chicken cooked beautifully and the dumplings were light and fluffy. Murphy enjoyed the meal by having too helpings of the chicken and the green salad with a parmesan dressing.

"This is great, Charlie," he praised. "How come you never made anything like this before?"

She shrugged. "Probably because I found the recipe about three years ago, and since it seemed so foolproof I've made it more times than I can count." She stood to pick up the plates and pushed Murphy back in his chair when he began to straighten up. "Oh, no, this is your day. You just sit back and relax." She stacked the dishes and put them on the kitchen counter.

"I have to admit the smells coming out of here really jacked up my appetite," Murphy confessed, listening to the homey sounds of silverware against crockery. "You never did explain what happened to the cake you were baking." He looked down at the shallow bowl set in front of him with what looked like cake chunks and some kind of chocolatey peanut sauce poured over it.

"I probably should have put candles on it, but there wasn't very much room," Charlie said dryly, placing her own bowl in front of her. "Happy birthday."

Murphy stared down at the bowl, then back up at her. "I realize I'm being rude, but what is this?"

"Candy bar cake." She dug her spoon into the mixture and lifted it to her lips. "Hmm, not too bad."

He shook his head in disbelief. "Is this Lena's recipe?"

"Yes. I'm going to kill her for giving it to me."

"What precisely *did* happen to the other layer?" he asked cautiously.

Charlie nodded, savoring her unusual dessert as she explained what had happened to the second layer. "I suggest you don't laugh if you don't want to end up with this on top of your head," she warned.

Murphy held his breath and tightened his lips to keep the laughter from escaping.

She finally relented. "All right, maybe it *was* funny, but at the time, I wasn't in the mood to see the humor in it."

Murphy chuckled as he dug into the concoction. "You know what? I think I like it better this way," he said honestly.

"An excellent choice of words," she replied, at last relaxing.

Murphy eyed her with the look of a man who had been away from his woman for almost a week. "Now what?"

Charlie smiled. "Now I kidnap you for the weekend," she announced.

"Sounds fair, as long as you don't drag out any whips and chains."

"Are you kidding? This is my first kidnap attempt, and I'm going to do whatever comes to mind." She arched an eyebrow and affected a sultry look. "But you won't have to worry because I intend to make this a birthday celebration you'll remember for the rest of your life."

Murphy felt his heart speeding up. He was sure Charlie meant every word.

CHAPTER TWELVE

"Boy, when you decide to kidnap someone, you do it with style," Murphy complimented the next morning during their walk on the beach.

When they reached the sandy edge, Charlie slipped her arm around his waist, linking her finger through a belt loop of his jeans, very much aware of the rhythmic movement of his hips as he walked. His own arm was draped over her shoulders. The day may have been gray and cloudy with a hint of rain, but as far as they were concerned, the sun shone brightly.

"Thank you, kind sir." Charlie couldn't keep the broad smile from splitting her face that was rosy from the chilling wind.

From the very beginning, she had been in charge of Murphy's birthday expedition, including driving him to the inn the night before. They settled into a beachfront room that was perfect for lovers, complete with a working fireplace and champagne on ice near the large four-poster bed. Snuggled under a large down comforter, they cuddled in bed, sipping the wine from one glass and talking. She couldn't remember the last time they had talked so intensely and she enjoyed it.

She loved Murphy and intended to show him exactly

how much. She was still leery of telling him so for fear he might not believe her. After all, her past track record hadn't been the best, and she wanted to use her time in proving to him she had changed. She looked down at the sand she kicked up with the toe of her running shoe and thought of something so funny she laughed under her breath.

"Did you know you snore?" she asked, still grinning.

"I do not!" He pretended to look hurt.

"Do, too."

Murphy halted and put his hands under her arms, lifting her up and swinging her around in a circle.

"Murphy!" Charlie laughed, holding her head back so she could feel the wind against her face. "Put me down."

"Tell me you made it up, that I don't snore."

"But I didn't make it up. You *do* snore!" She couldn't stop giggling.

"So lie to me! Give a guy a break."

"All right, all right, you don't snore—you just breathe heavy. Now put me down. I'm getting dizzy," she pleaded, still laughing.

Murphy's idea of putting Charlie down was to slowly slide her down the length of his body until her pelvis lightly rocked against his. "You're down," he said huskily.

"You're not." Her voice was equally breathy before she stepped back and suddenly spun around, then sprinted down the beach. "Same old game, Murphy . . . If you want me you're going to have to catch me!" she taunted over her shoulder. "If you can!"

"You little . . ." He laughed, running after her, but his heavier body had more trouble on the soft dry sand.

Her head start would have been his undoing if he hadn't soon swerved to run along the damp packed sand at the water's edge. As it was, he still didn't reach her until she had just passed an outcropping of rocks. "Gotcha!" He jumped forward to take her down in a tackle worthy of the Super Bowl.

Charlie shrieked as she was rolled over onto her back. Her smile on her face told him she wasn't hurt. "Hey, unnecessary roughness!"

Murphy crab-walked over Charlie until they were nose to nose. "You're a tease, Charlie Wells." His mouth brushed over hers. "A very tasty and sexy tease." He lowered his body until it lay over hers.

"Since you've caught me, now you can have me," she murmured, lifting her hands and pressing them against the sides of his head. "I hope you won't let go of an excellent opportunity," she added, flicking out her tongue and tracing the warm contours of his mouth before darting inside. He tasted warm and pleasant. She angled her face and began kissing him in earnest.

"Ever make love on a beach?" Murphy asked, turning his head to nip her ear and draw her gold fan-shaped earring into his mouth.

"No, are we going to try something new?" She tunneled her hands under his heavy fisherman's knit sweater and ran them over the skin of his chest.

"Damn right, we are. Your hands are cold."

"Give me a minute and they'll be warm."

"Mmm, I think you've got an excellent idea." He did the same under her sweater and fumbled with the tiny catch on her bra. He had watched her put that lacy wisp on earlier that morning, and all he could fantasize about was taking it off. Her breast immediately swelled under his caressing touch and the nipple teased his palm. "I'm sure glad you didn't wear long underwear." His other hand slipped between them to unsnap and unzip her jeans.

Charlie smiled up at him. "Aren't you afraid someone will find us?"

"Naw. Besides, who else is stupid enough to come out on a cold, windy day like this?"

She unzipped his jeans and insinuated her fingers between the metal teeth. "Hmm, and here I thought things contracted in the cold," she gurgled, warming the bulging flesh with her hand.

"It must be your magic touch." He found the lace edge of her bikini underwear and found his way beneath.

Charlie hooked her feet around his ankles. "You really mean to make love here?" she asked, amazed and tantalized by the idea.

Murphy nodded. "You can scream all you want, because if anyone hears you they'll just think it's seagulls." His head swooped down and took her mouth with a fury she hadn't expected. It only served to fuel the fire burning between them.

That fury didn't stop with the mating of their mouths. Their bodies participated with a sexual energy that was fast and furious. No clothing was removed, merely rearranged to allow his entrance into her. Their hands were warmed against bare skin under their sweaters, and their tongues participated in a duel where there would be no winner because they both would climb the mountain side by side.

Charlie felt a spiritual lifting of her body that was new to her but not frightening. Nothing concerned with

Murphy could be frightening. When her body tightened just before shattering into pieces, she screamed out Murphy's name and she could hear him calling out hers. They lay there for long moments, breathing heavily in an effort to regain their senses.

"A blending of the souls," Murphy said in a ragged voice, resting his forehead against hers.

Charlie ran her fingertips over the damp surface of his back. "So beautiful," she murmured, turning her head to press a kiss along his temple.

"Men aren't beautiful, Charlie."

How could a man's smile feel warm on her skin? "You are. You're beautiful when you're playing the part of administrative director to the public in your three-piece suit with your hair neatly combed, and you're just as beautiful when you're in jeans, a sweater, and those beat-up old boots." She smiled. "And you're especially beautiful when you stand naked before me and you're aroused with wanting me. Just looking at you then makes me aroused and wanting you."

Murphy's groan held the hint of a tired laugh. "Honey, you sure know when to make a man feel on top of the world. While making love to you here was an experience I thoroughly enjoyed, I would prefer the next time to be in that huge four-poster bed we have back at our room." He lifted himself up and reached down to pull her to her feet. Keeping his eyes on hers, he pulled her jeans back up over her hips. Taking more care than needed, he snapped and zipped them.

"You take such good care of me." She favored him with the same loving treatment.

"Got to keep you in one piece, or I'd have an angry crowd of ladies demanding I take over your exercise classes," he teased, draping his arm over her shoulder as they retraced their steps to the inn.

"Oh, so all I am to you is an exercise instructor," she declared with mock anger, half turning to punch his arm.

"I'm not exactly built correctly to show them how to keep their breast muscles from sagging."

"No, but I'm sure you're very good with hands-on treatment."

"It depends on where my hands are."

Charlie scampered away and turned around so she could walk backward in front of him. Her hands were in fists in front of her breasts, her elbows stuck out at an angle. "We must, we must, we must develop the bust," she chanted, pushing her arms out, then straightening out her arms and swinging them back. "The bigger the better, the tighter the sweater; we must develop the bust."

Murphy stared at her, then began laughing. "Charlie, I don't think a majority of the women need to worry about that."

"That was a very popular verse in high school," she informed him, turning back around to walk with him. "After all, guys tended to look at a girl's chest before anything else."

"Many still do."

Charlie rested her face against his arm. "I love you, Murphy," she said softly, turning her face to kiss the tangy wool of his sweater.

It took all his inner strength not to stiffen at her announcement or start whooping for joy and spinning her around in another dizzy circle. He had to convince himself she didn't mean it in the strict sense of the word, that she was just uttering words in the aftermath of their wonderful lovemaking. He adored Charlie with all his heart, but he doubted she could truly love any man. At least, not the way he wanted her to love him. He couldn't open his feelings to her the way he had before because he refused to relive the pain again. He would just have to harden his heart and live day by day.

"And I love you," he said, injecting an all-too-casual note in his reply.

Charlie dipped her head, not wanting him to see the disappointment on her face. Her declaration was completely unplanned. She had always thought it would sound better over candlelight and champagne, but the words just leapt out of her mouth. Deep down she knew she wanted him to know. Of course, he hadn't really given her any indication that he loved her. Then an unbidden memory came to mind: that day long ago when she had told Murphy about her new job and the need to travel with the show. He had told her then that he had loved, and she rejected him. How could she expect him to carry a love for all these years and calmly return it when she decided she loved him? The idea hurt —a great deal.

"Shall we drive into town and have lunch there?" she asked, finally breaking the silence.

"Sure." He was relieved he hadn't said anything because it appeared he was right: her words weren't spoken from the heart.

Charlie was overly quiet during their lunch at a seaside restaurant and their walk through the small town that boasted many shops geared for the tourists who stayed at the large inn down the highway. She couldn't find any enjoyment in the unusual shops even when

Murphy bought her a pair of lovely abalone shell earrings and a matching necklace. Her thank you was polite but without the enthusiasm she usually displayed. It was so noticeable that Murphy couldn't miss it.

"You okay?" he asked after they left the jewelry store.

"Of course." She pasted on a bright smile. "I guess I'm just more tired than I thought."

"We could always go back to the inn," Murphy suggested with a leering wink.

No, that wasn't what she wanted just then. "Couldn't we look around some more?"

Murphy was puzzled by her sudden interest in the shops but decided to give in. Maybe he could find out what was bothering her once they were alone again.

During the drive back to the inn late that afternoon, Charlie made her decision. She would just have to show Murphy how strongly she felt about him. Hopefully, he would begin to love her again. He certainly didn't make love to her like a man who merely lusted after her body or was looking for some great sex. And he didn't act like a man who saw her as part of a string of affairs. Murphy wasn't like that. She knew he wasn't. Charlie was convinced he wanted a home and family, the family he hadn't had as a child. All she had to do was prove to him that she was the prime candidate for such a time-consuming job.

One good thing about Charlie was that she was never kept down long. She was the eternal optimist and knew that, given time, she could show Murphy she wasn't the same self-centered young woman he knew years ago. She would have given herself that same label not all that long ago, but she was learning that she wasn't the only human being on this earth and others' feelings counted for a great deal.

"I was such a selfish little bitch back then," she said under her breath as they entered their room.

"Castigating yourself doesn't make it any better, Charlie," Murphy told her.

She grimaced, wishing he hadn't heard her words. "No, it doesn't, does it? I guess I'm finally learning some things about myself that aren't very pretty. It's difficult coming to terms with them."

Murphy pulled off his heavy jacket and threw it onto a nearby chair. "There's always something we don't like about ourselves, but we learn to live with it. I think I'll take a shower. You coming?"

"I don't think so." She couldn't help it if the hurt she felt sounded in her voice.

Standing under the hot spray of water, Murphy thought back to what Charlie had said. Was she changing faster than he thought? Should he tell her how he really felt about her? No, if he said anything now, he doubted she'd believe him and would only accuse him of just mouthing words. He picked up the bar of soap and ran it over his chest. He wished Charlie had come in with him. He wished a lot of things.

The weekend was pretty much ruined. Their dinner passed in silence, as did the few hours they passed in the adjoining lounge, listening to the band and dancing to a few tunes.

"I wanted this to be so special for you," Charlie apologized as they walked back to their room.

"It is, Charlie," Murphy assured her, pulling her close to his side. "In fact, I wouldn't be adverse to any time you cared to kidnap me again."

She smiled. "We'll have to wait for another special occasion."

"Charlie, as far as I'm concerned, with you, every day is a special occasion."

His words left her warm and glowing inside. When they fell into bed an hour later, their weekend turned out not to be ruined at all.

"Lottie and Marvin are getting married?" Charlie gasped, hearing Lena's news the following Monday. "Wait a minute, there's got to be a mistake. You once told me that she's been putting him off for the past fifteen years. What changed her mind after all this time?"

Lena smiled. "Roxy Girard."

Charlie searched her memory for a face to go with the name. "Roxy . . . ex-Follies . . . platinum hair in a marcel wave," she recalled. "She claims she could have been another Jean Harlow if she'd been given the chance. But what does she have to do with Lottie's finally accepting Marvin's proposal?"

"Roxy decided Marvin was perfect husband material and set out to snare him by acting like the helpless female whenever she saw him," Lena explained. "Good old gossipy Shirley Reynolds saw what was going on and told Lottie that Marvin took Roxy out to dinner and he didn't arrive home until after midnight. Since Shirley and her husband, Fred, live near Marvin's house and she enjoys peeking out her window, she certainly knew what time he got home. After hearing that, Lottie cornered Marvin the next day and told him in no uncertain terms they were getting married in two weeks time."

Charlie choked, thinking of the meek-mannered man who obviously didn't have a chance. "And he had probably already given up the idea of Lottie ever marrying him. That poor man." She burst into laughter.

"Lottie just feels she doesn't dare waste any time," Lena told her. "Some of us thought we'd give her a bridal shower Friday night. You'll be able to come, won't you?" She couldn't help teasing, "Surely James wouldn't mind giving you up for one evening."

Charlie wrinkled her nose. "He'd survive. Is Roxy also coming? After all, it was due to her that Lottie finally came to her senses."

The older woman shuddered. "Naturally not. Lottie has always been the perfect lady. Insisting Marvin marry her is enough of a personality change without watching her go for Roxy's throat if Roxy decided to goad her."

Charlie shook her head. Lena was right. At seventy-eight, Lottie MacIntyre was the epitome of the proper Victorian lady. She wore high-necked gowns at all times, carried a parasol when outside, and kept her luxuriant white hair in a smooth upswept style. Charlie had heard that her husband had died twenty-eight years ago of a heart attack, and Lottie hadn't given a thought to remarrying even her most ardent suitor until it appeared someone else would snatch him away. Charlie enjoyed the soft-spoken woman who served tea and scones when she had callers, even if Lottie did call her Charlotte, claiming she could never call a lovely young lady Charlie.

"What time and where?" Charlie asked.

Lena stood up and prepared to leave the office. "Seven thirty at Maude's. Eat something ahead of time because Maude will probably make her special punch. It has the kick of a mule. How about a game of tennis tomorrow morning?"

Charlie grimaced. "Why not? Running around the court chasing after your returns will be good exercise. I'll see you on the court at eight." She paused, her face pink with embarrassment at her question. "Oh, Lena, what do you give a seventy-eight-year-old prospective bride?"

Lena smiled wickedly. "How about *The Joy of Sex?*" She opened the door and slipped out.

Charlie sat back in her chair. "You've got to be kidding," she muttered. "I haven't even read it." She returned to her paperwork, deciding to go shopping for a shower gift that evening. She figured placemats and napkins would be safe.

At lunch Charlie told Murphy about the upcoming shower and wedding and wasn't too pleased when he began chuckling.

"Why don't they just live together and not bother with propriety?" he commented, tackling his green salad.

Charlie toyed with the idea of seeing what blue cheese dressing would look like on top of Murphy's head. "Because Lottie wants something permanent."

"She didn't until it looked like Roxy might take him away from her. Don't get me wrong—I adore Lottie. She's one of the sweetest, most gentle women I've ever known. But marrying Marvin so Roxy can't have him isn't the way to do it." His voice lowered. "Love has to enter into it somewhere."

His words set Charlie throbbing. That magic word made her want to tell him that she agreed, but how could she talk about commitment and a permanent relationship when Murphy was still convinced she would leave in a second if she could dance again? She had realized dancing wasn't as important as having a man love her, but Murphy didn't know that. She had never been too patient, and she wanted him to see how much she'd grown up and changed right away. But that was something she couldn't force.

"I want to go shopping for a gift tonight," she said softly, looking down at her own salad. "Would you like to come along?"

Murphy caught the new note in her voice and wondered what caused it. "If you'd like the company, I'll go, but I should think you'd be happier going with one of the women."

Charlie was stung. He obviously didn't want to go with her. "If I didn't want you to come with me, I wouldn't have asked you."

He reached across the table to grasp her hand. "Honey, I'm sorry. I didn't realize it was so important to you."

She wanted to lie and say it wasn't, but she knew he would see through her. "I enjoy being with you and I know you feel the same. I thought you might help me come up with an idea for a gift, since all I can think of are placemats and napkins."

"Why don't you ask Lena or Maude for some ideas?"

"I did. I asked Lena and she suggested I give Lottie a copy of *The Joy of Sex.*"

Murphy laughed. "It sounds more like something Maude would come up with. Don't worry, between the two of us we'll come up with something."

That evening they searched through several stores

until Charlie decided there was nothing wrong with lace-edged placemats and matching napkins. She also found a lovely crystal vase that Murphy insisted on paying for, explaining they could give it to the couple for a wedding gift.

While they shopped Murphy thought about Charlie's reaction to his somewhat callous comments that afternoon. He had no idea they would have hurt her so much. He remembered a time when she would have laughed and agreed wholeheartedly with him. Now he definitely knew she had changed more than he had realized.

Friday evening, Maude's cottage was overflowing with shower guests to wish the prospective bride good luck.

Charlie enjoyed talking to the various women and inspecting Maude's mementos of her past career scattered about the room. Charlie chuckled when she found a photograph of Maude, wearing a skimpy costume, posing with a police chief. She drank sparingly of the punch, even though she couldn't imagine that something that tasted like a tart fruit punch was so potent that two glasses could put a person under a table. But then she noticed the other women going back for another glass of the rose-colored liquid. And the more they drank, the more uninhibited they became.

"Lottie, we've got to make sure that Roxy doesn't try to get her hooks into Marvin again," Maude slurred after they had feasted on the lemon-filled sheet cake.

"We'll be married," the other woman insisted. "And marriage is a sacred institution."

Maude gave her own profane view of that sacred institution. "Someone like Roxy won't see it that way. Now, I'm going to teach you a little something to try out on Marvin on your wedding night. Honey, after he gets a load of this he won't even think about straying from you!" She walked over to the stereo and put on a record.

"Oh, no," Lena breathed, guessing Maude's intent.

Charlie turned to her. "What?"

"She's going to teach Lottie to strip."

Charlie squealed. "Really?" She turned to the front of the room. "Maude, are you going to teach Lottie to strip?"

Lottie blanched.

"Hell, yes. Can you imagine any red-blooded man resisting a good show?" Maude boomed.

"I want to learn, too," Charlie insisted, setting down her punch cup.

"Honey, for you it would be a snap." Maude turned on the stereo.

In the end, everyone learned the good old-fashioned bump and grind. And with a few glasses of punch in her, even Lottie swiveled her hips. The more punch the women drank, the looser their dancing became. By the time the party ended, no one felt any pain and it was merely a question of whether they would be able to go home under their own power. A few husbands and friends came by to pick up most of the women, and Jason offered to drive Charlie home. She solemnly explained to him that she wasn't drunk like the others. Jason looked at her heightened color and heard her slightly slurred words and knew better as he steered her out to the car.

When he started up the car, she asked to be dropped

off at Murphy's cottage instead of being taken home. She had silently decided to try out a few of her new dance steps on him before she forgot them.

Murphy was in bed and very close to dropping off to sleep when someone knocked on his door. Grumbling, he pulled on a pair of jeans and headed for the front door to find Charlie draped against the door sill.

"Hi . . ." She drew the word out into a breathy sigh as she floated past him. "Did you have a nice evening?"

"Apparently not as nice as yours," he replied. "You're drunk."

"No, I'm not. Oh, I have a good buzz on, but nothing more." She spun around, throwing her purse on the couch and sliding her coat off. "Let me entertain you," she sang in her husky contralto as she casually unbuttoned her black silk blouse. "Boom, chicka, chicka, chicka, boom." She hesitated and looked at him with glassy eyes. "Is it two chickas or three?" A shrug of her shoulders slid the blouse down to her elbows. "I guess it doesn't matter. Boom, chicka, chicka, chicka, boom."

"Is this where I say, 'Take it off, take it all off'?" he asked, his eyes widening as he watched the silk slide to the carpet while she shimmied out of matching slacks until she was clad only in a black bra and panties with a matching garter belt holding up her sheer black hose. Her black high heels made her legs appear to go on forever. What had gone on at that shower? he wondered.

Charlie smiled, fingering the clasp to her bra, then edged down to the ribbon tied on her hip. "Congratulations, sir, you have said the magic words." The clasp was undone and her bra hung loosely from her shoulders. One ribbon on her panties was slowly untied, then the other was undone.

Murphy was having a lot of trouble breathing. Deciding she had gone far enough, he strode forward and swept her up into his arms, carrying her into the bedroom.

Charlie laughed when she was tossed into the middle of the bed and Murphy followed her down. Determined not to be far from her for very long, he grunted and groaned as he tried to push his jeans off without getting up.

"I missed you, Murphy," she murmured, putting her arms around his neck and pulling his face down to hers. Her searching tongue sought his and almost sent him over the top with her hungry kiss.

"I sure couldn't tell," he gasped when he finally came up for air.

Charlie laughed seductively. "If you're so unsure, I'll have to work at persuading you, won't I? All I could think about this evening was coming back here and making mad passionate love to you," she murmured, her fingers trailing along his collarbone and down his chest to the tiny male nipple that sprang to life under her loving touch. In order to ensure he wouldn't think of leaving her, even if he had had the strength to do so, her legs wrapped around his calves. "I want you," she said throatily, rubbing her body against his.

Murphy caressed the upper slope of her breast with his lips, bathing her taut skin with his tongue even as his hand found its way down to the blond curls that hid her feminine treasure. His fingers dipped in to find her moist and receptive. But he didn't want her just wanting him. He wanted her so hungry for him that she couldn't see straight. While she may have begun this seduction, he was going to give it a magnificent finale.

Charlie's eyes widened as Murphy's mouth continued lavishing attention over each breast as his fingers explored her femininity. The beginning spasms moving throughout her body were only a hint of what was to come.

"Make love to me, Murphy," she whimpered, running her hands over his back and around to his chest.

"I am," he muttered against the soft skin of her stomach. "And this is only the beginning." His mouth moved further down. Charlie's sharp indrawn breath told him he had reached the correct spot. He tongued, probed, and nibbled her into oblivion.

She whimpered, cried out, and practically screamed when she felt herself being overwhelmed. Colors intensified, the room swirled around her, and the world became more beautiful than ever. When Murphy finally released her to move up and surge into her waiting sheath, she gasped with the rightness of it all. Nothing they had shared before compared with their loving tonight.

She opened her eyes and looked into his tight features, taut from the passion they were experiencing. For long moments they looked into each other's eyes. She saw a blue so deep it could rival the midnight sky; he saw a blue that was smokier, with a touch of misty gray that made him think of drowsy mornings spent in bed. She lifted her head to rub her face against his. The musky scent of his body drifted up to her nostrils and left her feeling more light-headed than any alcohol could.

Murphy experienced the same kind of crazy feelings.

No one but Charlie ever left him feeling as if he was a man who could do anything. As long as Charlie was here to nurture him and give him the love and affection she had within her, he was on top of the world. He moved slowly within her, feeling her grip and release him only when she desired to.

He wasn't the victor in this sensual battle, but then, neither was she. No, they didn't win and they didn't lose; instead they gained something more valuable than could be measured in simple wins and losses. They gained each other.

Dawn was just breaking when Charlie awoke. She turned her head to see that Murphy was still asleep. He was probably tired after all she had put him through.

Murphy opened one eye. "You don't like to sleep much, do you? In case you haven't noticed, that pale light outside means dawn, not dusk."

"I can't help it if I woke up feeling wonderful." She lay back, stretching her arms over her head.

Murphy eyed the bare breast peeking impudently above the top sheet and decided he felt pretty wonderful, too.

"I wonder how many men will wake up this morning with a broad smile?" he commented, rolling over and covering her breast with his palm, rotating it over the taut nipple. Before they had fallen asleep hours earlier, Charlie had told him about the stripping lessons Maude gave the women and how all of them had learned the dance.

"A broad smile and sore backs," Charlie quipped.

"Feeling pretty saucy and sure of yourself, aren't you?" Laughing, Murphy pulled her face down to his.

The touch of his lips on hers was like liquid fire, pouring over her, branding her with his taste. His tongue slipped into her mouth, taking all she offered with deep, hard strokes in a kiss meant to go on forever.

Her hands roamed over his shoulders, across his back, up to tangle in the silky thickness of his hair.

It was as if they hadn't made love for days instead of hours. The spark always burning between them flared anew.

"Any more of this could kill me," Murphy groaned, pulling her over him.

She wiggled her hips. "You certainly don't feel dead to me."

He gripped her hips to stay her movement. "Are you seducing me again?"

"Yes."

He drew his hands away. "Okay, just checking."

"Murphy?" Her voice was soft in the predawn light. "I meant what I said before about loving you."

He sighed. He doubted she could understand that it just wasn't something he wanted to get into right now. "Let's not talk about it now, okay?"

She straightened up. "But I do! This isn't some kind of joke, Murphy. I'm serious."

"I believe you, Charlie, but it's just the time and place that makes you feel that way. Call it displaced hormones."

"That is not the reason!" she stated so fiercely the room seemed to vibrate around them. She leaned forward to grasp his arm, the quilt falling down to reveal her breasts, ivory in the dim light. "Murphy, you should know me better by now. I never say anything lightly. I realize you don't love me anymore. I can't blame you after all I've put you through in the past, but that doesn't mean I can't love you. I'm not the same woman you knew nine years ago—or even the one who showed up here several months ago."

He stared down at the coverlet half covering their naked bodies. If he hadn't looked at the cream and navy quilt, he probably would have looked into Charlie's eyes and lost himself all over again. He couldn't afford to do that, so all he could do was brazen the present situation out and hope for the best. He wanted nothing more than for Charlie to stay here with him for the rest of their lives, but he wasn't sure she was ready to give up what she loved so dearly if a miracle happened and it turned out she could dance again. He knew he had to give her the freedom to make her choice, and in order to do that, he had to make sure there wouldn't be any commitments on either side. God, how that hurt.

"Why don't we just take it one day at a time, okay?" he suggested quietly, still refusing to look directly at her.

She stared at him, unable to believe what she was hearing. "Fine," she said tautly, turning away to climb out of bed and search for her clothing. "Just don't expect me to meekly give in." The euphoria she felt earlier now tasted like ashes. She had just learned what Murphy's rejection felt like, and she decided that major surgery performed without anesthesia was preferable.

CHAPTER THIRTEEN

"I hate the rain, I hate the fog"—Charlie turned in her chair to face the direction of Murphy's office—"and I hate you."

Wrong. She really didn't hate him, but it made her feel better to say so. The night she had left his bed was more than two months ago, and she still wasn't sure whether or not her decision was right. Come to think of it, she didn't know if she had actually made a decision. Well, in a way she had. Murphy didn't believe she truly loved him, and he didn't believe she would continue to work at the retirement center for the next thirty years or so. She knew the best way to show him he was wrong was to work harder than ever. That might also be the only way she could prove to him that she did love him and it wasn't some kind of passing fancy.

There had been a lot of changes made in the past two months. Charlie didn't go to Murphy's bungalow in the evenings, and she made sure she was never alone with him again. Many days she shared a table with him at lunchtime, but there was always a third party present. She was the one having problems, wasn't she? So why wasn't Murphy as miserable as she was? How come he smiled all the time and acted as if nothing had happened? Come to think of it, maybe she *did* hate him for putting her through this. So what if she was the one putting the distance between them? It was all his fault that she felt she had to do it. If she hadn't, she'd still be sharing his bed and would never have a chance to work things out. Charlie knew sex wasn't the answer to the problem; it merely blurred the edges until she didn't know whether she was coming or going.

She rubbed her fingertips against her temples, wishing her headache would go away. She knew it wouldn't because she'd had it for quite a while, along with the insomnia that plagued her night after night. Charlie began to wish that Murphy would question her about her attitude, yell at her—*anything*. But he merely smiled sadly and told her he understood. Great, he understood. Now if he'd only tell her what she was trying to prove by this, she'd feel much better about herself.

The days hadn't turned out to be as bad as she feared. There was always a great deal of work on her desk. She'd also set up two new exercise classes that incorporated dance routines, and those took a great deal of time to choreograph. And there always seemed to be someone inviting her over for dinner or out to a movie, but it wasn't the same. She might not have lacked for company, but it wasn't the one person she wanted to be with.

Lena had inferred that if Charlie needed someone to talk to, the older woman was always there, but while Charlie was greatly tempted she couldn't bring herself to confide in her. Her mother used to praise her on how self-reliant she was when there had been times when she had wanted nothing more than to run in to her mother and cry her fears out. How could she when her mother had always said she could handle her own problems better than anyone?

During the long days, in an effort to keep herself as busy as possible, Charlie spent more time at the medical center. While Winifred Page still wasn't happy seeing her on the lawn with one of the animals, she didn't argue against it anymore. Even she, with her strict codes, could see that Charlie was only trying to help the patients by sitting there talking or reading to them and giving assistance in any way she could. In fact, on many sunny afternoons Snickers could be found dozing near a wheelchair or by one of the lawn chairs set up for the ambulatory patients. The snobbish cat may not have any patience with his owner, but he was all sweetness and light where the frail residents were concerned.

Charlie felt all these new changes coursing through her body. It was as if she were shedding her skin and leaving it behind, the way a snake shed its skin. It might not be a very nice analogy, but it was the only way she could adequately describe what was happening to her.

She glanced at the clock. It was too early in the afternoon to leave the office and too late to get herself involved in a few of the new projects she had thought up.

Charlie should have been happy, but she found herself growing more tense with each passing day. She had been at New Eden for a little over seven months and had been working on new exercise routines for the past two weeks.

She had also set up an appointment with her doctor the following week—without Murphy's knowledge. She hadn't told him because she knew that would definitely get his attention, but not the kind of attention she wanted. She didn't need a crystal ball to know he'd be upset and he would insist on going with her. But she wanted to be alone when she heard the final diagnosis.

Still, Charlie wondered how she would feel if the doctor told her she could return to dancing. She'd discovered that living and working at New Eden wasn't so bad after all. She had even set up a coed exercise class, and the men were even asking for a class all their own, teasing her that they enjoyed watching her twisting and turning in front of their old eyes.

Then there was Murphy. Dear, sweet Murphy who always seemed to be there when she needed him; who guessed her moods before she did. Oh, she still loved him, fool that she was. There was no doubt of that. But she had killed the love he'd once had for her. She knew he had enjoyed making love to her, but sometimes she wondered if that wasn't more physical than emotional. That was the way he seemed to look at it.

Charlie's time was running out. She had to tell Murphy about her doctor's appointment because she would have to take the day, maybe two, off. She, the woman who feared nothing, was afraid to ask him for the time off.

But an hour later, her luck changed. Murphy stopped by her office to explain he had to drive up to San Francisco the next day and would be gone for a week. He'd be back two days after her doctor's appointment. Charlie disliked subterfuge, but there was a time when it was required, and this was the time.

"I'm going to miss you," Murphy admitted that night when he took her out to dinner. "Oh, I know we've had some problems lately, but I hope this time apart will give us some time to think things through. We can talk when I get back. *Really* talk," he stressed.

Charlie nodded, feeling very much the same way. "Yes, we'll talk," she agreed softly. She felt light-headed with happiness and guilty at the same time. She just wished she had the courage to tell him about her appointment with Dr. Grissom. But she didn't want him to worry about what might happen and decided he was better off in the dark for the time being. Part of her thought about canceling the appointment and just going on the way she was, but that wouldn't work. She had to know, no matter what the outcome.

For the next few days, Charlie felt as if a part of her were missing. She moped around her office and around the cottage, feeling as if she'd lost her best friend, which, she realized, she had. She couldn't even generate any excitement over seeing her doctor.

The day before her appointment Charlie told Hazel she had an appointment in Los Angeles and wouldn't be in the following day and probably not the next. She left work at five o'clock and went home to pack and pace the floor half the night, wondering whether the doctor's news would make her happy or sad. She'd be a fool if she didn't admit that a tiny part of her wanted to return to dancing, but deep down she knew Murphy meant a great deal more to her. She had finally realized that he was much more important than showing an impressive list of credits to a choreographer. With a bittersweet smile, Charlie realized she had grown up.

"I have to admit I was surprised you didn't appear on my doorstep six months to the day," Dr. Grissom told her late the next afternoon after the somewhat painful tests she had endured that day.

Charlie smiled tightly. "I didn't want to appear too

eager." She clasped her hands in her lap to still their trembling. "I also figured you'd tell me to wait awhile longer."

The doctor leaned back in his chair, studying Charlie as if he were seeing her for the very first time. There was no mistaking her pale cheeks, overly bright eyes, and white lines of strain bracketing her mouth. She was frightened to hear his verdict.

"We've been together a long time, Charlie," he said conversationally. "And if I recall, I told you the first time I treated you that that weak knee of yours would give out sooner or later."

She winced. "Meaning, I'm definitely washed up."

He shook his head. "Actually, it's in much better shape than I expected." He paused.

"But . . ."

"If I were you I wouldn't count on its holding up under too much strain," he said bluntly. "Oh, you could return to dancing, but all it would take is one tiny misstep to leave you a cripple."

Charlie looked down at her hands. She was unhappy over his diagnosis, yes, but not half as stricken as she thought she would be.

"Talk about a written guarantee," she murmured.

Dr. Grissom nodded. "That's about it. How's your job at the retirement community?"

"Fine." She managed a strained smile.

"You were aware this could happen. I warned you it could go either way, but I was afraid my diagnosis would be what I just told you," he said gently. "I am sorry, but you're not alone. I hate to think how many dancers end up with the same problem. The wear and tear on ankles and knees are especially appalling."

"Yeah," Charlie replied softly. "I guess I'm better off than most since I have a decent job." She stood up and offered her hand. "You were honest with me and I appreciate it."

He grasped her fingers and squeezed them. "You may still have flare-ups with that knee, Charlie. You come to me when it happens."

"I will," she promised. "Thank you."

Charlie walked out of the medical building, swamped with conflicting feelings. Dancing would have meant losing Murphy. No dancing meant keeping him. Deciding not to stay in Los Angeles for the night, she headed for her car and began the two-hour drive back to Santa Barbara.

Murphy didn't believe in rushing business trips, but he fairly flew through this one with good reason: Charlie. It wasn't until he sat alone in his hotel room in San Francisco or dined by himself that he realized how much he missed her. And it wasn't just missing her in his bed. He missed talking and laughing with her and watching the world through her eyes. He tried calling her one night, but there was no answer. Figuring she might have been visiting someone, he decided to try again in the morning when he knew she would be in the office.

The moment he finished breakfast he returned to his room to call the office. The moment Hazel answered the phone he asked for Charlie.

"Why, she isn't here, James," the older woman explained. "She had a doctor's appointment and left for Los Angeles yesterday. I assumed you knew all about it."

Murphy finally understood the meaning of the phrase "his blood ran cold." That was exactly how he felt.

"Yes, you're right . . . She did mention it to me. I just forgot," he lied. "Did she say when she would be back?" He coughed to hide the hoarseness of his voice.

"I believe she said she'd be back in a day or two. Was there something important you needed to know? Could I help you?" Hazel asked.

"No," he replied dully. "Nothing." Without saying another word, he slowly replaced the receiver and remained sitting on the bed, staring at the wall. The time had come to make the break and Murphy wasn't ready. He had prepared himself months before, but when the actual time came he still wasn't ready to lose her. Murphy preferred not to think about the mornings when Charlie complained about her knee feeling stiff or her jokes about fitting in the community so well since she considered herself a washed-up dancer. All he could think about was that the doctor probably told her she was fine, and she would return to her dancing and he would lose her again.

"Dammit to hell!" he shouted, pounding his fist against the bed, then pounding it again and again and again. But it did nothing to alleviate the pain tearing through him.

Murphy didn't bother to remember all the times Charlie told him she loved him and the way she fitted in so well with the residents and his new life. He didn't want to remember her new ideas for activities and subtle comments that she would be there long enough to turn into a resident herself. All he knew was that she had gone to the doctor without telling him and would probably come back and move out without saying a word. It would be just like the last time. No, it wouldn't be like then because he hadn't loved her half as much then as he did now.

As he stood up and moved around the room, all he could think of doing was returning to New Eden to confront her and cut her out of his life before she had a chance to leave him. He wasn't going to be the loser this time. He would be the one to walk away even though he knew he would never get over the pain of losing her again.

Murphy picked up the phone to rearrange two appointments, which would allow him to return to Santa Barbara that evening. He wasn't going to take any chances in missing her. And during all that time, he refused to listen to his heart suggesting he hear what Charlie had to say.

It was late evening by the time Charlie arrived back at New Eden, a place she now considered home. She was so tired from her long drive that she dropped her clothes on the floor and crawled into bed, falling asleep before her head hit the pillow.

She got up early the next day feeling more positive than she had in a long time. It was funny—yesterday she was told her major career was basically over and if she tried to return to her first love she would most probably end up a cripple. Instead of feeling sorrow, she only felt relief that she wouldn't be breaking her back for parts or putting up with rehearsals and classes at all hours. For the first time in her life, dance came second and it didn't bother her one bit. As she dressed for work she thought about new ideas for outings and other activities for the residents and was eager to get to her desk and get to work.

"Good morning, Hazel," Charlie greeted the secretary cheerfully before sweeping into her office. She stopped short when she found Murphy seated behind her desk. Her eyes were so filled with stars she didn't notice his dark countenance. "You got back early. Oh, Murphy, I have so much to tell you! Now I won't have to tell you on the phone."

"How did your doctor's appointment go?"

Charlie stopped, surprised by the chill in his voice. "You know about it?"

He nodded. "It was time for it. After all, it's been a little over six months. But did you have to wait until I was out of town? Why didn't you tell me you were going to the doctor? And when were you going to tell me the happy news? When you handed in your resignation? Is that why you're so thrilled with life all of a sudden? Did the doctor say you're fine?" The questions rattled on like machine-gun fire.

"Well, yes, but—"

"I'll expect you to be gone from here by the end of the day." His words rang out like a death knell.

Charlie's eyes widened. "Murphy?"

"James, my name is *James!* Murphy hasn't been around for a long time." He bit each word out savagely. "I knew the day would come when you'd decide your dancing was more important than me. I shouldn't be surprised that you'd pick dancing over staying here. After all, there aren't any bright lights and fawning audiences up here. Go back to where you'll be happy." He sliced the air with his hand for emphasis.

"Murphy, *listen* to me," she implored, stepping forward, her hands outstretched. "You don't understand."

He stood up and moved away before she could touch him. "Good-bye, Charlie. It's been fun. This time don't bother to find me in nine years. I'll have better things to do than take up with an old lover." He walked out of the office without a backward glance.

Charlie groped for a nearby chair before her legs gave out. Her eyes burned with tears that refused to fall. She'd had no idea this could happen. How did it all go wrong so quickly? She came back here ready to tell Murphy she was ready to settle down, and he'd abruptly slid the rug out from under her. He hadn't even listened to a word she had to say. She hurt. She hurt so much she couldn't tell where the pain began or ended.

When she felt as if she could cope with standing up and walking again, she left the office without bothering to gather up her personal possessions. She had no use for any of it. She blindly made her way to the cottage, packed her clothes, put Snickers and Donnie in their animal carriers, and drove away without looking back. When the tears finally fell she was safely behind an anonymous hotel door where no one of consequence could hear her sobbing.

Murphy would have preferred drowning his sorrows in a bottle of scotch, but he saw that as a coward's way out. He couldn't despise himself any more than he already did. So far, Jason, Lena, Maude, and Sylvester had stopped by to find out what happened to Charlie and blasted him to hell and back for firing her.

"Her knee can't stand the strain of full-time dancing," Lena had informed him in a cold voice. "I don't care what you think you heard her say. I doubt the doctor released her. Not after what she's said has happened in the past. Besides, how do you know she came back to quit? Perhaps she had decided to stay on. She's been happy here, and she just might have realized that we would be her future. She isn't to blame for what happened. You are. You're just afraid of getting hurt again, so this time you did the hurting first. And you thought she was vicious once upon a time. Honey, you take the cake."

Murphy had winced at that deliberately placed barb. It was true. He *had* been afraid of losing her. He feared losing her so much that he went ahead and cut the ties first so this time he could say he broke it off. The trouble was, it didn't make him feel any better about it.

He turned toward the kitchen. Come to think of it, a stiff drink wouldn't hurt after all. It might even dull the pain a little.

Deep down he wanted to tell himself that Charlie would call. That she would explain what had happened, and they could hash out their differences. But he sincerely doubted that would happen. He knew Charlie only too well. He had thrown her out in the cruelest way possible. He couldn't expect her to come back after what he'd done. He had driven her away and knew he would regret it to his dying day.

Charlie found it difficult to rent an apartment because of the animals, but perseverance finally paid off and she found a small studio apartment in West Hollywood. It wasn't much to look at, but it offered a badly needed haven. She stumbled through each day in a daze. Nothing seemed to matter anymore. In time, she arranged to return to her dance classes and found herself favoring her tender knee during the more difficult steps for fear of further injury. For a dancer not to give her whole heart was just a lie to herself and the audience she would eventually play to, but Charlie refused to think about that.

When she felt ready to speak to him, she called Harry as a matter of courtesy but told him nothing of what happened between her and Murphy. She was sure he'd hear the story from his aunt soon enough.

Harry was silent for a few minutes before venturing in a gentle voice, "Would you like me to find you some work in commercials, Charlie? Something where you wouldn't have to dance?"

She sighed. "To be perfectly honest, Harry, I don't know what I want right now. Can I call you back about it?"

"Sure. You just take it easy. Call me when you're ready." He hung up soon afterward.

Charlie replaced the receiver and looked over at Donnie, who sat quietly on her perch. Even Snickers was behaving, sleeping peacefully on one corner of the couch. She knew she would have to go to work sooner or later. The apartment wasn't the most luxurious, but the high rent made it sound more like a penthouse than a small studio apartment. She couldn't expect her savings to last forever. But she didn't want to think about it just now. She just wanted to wallow in her misery and damn Murphy for his quick tongue. If he had only given her a chance to tell him what she was so excited about. If he had bothered to listen to her, he would have learned that she was going to stay at New Eden with him instead of returning to a career that now had no future for her.

It took Charlie three days to decide to call Harry back and ask for work.

"Even if dancing is involved," she told him in a flat voice.

"Charlie—" he began, but she didn't give him a chance to finish.

"The doctor said I can dance again, Murphy thinks I'm going back to it, so I might as well be damned the whole nine yards and do it."

Harry didn't agree with her statement, but he knew better than to argue with her when she was in this kind of mood. He told her he'd call her back later in the day. As it was, he called her barely an hour later and gave her a startling list of three audition times. They were all commercials with no dancing involved.

After all the months at New Eden, Charlie forgot how difficult it was to audition. She turned out to be the wrong type for one commercial, didn't like the director's attitude for the other, and won the third. It gave her three days of work and enabled her to tire herself out enough to sleep at night without thinking about Murphy. She had already grimly decided that he wasn't even thinking about her or worrying about how she was getting on. When Harry came through with an audition in a show that was replacing two of their dancers, she calmly jotted down the information and prepared herself for the part by attending the musical twice. Where once she would have been excited and eager to have the chance, now she couldn't find any joy in it.

Murphy wasn't doing much better. He had thought about seeking Charlie out; in fact, he had even gone so far as to call her house in L.A., but the man who answered the phone told him Charlie hadn't contacted him and appeared uneasy about possibly losing his sublet. Murphy muttered something and got off the phone as quickly as possible.

He thought about contacting Harry to learn Charlie's whereabouts, but he didn't think the older man would receive him very kindly. He had to decide just how badly he wanted to talk to her. He had been hasty in his condemnation of her. What if she couldn't dance again? What would she do with her life now? Look how helpless she was when she first came to New Eden. He uttered a harsh laugh. Charlie, helpless? It just didn't fit the image. She had always been self-sufficient; that was what he first liked about her. She had refused to let life get her down. But what if life had finally slapped her down so hard she would have trouble getting up again?

Instead of eating lunch that day, he took a stroll around the grounds. He was brave to do that since most of the residents fixed him with a disapproving stare. It seemed they blamed him for Charlie's leaving. They were right.

"It takes two to make an argument," he declared to one elderly woman who glared at him as she walked past him.

"Then the one who happens to be the jackass ought to smarten up and apologize," she stated bluntly before walking away.

Murphy sighed.

"You're not exactly in the lead for the Mr. Popularity

Award, are you?" Jason walked up and clapped his hand on the younger man's shoulder.

"Right now, I'm being compared to Scrooge, Simon Legree, and Bluebeard all rolled up into one neat package," he said wryly. "You shouldn't be seen with a desperado like me. It might ruin your image."

Jason chuckled. "No one ever said love was easy. Why don't you go after Charlie and talk things out?"

"If I knew where she was, I would go after her, though I'm sure she'd slam the door in my face before I got one word out," Murphy replied. "I guess I couldn't blame her."

Jason reached inside his shirt pocket and withdrew a folded slip of paper, handing it to Murphy. "You'll never know until you try," he said before ambling off.

Murphy looked down at the paper, finding an address and telephone number neatly printed on it. "Where did you get this?" he called after the other man.

"I have friends in low places. Actually, Charlie sent Lena a postcard a few days ago with her new address and the request she not let you know where she was. I wasn't held to that promise," Jason added. "Good luck. By the way, Lena and I have decided to get married two weeks from Saturday. If you're a good boy and do the right thing, we just might allow you to share the wedding with us."

Murphy looked down at the paper again. It was true: he would never know until he tried. He folded the paper and slipped it in the pocket of his jeans. Dammit, she was going to listen to him apologize even if he had to tie her up first!

* * *

Charlie entered the back of the theater and was immediately swamped by memories. Scents of sweat, makeup, and even fear permeated the air. She slowly slid off the fleecy warm-up pants and unzipped the matching jacket to reveal a red leotard and purple tights. Red leg warmers drooped around her ankles. She rummaged in her large tote bag for her shoes and stood off to one side of the stage after giving the stage manager her name.

Though the cavernous hall was cold, she found herself sweating freely. Her palms were clammy and she could feel the trickles of perspiration trailing down between her breasts. She, who never had worried about an audition before, was scared to death. She listened to the choreographer and watched the dance steps they were using—intricate, with a lot of turns. Lights danced in front of her eyes. She closed them, breathed deeply, and counted to ten. In a few moments, she felt calmer than she had in a long time.

Three hours later, Charlie huddled under the covers of her bed with Snickers curled up at her feet and Donnie pacing the length of the bed. She couldn't stop shaking and tears kept rolling down her cheeks. She thought seriously about pulling the covers over her head until the turn of the century.

Maybe she'd feel more like her old self then.

She groaned loudly when she heard a knock at the door. She feared it was the aspiring actor, presently a waiter at the health food restaurant down the street, who lived three doors down the hall. She had forgotten lechers like him lived in this crazy world. She remained quiet, hoping he'd decide she wasn't home and go away. The knocking continued.

"Being polite is a thing of the past," she decided grimly, crawling out of bed. "I'm going to be so rude he'll never come near me again."

She threw open the door and stepped back when Murphy's tall figure filled the open space.

"Hello, Charlie," he said quietly, searching her stunned features with hungry eyes.

"Wha—what are you doing here?" she stumbled. He was the last person she expected to see.

"I came to see you. May I come in?"

Charlie nodded and stepped to one side. Murphy walked in and looked around at the shabby furnishings. There was nothing to indicate her sunshine personality here. It looked sad and bleak—just like Charlie's face.

"Would you care for some coffee?" she asked politely, too politely.

"That sounds nice, but don't go to any trouble." He sounded formal.

"It's no trouble; I have some already made." She disappeared into the tiny kitchen and soon returned with two steaming mugs. "Did you have business down here?" She wanted to know how he got her address but was afraid to ask.

Murphy shook his head. "Jason told me where you were," he explained, knowing she was curious and not wanting her to think Harry had given away her location.

Charlie's brow wrinkled. "Jason?"

He smiled and shrugged. "He told me he has friends in low places, then explained Lena had heard from you. You forgot to ask *him* not to tell me where you were."

270

He lifted the mug to his lips and sipped the hot brew. His pulse was racing enough without the addition of caffeine, but if it kept him there longer he'd drink the entire pot. Glancing at her warily, wondering if she'd demand he leave without giving him a chance to talk to her, he took the easy chair to the right of the couch.

Charlie stared down into the dark liquid. "Why did you come?" she asked in a low voice. "I was just beginning to settle down again. Haven't we hurt each other enough? Or have you come to inflict more pain?"

He winced. "I deserve that . . . and more. I didn't give you a chance that day, did I?"

"And you are now?" She looked at him with flashing eyes. "Well, thank you very much. Why don't I just tell you what you want to hear and then you can go back to Santa Barbara secure that you were right. So far I've worked in one commercial, and I auditioned for a musical today. Does that answer your question?" she demanded. "Isn't that what you wanted to hear? Yes, I can return to my dancing, our affair is over, and you can leave here with a clear conscience. I promise not to look you up in nine years. Now, will you please go?" She swung away so she wouldn't have to face him with tears in her eyes.

Murphy was stunned by her attack. Of course, he deserved it and had only heard what he expected to hear. But why didn't it have the proper ring of truth to it? What was going on here? This wasn't the typical kind of place Charlie lived in. Where was her personal stamp on her surroundings? The colorful posters hadn't been taken off the walls of her cottage before she left New Eden, and these drab walls needed something to brighten them up. Was she planning on moving somewhere else soon, or did she just not care where she lived anymore?

"Just get out of here and leave me alone," she insisted in a choked voice. "I'm tired and I'd like to get some rest." She set the mug down for fear her trembling fingers would drop it and he would see just how agitated she was. She cried out when his hands descended on her shoulders and spun her around.

"Come on, Charlie, let's get it all out in the open, shall we?" Murphy spoke evenly, although his eyes glittered with dark lights. "Okay, you worked in a commercial. Was there any dancing involved? And don't lie because when you're backed up against a wall, you can't get away with it."

She shook her head, keeping her eyes lowered. The horrible beige carpet shimmered before her teary gaze.

"Fine! We've got that out of the way. Now, did the doctor actually come right out and say you could dance again?"

She nodded, still refusing to speak.

His hands tightened. Lena was wrong and he could feel the pain already clawing at his vitals. "All right"— his voice sounded strained from an effort at keeping it calm—"so you can go back to dancing again. You mentioned an audition; did you get the part?" he asked hoarsely.

Charlie sobbed aloud. "I couldn't go through with it," she cried, shaking her head back and forth. "I went to the theater determined to win that part, and when the time came for me to go on the stage and show them what I could do, I couldn't go through with it. I was so scared of getting hurt." Her fingers found the front of his sweater and clung to him with desperation. "Dr.

272

Grissom said I could go back to dancing but I would always have to favor my knee because one misstep or fall and I'd never dance again. There's still a chance it will act up, and for all I know, the time could come when I'll have to have surgery. But it didn't matter to me anymore. I didn't care about not dancing professionally anymore because I knew that time of my life was already over. It didn't bother me as much as I thought it would."

"Because you figured you had another job to fall back on," he said softly, guessing the unspoken end of her sentence. He wrapped his arms around her and drew her against the comforting warmth of his body. "That is, until I pulled the rug out from under you. Why didn't you fight back that day? You never let anyone browbeat you the way I did."

"You hurt me." Her words were mumbled against the soft wool of his sweater, and all the fight was drained out of her.

Murphy sighed. "I think we've done enough hurting to last us a lifetime." He steered her toward the couch and sat down, keeping her in his arms.

"We're better off without each other, Murphy," Charlie said wearily, resting her head against his shoulder.

"No!" he denied fiercely. "Our souls are too closely bound together, Charlie. If anything, we're only halves of a whole when we're apart."

She managed a watery smile. "Sure, and the good times go along with the bad. I know all the platitudes. I just wish you would go away and let me get on with my life while you get on with yours."

"I think the best way for us to get on with our lives is to do it together," he ventured cautiously.

"Oh, I see. You can't find another director of activities, right?"

"No, I can't find a wife."

Charlie stiffened, refusing to believe the sincerity in his voice. "Don't joke, Murphy. I can't take it right now."

"I wasn't joking," he assured her quietly, using his thumb and forefinger braced under her chin to tip her head up. "I love you, Charlie. I always have and, God help me, I always will."

"You make it sound like a curse."

"In some ways, it is." He decided he was better off being blunt about it. "But it's also a blessing. If I haven't killed your love for me with my boorish ways, I'd like us to get married."

"It isn't the most romantic proposal I've heard," Charlie told him, although her heart raced at the idea of living out her life with him.

"And we won't have the kind of marriage you read about in fairy tales either," he said candidly. "We're both bullheaded and strong willed. We'll argue about the most ridiculous things, such as whose turn it is to take the trash out and who left the top off the toothpaste tube. You may even insist I sleep on the couch, to which I will wholeheartedly protest, but we'll also share a lot of love. And I think that will balance things out nicely." He looked into her eyes.

"Do you honestly think we can make a go of it?" she whispered, so afraid he might be trying to talk himself out of it.

Murphy nodded. "It won't be easy," he warned.

"We'll both have to compromise at times, but we'll end up stronger for it. I think we have a lot going for us and that's what counts. I want to marry you, Legs. I hope you'll want to have my children eventually."

"*Our* children," she corrected him in a daze. "I'd like that."

"Browning said it best, 'Grow old along with me! The best is yet to be,'" he quoted, adding whimsically, "Who knows? We might be able to get a special rate at New Eden in thirty or forty years."

Charlie sniffed, swiping at her tears with the back of her hand, but Murphy forestalled her by covering her face with tiny kisses guaranteed to make the smallest of tears disappear.

"Jason and Lena have finally decided to make honest people of each other, and it appears they wouldn't mind sharing their wedding with us," he said with a hopeful gleam in his eye.

Charlie's eyes widened. "They *are?*" she squealed. "That's wonderful!"

Murphy smiled for the first time since he had entered her apartment. "I gather that means you won't mind sharing the limelight." His expression sobered. "I don't believe in divorce, Charlie. Once you're mine, I won't let you go. I'm sure you're thinking of me as an arrogant bastard, but I believe in doing whatever possible to make our marriage work."

Charlie's eyes glowed. "I admire you for sounding realistic instead of coloring your words with hearts and flowers. It's true, there isn't a perfect marriage, but I love you enough and now I know you love me enough to make ours pretty close to one. Now, if we've got all the practical details worked out, would you mind carrying me into the bedroom and making mad, passionate love to me? I have this insatiable urge to be ravished."

Murphy grinned that pirate's grin she remembered from Halloween. He stood up and scooped her into his arms with ease. "Honey, you're going to be ravished like you've never been ravished before. And after I have you in my power, we're going to discuss finding a new home for Snickers." He walked into the bedroom and put her on the bed.

"A new home? Murphy, I love that cat dearly. You can't ask me to give him up!" she insisted, watching him undress hastily.

"Want to bet? You may love that cat, but he certainly hates me." He dropped down on the covers to begin undressing her. His mouth covered hers in a soul-consuming kiss. "And I hope you'd prefer having me around over him."

"He's not all that bad," Charlie breathed when he finally let her come up for air.

"Then it will be a snap to find him a new home."

"Not if I have any say in this."

"You will."

"When?"

"When you say something I want to hear."

"Such as?"

"Such as, 'Murphy, I love you madly and make love to me before I go crazy.' " His hand covered one breast.

Her eyes glazed over. "That sounds fine with me."

"You're agreeing with everything I've just said?" He was surprised she gave in so easily.

"No, just with loving you and you making love to me. The other we can discuss later." Her hand found his zipper.

"Good idea. Much later."

EPILOGUE

"What the hell do you think you're doing?" Murphy's shout of outrage didn't faze the woman it was directed at.

Charlie glanced over her shoulder. "Oh, hi! You're home early. Did you have a good game with Jason?"

"I'm glad I decided to quit at the ninth hole," he grumbled, grasping her around her almost nonexistent waist and lifting her off the chair. "You could have fallen and hurt yourself. What do you need so badly you almost risked breaking your neck to get it?"

"I was looking for a can of grapefruit juice," she replied cheerfully, pecking him on the cheek. She was used to his anger these days, and it didn't bother her one bit.

"I put it in the refrigerator this morning so you wouldn't pull a stupid stunt like the one you just did. I don't want to see you on another chair again, or I'll handcuff you to the bed," Murphy threatened, pulling her against him. He couldn't admit to her how frightened he'd become seeing her standing on the chair and visualizing her falling and hurting herself. Now that he had her, he meant to do everything in his power to keep her whole.

"Hmm, I love it when you talk kinky," Charlie crooned, linking her arms around his neck.

He shook his head as he pulled on the untidy ponytail at the back of her head. "Why is it so hot in here?" He released her to walk over to check the thermostat. "Charlie, it's almost a hundred degrees! Why don't you have the air-conditioning on?" he demanded, spinning around to look at her.

She rolled her eyes upward. "Probably because it doesn't work."

He began raging. "Then call someone to fix it! Dammit, you're pregnant and shouldn't have to suffer through this heat wave."

"You are so right," she agreed, her words having a bite to them. "Next winter you can sleep alone, buddy, because I won't go through another summer pregnant. As for the air-conditioning, I already called four repairmen and it appears everyone's air-conditioning isn't working. No one can come out until the day after tomorrow."

"Then tell them you're pregnant."

Charlie made a sound of disgust. "I did. One said so's everybody else, two said congratulations, and the fourth said his wife was pregnant, too, and she has to wait her turn like everyone else." She opened the refrigerator door and withdrew two cans of Diet Coke. "If you can do better, go for it." She handed one of the cans to him.

Murphy gazed at his wife of eighteen months. Even six months pregnant, looking as if she had swallowed two watermelons, she was beautiful. The residents of New Eden spoiled Charlie shamelessly, and the nursery was filled with all sorts of knitted sweaters and booties for the upcoming arrival. There wasn't one person who wasn't looking forward to the birth.

He'd be a fool if he said the past eighteen months had been newlywed bliss. They'd had their problems like any other married couple. There were days when Charlie had mourned the loss of her dancing career, and teaching two classes at a local dance studio hadn't always been enough for her along with her job in the community. Then there were times when Murphy still feared she'd up and leave when he least expected it. It wasn't that he didn't trust her, but old fears were hard to put to rest.

They argued, but they never went to bed angry. They compromised and they loved as deeply as two people could. Murphy wouldn't change their marriage for anything.

"It hasn't been all that bad, has it?" Charlie asked softly, reading his thoughts easily, as she had learned to do over the months.

He smiled and shook his head as he led her toward the new master bedroom. The previous master bedroom had already been redecorated into a nursery, and another room was also added on just after Charlie's pregnancy had been confirmed. Standing her by the bed, he turned her around to slip the sleeveless dress over her head and gently push her onto the bed.

"Active today?" He stretched out next to her, rubbing her swollen stomach gently.

Charlie made a face. "I feel like a beached baby whale. And I admit the heat hasn't helped."

"You could go over to the pool and at least put your feet in the water," he suggested. "Wouldn't that help?"

"Are you kidding? I'd feel even worse around all

those thin women. And if I look cross-eyed or happen to breathe the wrong way, they're swarming all over me, asking if I need something or if I'm feeling all right. Oh, I'm not complaining, but I can drink only so many cups of herbal tea before I begin to float away," she wailed.

"Poor baby," Murphy sympathized, burying his face in the curve of her neck and smelling the floral scent of her cologne on her damp skin. "It's been rough for you, hasn't it?"

"What do you know?" she asked sullenly. "I feel like I've been pregnant all my life." She stared at him with accusing eyes. "Are you sure you had no idea twins ran in your family? They certainly don't run in mine."

"Of course not," he denied.

Charlie snuggled closer into his embrace, needing his love to cover her like a comforting blanket. "I know one thing," she said softly, "if one of them is a girl, I promise not to talk her into dancing. Come to think of it, I won't do it if both are boys."

Murphy chuckled. "Same goes for me touting an acting career." He paused to take a long drink from the cold Coke can standing on the night table. "Of course, it might be a good idea not to have another you in the dance world."

Charlie lifted her head and eyed him suspiciously. "Meaning?"

He didn't hear the cold front coming from her question. "No offense, honey, but while you were good, you weren't great. You certainly weren't another Pavlova."

Charlie struggled to sit up, no easy feat in her advanced condition. "Are you implying you were a better actor than I was a dancer?" Danger was spelled out loud and clear in her eyes.

Murphy shrugged. "I had no difficulty getting parts," he bragged. "Hey, I bet I could go back today and find work."

"Ah, yes, the perennial killer, such as the part you played in *Mallory for the People.*" She named a television movie he had once done. "True, not just anyone can pick up a phone and breathe heavy into it."

He sat up. "You said that was my best role."

"That's because you're such an expert at heavy breathing."

"Why didn't you tell me before that you thought I wasn't such a hot actor?"

"How could I? Everyone knows how fragile actors' egos are. I didn't want to be the one to damage yours. I figured you'd find out soon enough."

"At least I didn't fall on my can during a performance!"

"And I didn't go through thirty takes because I got the leading lady's name wrong every time!"

Charlie started to snap out another retort when she realized how she sounded. She pressed her fingertips against her lips, but she couldn't stop her laughter from spilling out. Murphy caught her mirth until they both laughed so hard their sides hurt.

"One thing is sure," he commented, pulling her back into his arms, "I never thought being married to you would be boring."

Charlie drew her head back in order to see his face. "Murphy, I love you so much it hurts," she murmured, humbly grateful for a second chance to have the life she should have worked for in the beginning. She wouldn't trade her husband for all the shows in the world.

He smiled and held her tenderly. "Sweetheart, if anyone knows how to defuse a disagreement, you do. Tell you what, five months from now, we'll give Jason and Lena the thrill of their lives by allowing them to babysit while you and I go away for a weekend of pure debauchery. How does that sound?"

Her face lighted up. He still loved her—even if she did look like a turkey ready for Thanksgiving dinner. "That sounds wonderful. And maybe by then a certain lusty buccaneer will appear and carry me off to ravish me like he did two years ago."

"Don't worry, he wouldn't miss it for the world," he assured her, kissing her and drawing her lower lip between his teeth. The doctor had advised them against full lovemaking a month ago because Charlie's slim body was nurturing two babies. But that didn't upset Murphy. He didn't have to possess her body to prove he loved her, and there were so many other ways to love a person.

He continued holding Charlie in his arms and whispering nonsensical words in her ear and listening to her giggle. This was what love was all about. The woman he cared about beside him and the prospect of children further enriching their lives. If he lived to be a hundred, he couldn't ask for more.

Catch up with any Candlelights you're missing.

Here are the Ecstasies published this past September